FEARLESS

FEARLESS

HELLCAT RELEASED™ BOOK FIVE

MICHAEL ANDERLE

LMBPN Publishing
PMB 196, 2540 South Maryland Pkwy
Las Vegas, NV 89109

Version 1.00, September 2022
ebook ISBN: 979-8-88541-469-2
Print ISBN: 979-8-88541-470-8

THE FEARLESS TEAM

Thanks to the JIT Readers

Dorothy Lloyd
Zacc Pelter
Diane L. Smith
Christopher Gilliard
Jan Hunnicutt
Kelly O'Donnell

If I've missed anyone, please let me know!

Editor
The SkyFyre Editing Team

DEDICATION

To Family, Friends and
Those Who Love
to Read.
May We All Enjoy Grace
to Live the Life We Are
Called.

— Michael

Sweaty, beautiful bodies writhed in a frenzy to the heavy beats of music on the darkened dance floor of the Atlantica Central Station club. Dim red lights barely illuminated the room. Brighter rays, a full gamut of colors, strobed through the darkness highlighting the mass of humanity filling the area, trying to forget their troubles.

Dante and Nasreen sat at a balcony table in the club's VIP section, surveying the scene beneath them. Complete with Station flags on either side of the balcony, the fancy chairs and tables of the section were reminiscent of a low-rent dictator's perch.

A dancer below might look up at the Marauder and envy the status and money that gave Dante access to the VIP section. They would never pick out how tightly his fingers gripped his wine glass filled with a non-alcoholic light rose-colored drink in the darkness. He couldn't afford to be distracted now by the slightest touch of intoxication.

One man's glance had Dante reaching into a pocket for his razorfist before he realized the clubgoer wasn't looking his way but instead past him to a woman waving from another balcony. Dante drew a deep breath. *First crisis averted.*

Dante had earned fame as both Dante Shale and the made-up persona of Jordan "Hellcat" Raksha. That fame had helped him when he took down Cormac Slaine and SSS for betraying him. Now it left him worried about assassins spotting him in clubs and creating a mess for him to clean up despite his disguise.

He tried not to scratch his face. The disguise Nasreen had applied changed his face enough that he didn't look like himself without being too obvious. That didn't make it any more comfortable. He wondered how many years she'd spent in her earlier spy career wearing uncomfortable disguises.

"Everything clear out there?" Dante asked under his breath before checking out the nearby empty tables.

Nasreen had reserved them all using different dummy accounts to ensure this part of the VIP section would be empty. Dante and Nasreen didn't want a fight. They wanted complications and collateral damage even less. The best place for a clandestine meeting would have been away from all these people. Unfortunately, there was no way their expected contact would meet them in a place like that.

"Lots of people coming and going," Braelin drawled over comms. "No one who looks like they want to kill anyone." He laughed. "No. That ain't right. One poor bastard got caught looking at another woman's ass by his girl. He might not make it through the night."

"That's not our problem," Dante replied. "*You* better not be staring at her ass. You're supposed to be out there making sure you're watching the club to save our asses."

"I wasn't staring. I looked that way because it drew my eyes. They didn't linger."

"We're clear from my position," Jolo cut in with ice in her tone. "I agree. Make sure you're looking at the right thing, Braelin."

He groaned. "I wasn't looking at her ass. I swear it!"

"Nothing of note from my position," Mugoi added with a hint of amusement.

A huge yawn preceded the next answer from the last member of the ground team, Hyde. "Keep drinking your wine and staring at Joelle's ass, Shale. We'll do all the real work."

Dante's nostrils flared. "I'm not drinking any wine, and I'm not staring at Nasreen. Everyone needs to focus and remember why we're here. This isn't a night out on the town."

Nasreen arched a brow and shook her head, not sparing him too long a look before a cool, detached survey of the crowd. He appreciated her professionalism. Not being Dirtside or on an active raid made it too easy to relax. They couldn't. One missed movement might end with a dead team member or a lost chance to spot their contact.

Midas, his AI implant, had also kept quiet. Dante appreciated the AI's restraint. Between the comms and the bustle of the club, too many overlapping noises and voices demanded his attention. A lifetime of risking his life in dangerous situations and battles normally helped him focus on what was important in any given environment.

The problem was the overlapping voices reminded him far too much of their current enemy, the mysterious Omega Syndrome. When they'd hijacked Midas a year ago and used his voice modules to speak in a threatening chorus of voices, they'd warned they'd be watching Dante and Nasreen.

While always worried about them, Dante hadn't known their true name until the recent kidnapping incident and his first encounter with the anti-Omega Syndrome resistance group Firewall. He still knew far too little about who the Omega Syndrome were other than the true power behind the Atlantica Stations and the festering corruption at the heart of orbital human civilization.

Mugoi, Braelin Klement, and Jolo Neburu had been Dante's

apprentices for a year. They had a while to go before they reached his level, but they'd turned in impressive performances on past missions. Their recent pseudo-kidnapping-slash-recruitment attempt at the hands of Firewall and subsequent rescue by Dante, Nasreen, and Hyde had led to tonight.

Dante scanned the crowd, hoping and worried an enemy would come their way. Mugoi had traced Firewall comms and sent them a message on a secure channel to discuss a meeting about their mutual enemy. Unfortunately, there was the minor issue of Dante's team having killed Firewall members during the rescue op.

He would have rather been Dirtside with a pulsecore carbine in hand fighting a Nightmutt. That would have been straightforward. Instead, he was playing spy games in a crowded nightclub waiting for a contact who might be as interested in blowing out his brains as talking.

Nasreen picked up her drink. "Try to act more natural. You're standing out too much."

Dante stared at her like she'd said he had two heads. "This *is* me being natural."

"Then be…less like you. Your body language screams suspicious. Our disguises aren't perfect."

"If someone was going to kill me because I scowled too much in a club, I would have been dead years ago."

"I see." Nasreen demonstrated a pose of perfect unassuming languidness, a leg draped over the other. Her mouth curled up in a sly smile. The high-slitted, clinging blue dress supported her in all the right ways while being long enough to hide deadly toys. Dante had been surprised by how much she'd hidden before they came to the club.

"This hiding and waiting is your game, not mine," Dante replied. "I'm the man with the public reputation for being an asshole. I should be up here glaring at people and saying they suck at dancing."

"Try to think of it as less a public reputation as an asshole and more a reputation for honesty." Nasreen's gaze slid back and forth, taking in the entire crowd. "This doesn't have to go badly. We're on the same side as these people. It's to our mutual benefit to cooperate."

"They might not believe that after what happened last time."

Dante glanced her way with a forced smile. They were supposed to look like a couple out on a date at a club, not two Marauders waiting for a resistance contact to arrive. Tucked away in their VIP balcony, no one could hear what they were discussing.

"This is annoying," Hyde offered over comms. "Give me mercs to kill before I die from boredom, *Papi*."

Dante wouldn't give him the satisfaction of objecting to the nickname. Even Cormac Slaine couldn't get the cyborg not to use it.

"Remember, we're not waiting for trouble," Nasreen cautioned. "We're waiting for allies."

"Yeah. I'll take killing those assholes, too. Just because they call themselves a resistance doesn't mean they don't need killing."

Leaving Hyde outside had proven wise. The apprentices and Hyde had been stationed outside the club to watch the entrances and exits. Dante didn't want or need a fight. The meeting was supposed to be about recruiting help, not making new enemies. He doubted Firewall would accept another incident with his team killing their people.

"A more entertaining night by your standards might bring carnage, Hyde." Mugoi sounded as bored as Hyde despite its words.

"Ha!" Hyde barked. "Now you're getting it. Those implants aren't all a waste of money." Glee infused every syllable. Hyde was a more grateful and relaxed man than the ruthless cybernetic monster he'd been when still working for Cormac Slaine. That didn't make him kind, normal, or a man above hurting people for fun.

"It's you who isn't getting it," Mugoi replied with a hint of disdain. "You need to think long-term. I understand that's difficult for you. These people are necessary to handle our enemies. They can help us. Our new enemy isn't someone we can punch past even if you had your old body."

"You think those Firewall idiots can help us?" Hyde scoffed. Hateful mockery infused the sound.

"Those *pendejos* are shit who can't help themselves. They were ready and waiting for trouble, and they still got their asses kicked when the team showed up to save your little apprentice asses. They first kicked your ass, huh? What's that say about you? Why have all the hardware if you can't kill someone trying to take you out?"

Braelin groaned. "Hey, they ambushed us with lots of guys. We gave as good as we got, and that was with all the pints we had in us. Nah. We gave better. Mugoi kicked tons of ass."

Jolo's smooth voice came next. "An alliance is about more than combat ability, and Mugoi did a fine job, all things considered."

"Mugoi's got skills," Braelin added. He chuckled. "Sometimes more than me. Like on Tuesdays past nine when we're in El Dorado. I ain't saying that little shiny cyborg is better than me all the time, mind you."

"You're competent for a non-augmented human, Klement," Mugoi replied. "That's all one can ask. You can see the big picture, unlike certain people."

"I agree," Jolo added. "I suspect if you were there when Firewall attacked us, you wouldn't have performed as well, Mr. Curtidor."

Dante could always tell when they wanted to get to him. Hyde didn't mind his true last name. Somehow when Jolo said it, despite the elegant delivery it came off as a devasting insult.

Hyde groaned. "What's this shit?"

"There's no *shit* involved," Jolo countered. "I'm stating a fact."

Hyde's unnerving snicker followed. "We all going to sit around a campfire Dirtside and sing songs about how much you love each other next?"

Dante glanced at Nasreen in surprise. She remained focused on watching the area. Braelin's admission and Mugoi's response startled him. His apprentices had spent almost as much time fighting each other as training in the last year. Now, they were defending one another.

He'd noticed it more recently. Mugoi would go after Hyde instead of Braelin. The apprentice's competitive nature targeted the other cyborg on the team with laser focus. At first, Dante believed it was because they were both cyborgs. Now, he was far more convinced it was about the apprentices having bonded during their time in captivity.

Mugoi's restrained scoff cut through the comms like a knife. "You question our competency, Hyde. You let street scum take you down. What does that say about you?"

"They didn't take me down," Hyde growled. "An explosion took me down, you little—"

"Enough," Dante cut in. "Focus on the task at hand. We need these allies. Unless someone shows up and attacks us, we'll approach this meeting with that idea in mind. If you all don't shut up, I'll shove a pulsecore up your asses to shut you up."

"Ha-ha." Hyde cackled. "Okay, *Papi*. I'm quiet now."

Dante's attention cut to a corner near the stairs. A red-faced blonde staggered around the corner, her eyes unfocused. A strap had slipped on her low-cut scarlet dress, threatening to let the rest of her top slide down. She broke into a huge grin when she spotted Dante before winking.

The woman staggered toward the table, her hips swaying to a song only she could hear. "Hey, aren't you a guy?"

Dante didn't have time for this nonsense. "Yes, I'm a guy last time I checked."

"No, no, not a guy. *That guy.*" She tittered with a hand to her mouth. She traced an invisible man with her hands. "Like that *that guy.* The famous guy." She purred. "I like famous guys. I *really* like famous guys. My other date was boring and stupid. I don't care if you're not famous. I think you're a good time. I need a good time."

Dante chuckled and motioned at Nasreen, unconcerned about the apparent failure of his disguise. "I think you've mistaken me for somebody else. I'm here with my friend. I'm not looking for any fun."

"Because she's so frigid?" slurred the drunk woman. "I can heat you up if she can't."

Dante maintained his smile. He was glad Hyde and the apprentices couldn't hear the woman's half of the conversation. His newfound friend remained a problem. An offended woman who started yelling would only draw more attention.

The woman sashayed toward him. Before he could say anything else, Nasreen threw up an arm to block the new arrival. Her other hand stayed hidden underneath the table.

"I'm going to ask a question," Nasreen whispered venomously. "You're going to answer that question, or you're getting the hell out of here."

"You are frigid, aren't you?" The drunk woman stared at Nasreen's arm. "It's not my fault your man's bore—"

"I want to go to Celestial Seoul," Nasreen interrupted. "From El Dorado. What's the best route?"

Dante kept a cool expression, despite his surprise. He'd assumed the drunk woman was nothing more than a party-going girl enamored of his charms despite his disguise. The realization she might not be stung more than he expected. He'd take that secret to his grave.

Nasreen's inquiry was far from random. When they'd sent a

follow-up message to Firewall, she'd given them a sign and countersign to identify their operative.

Dante still couldn't see what was in her other hand. He had no doubt it was a blade or a wrist-mounted launcher. Nasreen had seen right through the woman. For all her progress in training as a Marauder, she'd spent most of her life as a freelance spy. Those skills hadn't vanished because she'd played more with pulsecores, Reapers, and Nightmutts Dirtside.

The drunk woman leaned over the table, trying to bait Dante into looking down her dress. She swayed as if she might collapse any second. "Your girlfriend's a bitch. Come on. Ditch her. Why don't you party with me, big guy?"

Dante focused on her face and frowned. "My friend asked you a question. Answer it, or get the hell out of here. Don't make us call security."

The corners of the woman's mouth twitched into a mocking smile. She looked between the two before pulling out a chair and seating herself. "The best way to go to Celestial Seoul from El Dorado is by way of Dirtside through Bucharest on Wednesdays."

She'd sat but kept her arms near her sides. One hand hovered near the front of her dress. All the amusement and lust in her face from earlier was gone. Her gray eyes focused on Nasreen as she awaited her response. Dante's partner lifted her empty hand from underneath the table to join her other hand on the tabletop. The drunk woman mirrored her.

Nasreen narrowed her eyes. "You're late."

The woman shook her head. Her slurring and accent had changed when she replied, with hints of a Slavic background surfacing. "We never committed to a time. You offered a time. After what you did, you should be happy I showed up."

Dante cleared his throat. "That was a misunderstanding. We're sorry about that. We were trying to save our people."

"A misunderstanding? A fatal one." The woman's nostrils flared. "We'll set that aside for the moment. We have a mutual *friend*, and working together means giving that friend what they deserve. We can overlook sacrifices."

"What's your name?" Dante asked.

"Does it matter?"

"Yes." Dante shrugged. "I don't want to always say 'Hey, you.' It gets annoying."

The woman's stare bored through him. Anger and resentment burned behind her gray eyes. "You can call me Tether."

Dante snorted. "Call me a hypocrite, but I want to know your real name. Not your handle or your nickname."

Nasreen nodded her agreement. "It's only fair. You know ours. It's not like your people didn't target us. We want your help. You want ours. We need to make sure we have a balanced relationship to keep everything proceeding smoothly."

Tether shook her head. "We wouldn't have lasted this long against our mutual friend if we wandered around giving up too much information. You two have pulled off impressive successes. We acknowledge that. You also aren't subtle and don't get what you're up against."

"We understand well enough," Nasreen replied. "That's why we contacted you."

Tether laughed, the sound coming out harsh and bitter. "No, you don't. Because you're not committed like we are. You think this will be like that little tool Slaine you helped take down Dirtside. You think you can take these people on and win easily."

Dante shook his head. "No, we don't. That doesn't mean we're going to wet our pants because they have deep pockets and resources."

She slapped her hand on her chest. "I'm dead."

"If you were going to lose your nerve, you shouldn't have come."

"No. You still don't get it." Tether leaned back in her chair and drew a deep breath. Her gaze slid between Nasreen and Dante with an air of irritation. "We're not like you. This isn't a game. When we join the organization, we give up our names for aliases.

"Subsequently, all our information gets expunged. We stop existing in the system. *They* control the system. Only by giving up everything can we have a chance. Tether is the closest thing I have to a real name. Deal with it."

Dante couldn't question the reach of the Omega Syndrome. Hyde's vague warnings about "big spiders" controlling the Stations had hinted at their existence before their dramatic invasion of Midas. In a sense, the Omega Syndrome had reached into Dante's brain to threaten him. Taking them lightly or assuming they weren't capable of something would end badly despite recent internal implant upgrades to help better protect him.

Tether drew a deep breath. Although her cheeks remained as red as when she'd first staggered around the corner, every other movement had become sharp and precise. "Can we dispense with the pointless questions now? I'm responsible for onboarding you into Firewall. The less time we waste with bullshit, the quicker that can happen."

Nasreen shook her head. "We're here to discuss what we can offer one another, not join up."

"Yes," Dante added. "We're not picking out stupid names while you erase our backgrounds. I've died before. It didn't take."

Tether jerked back in her seat with a brief flash of panic in her eyes. "The only way you can help take on our mutual friend is by going that far. I thought you understood that by now."

Nasreen offered her a dismissive look infused with pity. "We are looking to ally against—" Tether's back stiffened. She tightened her hands into fists. "Our mutual bad *friend*."

Tether relaxed. She swallowed. "I thought you were going to say their name. You can never say their name in public. They're listening for it. You don't understand how much they hear and see."

"I'm living proof you can operate underground without

permanently erasing yourself." Nasreen motioned at Dante. "So is he. This isn't the first time I've had to discuss something sensitive and be careful about it. Let's get back to discussing how we can offer each other mutual aid while remaining separate."

Was saying Omega Syndrome aloud that dangerous? Dante doubted it. He accepted that Hyde's big spiders were far more of a threat than Cormac Slaine and SSS. That didn't mean they were omnipotent and omniscient.

"No," Tether declared. "We don't do alliances. You're either all in or a threat. That's the only way we can win against them." She stood, straightened her dress, and fixed the strap. "You shouldn't have wasted our time. Don't contact us again. If you do, we might have to take extreme measures."

"Hey!" Dante stood. "Don't be so quick to run. We've proven what we can do. You need us as much as we need you."

"You've proven nothing." Tether sneered. "Don't you get it? They *let* you take down Slaine. He'd become a liability. You're nothing more than another tool."

Nasreen looked unperturbed. She folded her arms. "You're being shortsighted. Winning against a powerful organization means getting help wherever you can find it, not trying to put too many conditions on that aid."

Dante agreed. He'd once been devoted to getting his revenge on Ambrose and Hyde. Now he was working side-by-side with both men.

"You don't understand," Tether repeated.

"Armored hovercars converging on my side of the club, Captain," Mugoi reported. "While they are trying to conceal their weapons, multiple men in long coats are now emerging. I've glimpsed batons."

"More coming down the street," Jolo added. "They're stopping closer to Hyde's position."

"I've got assholes, too," Braelin reported. "All slow and lazy-like. I see DeFrieze in one of the cars."

"They're trying not to draw too much attention," Dante concluded. "We can use that."

"Finally!" Hyde shouted. His voice verged on singsong. "Let's tear shit up. I was about to fall into a coma out here I was so bored."

Dante turned to Tether. "We have trouble coming. We need to get out of here."

Tether whipped a knife from underneath her slinky dress like it'd been invisible. "You bastards. You sold me out. You're insane if you think I'm going anywhere with either of you."

Dante sighed and pulled out his razorfist. "We don't have time for your fucking paranoia. We need to escape while we still can."

Sir, Midas chimed in, sounding more like a British butler from a period drama than normal. *Please note the following.*

The AI added a helpful green arrow at the edge of Dante's vision, pointing at men in long dark coats slipping into entrances. They no longer concealed their batons but kept them on their belts. People in the crowd parted to let them through. Others headed for other exits. No alarms rang. The crowd might have taken them for club security.

DeFrieze's men looked back and forth taking in the crowd. Their lack of urgency only lit a fire in Dante's veins.

Midas highlighted an emergency exit. No Block 9X had entered from that part of the club. That made sense. It was the one closest to DeFrieze. Where DeFrieze was, there'd be Irondog cyborgs.

Nasreen pulled a tranq dart launcher onto her wrist. Even knowing she'd stowed it beforehand, Dante was even more confused about where exactly she'd been hiding it than he was with Tether's weapon. Women's bodies could be a greater mystery than any evil conspiracy.

Dante frowned at one of the men wading through the thick crowd. "I recognize him. I'm so glad DeFrieze brought his experienced crew."

"Of course he did." Tether jerked her head back and forth. "They're covering almost all the exits. They aren't stopping everyone. That means they must be looking for me."

"Shall we engage, Captain?" Mugoi asked eagerly.

Hyde growled. "Let's bust the heads of these *pendejos* open and beat the others to death with their friends' brains. That'll get them running."

"Hold position," Dante ordered. "There are too many people here and not enough people getting the hell out. We start the fight early, and we'll cause too much collateral damage. We weren't here to fight them. We were here for the meeting. We can still get out of here if we move fast and not stir them up. They think they have the upper hand. Let's use that."

Tether inched away from the table. "You're trying to make sure I don't run."

"You want to run, be my guest." Dante slipped on the razor-fist. He didn't extend the blade. "As long as you don't mind a bunch of innocent people getting killed, Miss Freedom Fighter."

Should I contact the authorities? Midas asked.

"Hell no," Dante replied. "We can't risk the locals working for the…our mutual *friend.*"

Dante didn't care if he looked like he was talking to himself in front of Tether despite the dirty look she gave him. She'd assume he was on the radio with his team anyway. The truth would take too long to explain.

"This ain't good," Braelin advised. "More guys hopped out near DeFrieze. They ain't in no hurry, but he's heading in Hyde's general direction along with guys with weird goggles."

"The goggles guys are Irondogs," Dante said. He'd been right with his earlier assumption. "They think they've got this place locked down. We've got a window to get out of here without a major confrontation." He glared at Tether. "If we move together right now."

Hyde growled, "Fuck this. I'm going to finish what I started. His knockoff trash isn't going to be tougher than last time."

"Prepare to fall back to the extraction point, Hyde," Dante replied. "*Everyone* prepare to fall back. Ambrose, we need pickup *yesterday*. Head to the evac zone on the east side of the club. We'll meet you on the roof per the plan."

It was a calculated gamble. Ambrose might be heading toward a destination near DeFrieze and his cyborgs, but the building positions would cut down on reinforcements from other sides.

"I'm on my way," Ambrose replied over comms. Dante was grateful he'd been paying attention.

Dante gestured for Tether to follow. "We have a shuttle on the way. Come with us."

"No," she snapped.

He'd worried about this reaction. He didn't have time for it.

The mercs in the club froze in place. One looked toward the front of the building. A second later, they lifted their batons. One pointed at Tether on the balcony.

"Screw it, Shale," Hyde replied. "Don't worry. I'll kill them all outside. You should have heard the scream of the first guy. Then Igento can come and get us whenever."

"A whole shit ton of guys are running out of their cars and not trying to hide their weapons," Braelin reported. "It's like something stirred them all up."

"Yes," Dante muttered. "A damned mystery for sure." He glared at Tether. "Unless you think you can take on all of Block 9X by yourself, you're going to come with us to the east entrance right damned now."

Tether kicked off her heels and ran toward the balcony railing. She vaulted over to the screams of patrons below but caught a flagpole to break her fall. With a quick back-and-forth swing to build up momentum, she jumped to the floor and landed in a crouch.

"Shit. Why can't anyone fucking listen?"

Dante glanced at the railing before rushing toward the stairs. He didn't trust his agility that much. Nasreen sprinted after him with an annoyed look as Tether raced for the east exit.

"We're coming your way, Hyde," Dante announced. It was too late to rein the man in. Dante might as well make use of his homicidal tendencies. "Make sure they aren't on our ass the second we step out of the building."

"I've got you, *Papi.*"

The Block 9X mercenaries inside the club shouted at Tether and shoved people out of their way. People spat and cursed at them. Despite that, no one tried to fight back against the large scowling men with batons. On a deep level, most people living in the Atlantica Stations understood that looking the other way was the easiest way to avoid getting swept away by the deep corruption soaking orbital humanity.

A cluster of drunks slowed Tether's process. She pushed them aside. One man tried to complain. He backed away with his hands in front of him when she flashed her knife. The delay cost the operative her escape. Two mercs blocked the exit with predatory grins and raised their batons.

Dante and Nasreen hit the bottom of the stairs. The crowd's shifting to avoid Tether and the mercs had forced more people to their part of the club, slowing their progress. People focused on the knife-wielding woman in a slinky dress squaring off against the two larger men and didn't get out of Dante's and Nasreen's way.

A merc swung at Tether. She ducked the blow with ease and slashed the man's arm. The merc grunted and stepped back dripping blood. She rushed forward, feinting another blow at his arm, and sidestepped his counterattack to shove her blade into his neck. A gurgle ate his scream. She yanked the knife out and rolled around his falling body, using it as a shield against his partner's blow.

Nearby crowd members tried to move away from the fight.

The inconvenient location in front of the closest emergency exit trapped a ring of wide-eyed party-goers unaccustomed to witnessing arterial sprays from men's necks outside of gritty crime dramas.

Tether stayed light on her feet, dancing back and forth to the mercenary's wide swings. He growled in frustration, and his blows grew more desperate and quicker. Her dodges were effortless.

"Get the hell out of my way, you bastard," she spat. "Or you're dead."

The merc jumped backward. He hadn't cleared her way. He was still blocking the exit when he lifted his baton and a carbon filament blade popped out. Three reinforcements closed in on the fight. They all carried extended blades.

His jaw tight, Dante extended his razorfist blade. With a hiss, Nasreen fired her tranq launcher. She hit one merc in the neck. He collapsed in a heap. The sea of humanity shifted, blocking further shots.

Tether's quick footwork and shoulder twists saved her from the first swings. The furious merc tried a double-handed swing toward her neck. She bobbed underneath the blow, and his blade stuck in the wall, giving her time to plant her knife through his eye. This time the leftover crowd greeted the blow with a collective groan.

Dante put his shoulder forward and charged through the crowd, scattering people along the way. He'd closed in on Tether when the reinforcements burst from the crowd toward the operative and the dead mercenaries.

Tether yanked her blade from her latest victim and jumped backward. The move saved her from the first mercenary. It didn't save her from a second who'd circled to her side. His blade moved, the shifting lights of the club bathing it in different colors before it cleaved through her arm with a *squelch* and *crunch*.

Her limb flew to the floor. Blood splattered everywhere. Her piercing cry cut through the loud music.

Witnesses screamed and yelled. The death before had hypnotized them. The dismemberment shocked them back into reality and a land of terror. They stampeded away from the fight.

The merc smiled and brought back his blade to cut off her head. A tranq dart to the back of his neck dropped him to the floor. His blade ended up embedded in his shoulder, adding more blood to the floor.

Dante arrived at the circle's edge. He charged into the closest reinforcements and shoved his razorfist blade into the heart of one man. With a tug, he pulled the man's filament blade out of his hand and flung it into the face of the second. The victim moaned before pitching backward.

Other mercs waded through the panicked crowd with murder in their eyes. The long coats worried Dante. Block 9X had proven they had no problems using illegal weaponry aboard the Station. A man whipping out a pulsecore might kill dozens of people in the crowded club.

Nasreen helped the groaning, pale Tether to her feet. Dante pulled an autoclamp from his pocket and tossed it to Nasreen. It paid to be prepared.

She pressed it to Tether's bloody stump and ran her fingers along the activator buttons. With a *whir* and *hiss,* the clamp expanded around the wound and sealed it while spraying anesthetic and antiseptic compounds.

Tether let out a quiet moan and swayed as her eyes fluttered. Dante hoisted the Firewall operative into his arms before opening the door into the false darkness of the Station outside. Screams and shouts echoed in the distance. He'd trained his team well. Now was his time to trust them.

Nasreen downed more mercs with tranq darts. The others ducked behind tables along the edge of the dance floor. One man grabbed a scared woman as a human shield. Nasreen backed toward the door and swung her arm back and forth.

Sir, Midas reported. *A public security alert is being broadcast for this area. It's reporting a terrorist incident. Public security forces are on the way.*

"We need to get out of here!" Dante shouted. Chopping off a woman's arm was too much for the jaded crowd. He didn't trust that any security forces would be on his side. "Everyone make sure the evac path to the shuttle is clear."

Hyde let out a jolly laugh. "I've killed lots of knockoff losers. There are lots more, though. Don't bitch too much. We've got this."

There were dead bodies, blood everywhere, and a woman missing half an arm. At least someone was having a good time.

CHAPTER TWO

The tight, mazelike layout of the nearby buildings boxed in Dante, Nasreen, and Tether while limiting enemy reinforcements. In the melee-heavy battles that dominated Station encounters, funneling enemies into tighter formations meant a smaller group could win against a superior group, a twenty-third-century version of the Battle of Thermopylae.

That was the theory anyway. Basing modern battle strategies off the losing strategies of eugenics-obsessed Bronze Age warriors was questionable. The body flying at Dante as he exited the club offered the first evidence that this battle plan had gone south.

The mercenary flew past with his neck bent at almost ninety degrees and his face smashed to a pulp. Dante ducked with Tether still in his arms. The body *thudded* against the wall behind them and dropped to the ground with an unceremonious *thump*.

Nasreen spun and slammed the door closed. She yanked a small thin silver square out of her pocket and smacked it atop the lock. That'd cut off the forces from inside but also their escape route. The situation had shifted to triage over careful strategy.

A mob of mercenaries with carbon filament blades had formed a half-circle in front of a laughing Hyde with gouges in his armored body. The cyborg showed more joy than he had in weeks, if not months.

Three men in dark goggles lay on the ground in pools of blood, one with a missing arm and others with exposed metal or tubing. One of the defeated cyborgs crawled toward Hyde on twisted legs. Metal claws extended from his right hand. Hyde stomped on his head and caved it in, producing a scarlet spray before slamming his boot into the chest of another mercenary with a loud, sickening *crunch*. His latest victim flew backward and impaled himself on another man's blade.

Hyde scoffed, "Those guys we fought before were tougher than this. I'm insulted."

Piles of bloodied and broken bodies littered the nearby street. A glowering DeFrieze stood behind his advancing men, holding a blade. Other Block 9Xers tried to flank Hyde as Braelin and Jolo offered their streak of punches and shock baton swings to the available live targets. Mugoi flowed from man to man with quick and precise punches and chops to the neck and knees, downing men in a staccato chorus of screams, grunts, and cries.

Dante liked what he witnessed. Skill and a homicidal cyborg were effective force multipliers. That didn't mean they guaranteed victory. Until they boarded their shuttle, their lives were at risk.

Midas' conveniently provided distance counter and green crosshairs marked Ambrose and the approaching shuttle flying toward them. Based on previous planning, the team would need to evacuate to a nearby rooftop for extraction. Dante was rethinking the more open front of the club, even if that meant being swamped by the small army DeFrieze had brought with him.

Nasreen turned and downed a mercenary running around the

corner with a nasty dart to his cheek. She spun for a matching disabling shot on the opposite side reinforcements. "We need to move before they overwhelm us."

Dante traced a wide curve as he jogged toward his people with Tether still in his arms. Jostling a woman who'd lost an arm and needed better care wasn't optimal.

Tether's eyes fluttered open. She let out a loud moan before her eyes closed again.

Her heart rate and blood pressure are unstable, Midas announced. *Based on the estimated amount of blood loss, more emergency first aid is recommended.*

"Thanks," Dante scoffed. "I needed an advanced AI to tell me that getting an arm chopped off is hazardous to a woman's health. What would I do without you?"

You would have long since died. Midas didn't need a sass module for an effective mental snort. *I also believe a more advanced medical diagnostics upgrade would be helpful in better evaluating survivorship in situations such as this. As it is, you were reluctant for me to buy the level three first aid upgrades that are now proving so useful. You claimed they were unnecessary.*

"Let's finish escaping the assassin squad before we talk about your damned upgrades and 'I told you so's.'"

"You're all going to die here!" yelled DeFrieze. "You shouldn't have fucked with Block 9X. You thought you were all so damned clever. You didn't know who you were messing with."

Mercenaries flooded the street from both sides. One group flowed around DeFrieze like he was a stone in a river. The operations leader for Block 9X stayed in place, his twisted smile more smug than sinister. Dante would have loved to kill him. He filed that away for the future.

Braelin bellowed and charged in Dante's direction. The nearby mercenaries hesitated at the sudden shout, which allowed Braelin to brain one man before they thought to swing a blade.

Nasreen put down a second before reloading. They'd carved out the beginning of an escape path.

Mugoi jumped and crushed a man's face with his hardened knee. Using the man as a springboard, he leapt from him to kick a second mercenary in the face before cartwheeling to avoid a blade and landing. A sweeping kick downed a third, whom he finished off with a stray blade. Without the blood covering Mugoi's beautiful face and the screams of the dying, all the graceful movement might have reminded Dante of a dance.

The cyborg offered a thin smile to Braelin. "Are you counting?"

Their mutual kidnapping might have limited the old habits. It hadn't smothered them completely.

"This ain't the time, my metal buddy." Braelin shoved his baton into a man's stomach and followed up with a powerful left hook.

Hyde decapitated another merc with a borrowed carbon filament blade. "I've got more than all you combined!"

Jolo also traded a baton for a blade. Restraint didn't mean much when the people fighting you were trying to kill you. She sliced across a man's leg, leaving him screaming before cutting his neck with a backswing. He fell back, blood spraying everywhere.

The mountain of broken and cut bodies reminded Dante more of a medieval siege than a showdown outside a club on an orbital Station. That didn't stop Dante from smiling. His apprentices had been captured by Firewall when they were surprised. This fight proved their skill. When they were ready, armed, and waiting, they were a threat to far greater numbers.

A wall of new Block 9Xers rushing around corners and onto the street pulled a frustrated grunt from Dante. The prohibition against serious firearms on the Station kept everyone safer, but it meant flooding an area with combatants was a viable strategy.

Dirtside, a single pulsecore carbine could have taken out the new reinforcements with a handful of shots. All DeFrieze needed was to not care about his men for the strategy to work.

Sirens blasted from the other side of the building. The sound echoed in the nearby space through the buildings and alleys. Flashing lights danced on the walls. Station security had arrived.

The mercenaries were bad enough. Dante's team couldn't take them and Station security together. Ending up in custody would make them easy prey for the Omega Syndrome.

Mugoi jumped from the street to a wall. The cyborg pushed off the wall to launch into two men rushing toward Dante and Nasreen. It collided and knocked them over before spinning to land on its feet. Before the mercenaries could stand, Mugoi *cracked* their heads against the street with ax kicks.

Hyde's bloody tornado of violence continued as he crushed two men's heads together. He grunted as a man nailed him in his armored side with a shock baton. His knees buckled, and the mercenaries pounced, trying to stab and beat him into submission.

A flurry of darts from Nasreen sent the first wave to the ground and allowed Hyde enough time for a new strategy. He grabbed a half-dead Irondog and smacked nearby opponents with the hardened body of the disabled Block 9X cyborg. Hard bone met harder metal and broke with loud *crunches*.

Heavy, clanking steps announced two huge Irondogs coming around the corner. They'd not bothered with coats over their bulky and misshapen forms. One man punched the nearby wall, smashing a deep hole to demonstrate his strength in a feeble attempt to intimidate the team. The two new cyborgs hadn't bothered with natural-looking eyes. Solid silver stared out at the world.

"Ha!" Hyde cheered and smashed his fists together. "Come on! Bring it!"

Losing his old body had humbled Hyde. He'd spent a year in a glorified metal skeleton before the recent upgrades provided by Nasreen. Despite that, his upgraded form lacked the sheer power of his original body. Dante wasn't so sure he could win against the new arrivals.

The distant shadow of Ambrose's shuttle grew into a recognizable silhouette. Ambrose swept the craft around in a wide arc heading toward a rooftop. Their ride was there. There was one small problem.

Dante had planned for the possibility of abrupt evac under fire. He'd accounted for superior numbers of ruthless killers. He hadn't assumed he'd need to carry anyone up a ladder. Punching through the enemy toward the front and a street pickup would end with them surrounded by Station security.

Nasreen pulled out a knife. "They brought more guys than we thought they would." She sidestepped a charging mercenary to knee him in the balls before stabbing him and shoving him forward. "This is endless."

One of the silver-eyed Irondogs charged Hyde who borrowed a page from Mugoi's book with an agile spin. He jumped and wrapped an arm around the Irondog's neck before twisting. Gut-wrenching squelching and tearing rose above the din. Dark oil and bright fluid mixed with crimson blood to shower Hyde and the nearby Block 9X. Hyde had torn the man's head clean off. Dante didn't realize he was still that strong in his new body other than mentioning a couple of recent upgrades.

The Irondog didn't have the decency to die. Just like Hyde when he'd lost his body last year.

"Too many of you dumbasses don't reinforce your necks," Hyde mocked.

"I'll kill you when I get a new body," the Irondog growled. "You're dead."

Snickering, Hyde threw the head toward DeFrieze. The ops

leader ducked. The head bounced off a wall and *clanked* against the street.

The remaining silver-eyed Irondog proved better prepared than his friend. He extended two blades from his wrist with a leering grin. He slashed at Hyde but didn't close in for a grapple. Other wary mercenaries spread out and tried to press through the line, only to be met by Nasreen and the apprentices.

Sheer numbers meant heading for the ladder guaranteed Block 9X would run them down. The shuttle was almost there, but it might as well have been at a different Station.

Hyde grunted as his opponent slashed into his torso, producing sparks. "That's all you got? Pathetic."

"I'm gonna stomp your brain into a mush," the Irondog taunted. He thrust again. Hyde headbutted him and sent him stumbling back.

Dante eyed the ladder and the approaching shuttle. Tether had grown paler during the battle. Even if he set her down to help push back the mercs, it wouldn't do any good when she couldn't move on her own. The reinforcements weren't helping.

DeFrieze looked over his shoulder, mouthing something that Dante couldn't make out. "Damn it. Units One through Three, push them back! We outnumber them."

Dante didn't understand why the mercs weren't rolling over them with all their forces. Clarity arrived seconds later when Station security pushed around the corners clad in full armor and helmets. They carried huge riot shields locked together, and long spear-like stun poles poked out from the formation. A modern phalanx had joined the medieval carnage.

Block 9X mercenaries hacked at the shields with their blades and batons. The attacks left cracks and gouged out chunks, only for men to go down to security stuns. Station security might not be on Dante's side, but they weren't on Block 9X's side either.

The shuttle slowed and hovered over the building. Their ride was there.

Hyde smashed a fist into the head of his cybernetic opponent. He followed up with a quick jab. Blow after blow followed, crushing in the enemy's face. The laughing Irondog sliced at Hyde's neck before taking a chunk out of his armored side.

The steady advance of the security phalanx left Block 9Xers encircled. Their best move would have been to double up on Dante's team and make a run for it. Instead, most of their men turned to meet the new, more numerous threats.

"This is our chance," Dante shouted. "Hyde, I need you to pull back and carry our friend up the ladder. Braelin and Jolo will follow, then Nasreen. I'll cover with Mugoi."

Hyde staggered his opponent with a punch that sent him into a nearby wall. "We've got this. We've got help. Let's finish these *pendejos* off."

A bellowing loudspeaker echoed from all around them. "All combatants are to cease fighting and lay down your arms immediately. You will kneel, face the nearest wall, and place your hands on your head. Deactivate any active combat augmentations. Any resistance may be met with lethal force."

Dante nodded at the ladder. "They're not here to help. Now make an opening and take the woman, damn it."

The 9X Irondog yanked himself out of the crater and roared. He shoved nearby mercenaries out of the way before jogging back into battle. A grinning Hyde snatched up nearby mercs by the necks and brought his arms back. He didn't throw them at the cyborg. Instead, he flung them into their nearby non-augmented friends leaving a confused tangle of limbs.

When the Irondog finally closed in and slashed at him, Hyde turned into the blow, letting the blade sink into a shoulder. He scoffed, grabbed the other man around the waist, and tossed him toward DeFrieze. The heavier body didn't reach the ops leader. Instead, it knocked down clustered mercenaries like old-fashioned bowling pins.

Dante's team moved immediately. He ran toward the ladder,

holding out his arms. The apprentices broke after him. Hyde scooped Tether out of Dante's arms. When the mercs gathered their wits to follow them, Dante greeted the first with a razorfist into his face. The security forces broke through the mercenary formation, turning the mercenaries into prey.

Hyde jumped onto the ladder and scampered to the roof, holding Tether against his body like a baby. The ladder and rungs groaned under the weight of his body. It didn't break away before he hit the roof and rushed toward the open shuttle.

Braelin and Jolo evacuated next. Dante jabbed at a hesitant mercenary who kept checking over his shoulder, concerned about the closing security forces. Mugoi circled his opponent with blinding speed and knocked him to the ground with an elbow into the back.

Advancing security troops captured the mercenaries' focus. Dante grabbed the rungs and hurried to the roof under DeFrieze's baleful glare. He had pointed his shock baton at his escaping target. Security stun poles had left heaps of stunned Block 9X mercenaries all over the street. In another time, when he didn't have a dying woman to worry about, Dante would have enjoyed watching Block 9X getting their asses kicked.

Dante hurried onto the shuttle and dropped into a seat in the back, drawing a deep breath. The Atlantica Central Security Forces had come prepared for a major ground battle. They had not anticipated a waiting shuttle with a skilled pilot. Ambrose pulled away before they could scramble any interceptors.

Hyde laid Tether on the floor. Nasreen knelt behind her with an autoinjector from the shuttle's first aid kit. She placed it against the operative's shoulder and pressed the activator. The injector slid forward with a *click*.

Tether was paler than before. Dante didn't need commentary from Midas to know how bad the situation was.

Hyde looked down at the wounded Firewall operative. "We don't need those losers."

Dante shot out of his seat. "What the hell was all that?"

Hyde stared at him. Disbelief spread slowly across his face like he couldn't comprehend what he heard. "Huh?"

"You started the damned fight when I told you to hold your position." Dante flung his arm toward the deck and the club's general direction. "They weren't coming in hot. You went and started a fight, and they went to full alert mode. You messed up our evac."

"So?" Hyde shrugged. He glanced down at an exposed tube in his side leaking a light blue fluid. "They brought an army. We thinned their ranks for next time. And don't pretend there won't be a *next time*."

"We could have made it to the extraction point without fighting through an army." Dante pointed at Tether. "You spooked them, and they spooked her. If she dies, we kiss any chance of an alliance with Firewall goodbye."

"Fuck Firewall," Hyde sneered. "They're the sloppy bastards who got followed."

Dante couldn't be sure it wasn't his team's fault. Evidence pointed away from that. Block 9X hadn't shown up until after they'd run into Tether. The mercenaries would have been better prepared to deal with the shuttle if they'd known Dante's team would be there.

Dante stared at the autoclamp spread over the bloody stump of Tether's arm. A trail of blood led to the shuttle's hatch. "You, of all people, should know better. You warned me about the big spiders before that shit with Midas. Firewall might be the only allies we can trust to take down this conspiracy."

Smug smiles had replaced earlier looks of concern from Jolo and Braelin. The louder Dante grew, the more they smiled. Mugoi sat in his seat with a cooler, more inscrutable expression but no doubt enjoying Dante going after Hyde as much as the others.

Dante jerked his head at the apprentices. "Don't think it's just him. You all screwed up. Everyone needs to learn to follow my damned orders and stop doing a piss-poor job at multitasking."

"Sir," interrupted Midas, using the voice module so the entire shuttle could hear him.

"What now?" Dante snapped.

"The sensors in the clamp indicate she's experiencing a critical worsening of ventricular fibrillation," the AI reported. "She's likely to experience imminent cardiac arrest if this continues. Breathing is becoming irregular."

Nasreen pulled a small black disc from the first aid kit. She slipped it under Tether's dress onto her chest and tapped the automated defibrillation button on the top. She pulled her hand away.

"Please release your hold on the patient," a low feminine voice declared. "Attempting rhythm restoration. Electrical shock in progress in three, two, one."

Tether's body tensed. Her back arched before she slumped back to the deck.

"Midas?" Dante barked.

"VF unchanged," Midas replied. "No indication of a return to normal rhythms. Please note I can remotely activate the device."

Dante looked at Nasreen. She nodded back. They didn't have much choice. They couldn't land at a hospital for treatment given the situation.

"Do it," Dante ordered.

Tether's body seized with another surge of electricity. The only blessing in the entire situation was she was unconscious. He'd seen far too many wounded Reapers and Marauders interfering with their own first aid with their panicked pain-induced thrashing.

"Functional rhythm restored," Midas reported. "Pulse still low. Breathing shallow."

"I'll take the small victory," Dante replied.

He looked over the rest of his team. Hyde didn't appear to be in pain despite his leaks and the gouges in his artificial body. Cuts, scratches, and bruises covered most of the team. They'd gotten lucky there was only one major injury. "Ambrose, take the long way to the backup safe house. We can't take another fight."

CHAPTER THREE

Tether lay quietly in the safe house bed, pale as before and still unconscious. Even without her injuries, they were shoving enough painkillers and emergency nanobot solutions through the IV that she wouldn't wake up for a while. They'd added more monitoring devices to supplement the rudimentary sensors in the autoclamp. None of it was a substitute for a proper hospital or clinic.

All the violence Nasreen and Dante had experienced through their respective careers had offered a practical hands-on course in field medicine. That knowledge only went so far. While she couldn't speak for Dante, Nasreen had never had to save someone with their arm cut off. Before she'd started working with him, violent encounters marked the failure of her jobs, not successes.

Nasreen stood beside Dante with her arms folded. While not a worst-case scenario, things weren't much better. They'd been so focused on survival and escape that she'd not thought to question the dangerous decision and its ramifications.

She turned to Dante. "I don't know if this was a good idea."

He turned to her. "You think we should have left her to die? That's one surefire way to piss off Firewall."

"They are pissed off right now."

Dante scoffed, "I can't say you're wrong. That doesn't mean we still can't use them. I'm working with Ambrose and Hyde. If I can work with a guy who left me to die and another guy who tried to kill me on more than one occasion, I can work with idiots who like codenames."

A shiver ran up Nasreen's spine. On most days, her old fear of Hyde lay deep in her subconscious. Losing his original body and being humbled to the point of needing her assistance had changed their relationship. Once in a while, the terrifying early minutes of their first encounter bubbled up and reminded her that she was working with a man who'd once been a metal nightmare personified.

"Part of this was Hyde's fault. You were right to chew him out over jumping the gun." Nasreen motioned at Tether. "It was also her fault. She refused to go with us and panicked.

"If she'd moved when we first told her to, we would have made it out of the building without her losing an arm or much of a fight. Now, even if we save her, she still might blame us. Because we brought her here, I think we need to burn this safe house after we finish here."

Dante frowned in consternation. "That seems like an overreaction."

"We can't be too careful when dealing with either the Omega Syndrome or Firewall."

Nasreen didn't blame Dante for what had gone down. His training had assured the team survived the encounter despite the ridiculous odds. A year ago, she wouldn't have been able to maintain discipline against that many killers. A far smaller group of suspicious Reapers had almost killed her Dirtside when she'd first met Dante.

He stared at Tether's wounded arm, not replying for a long

moment. "We both have been in situations where we didn't know who we could trust. We both have had to make split-second decisions. And we both haven't always made the right decisions. That doesn't mean we're idiots who should have been left to die."

"All those premises are true. I'm not so sure about the conclusion." Nasreen pulled out her sphere and entered a quick command, scanning through the results. "No one has tripped the alarms at the other major safe houses, and I haven't used this location in a while. It'd be annoying to lose it, but not fatal to our plans. It's a waste of money. We both have plenty these days."

"No," Dante snapped, looking toward the wall. "It's not a good time. We'll discuss medical upgrades later. Yes, yes, I'm impressed with how much you helped."

Nasreen didn't glance his way. She knew he wasn't talking to her. She'd gotten used to him staring off and having mental conversations with Midas or the more obvious one-sided verbal chats he preferred.

She wouldn't have kept an AI as self-aware and idiosyncratic as Midas. Her implants lacked personalities. She also couldn't doubt how useful Dante's AI had been in their war against SSS and their new desperate struggle against the Omega Syndrome.

That described the entire team. They all had their quirks. Those quirks also made them an effective team far more lethal than their numbers would suggest. She and Dante wouldn't have been able to take down SSS by themselves. The apprentices and Hyde all had their roles, too.

"Things used to be easier when all I cared about was killing one guy." Dante narrowed his eyes.

"One guy?" Nasreen managed a dark chuckle. "You had a whole list of people to kill."

"Sure, but Slaine was at the top of that list." Dante shrugged. "Now things are way more complicated and annoying. I don't know who I'm supposed to be killing. That's why I took the risk to save her and why we need to make sure she survives.

"Firewall knows more about the enemy than we do. I don't care if they don't want to run raids with us. We need their knowledge. We know the Omega Syndrome is watching us. They know by now we used their toy mercs against them. The war's heating up, and we don't have enough troops and intel."

"I know all that." Nasreen sighed. "I'm not saying we don't need their intel, but Hyde's right."

Dante's eyes widened in shock. "That's a sentence I never thought I'd hear from you."

"I'm not saying he didn't screw up. I'm saying he's right that Block 9X showed up for her, not for us, and they were somehow able to trace her to begin with. We have to be careful about what we share with them. They've survived, yes. Are they perfect? Obviously not. They have holes in their operational security."

"Can we be sure it wasn't us?" Dante asked.

"With the route and preparations we took? And the timing?" Nasreen shook her head. "They had plenty of opportunities to set up better and more effectively if it'd been us they were following."

"That makes sense. Wait. What are you bitching about, Midas?" Dante frowned at the bed. Blood stained the sheets. "Why is she still bleeding so much? I was too busy trying to save her life and not die earlier to notice. She's still losing blood."

Nasreen crouched near the autoclamp. She brought out her sphere to interface with the medical device and checked the diagnostic reports. "The wound isn't sealed all the way. The clamp has only slowed the blood loss. I don't know if it's enough.

"With the loss she's suffered and the continued bleeding, she's not stable. We'll need more synthetic pints to offset what she's lost if I'm reading things right." She shook her head. "We don't have enough here."

"How the hell is that happening? Is the clamp faulty?" Dante gritted his teeth. "We need to seal this wound." He shot up. "Damn it. Of course."

"What?" Nasreen frowned. She didn't like being a step behind in a volatile situation.

"It's a Komodo Edge," Dante explained. "Why didn't I think of it sooner? It's so damned obvious."

"What are you talking about? What's a Komodo Edge?"

"Komodo Edge as in Komodo dragon."

Dante's explanation only confused the issue. Nasreen held onto a massive encyclopedia of facts gathered in her years as a freelance spy, including many stored in her AI implants. That didn't help her understand what an extinct Dirtside animal had to do with mercenary weapons.

His lips parted as understanding dawned on his face. "It was named after the old Dirtside animal because of how dangerous their bites were. The gist is the blades have a special fractal edge that makes fixing cut tissue difficult. In some cases, standard autoclamp treatment can make it worse.

"I haven't seen one in years. They're highly illegal and expensive. Even most Reapers don't use them. Not much point in fancy bleeding edges when dealing with Dirtwalkers that you're going to blow away with pulsecore rounds."

"When you have Omega Syndrome money, you can afford the most luxurious forms of cruelty," Nasreen observed.

"Yes. Something like that."

She wasn't worried about saying the name in one of her safe houses. The last year had shaken her confidence at times. Nothing that had happened had convinced her she didn't know how to sweep an area and protect it from surveillance. They'd also said the name plenty of times, and no murder squads with Komodo Edge blades showed up to take their heads or arms off.

Dante stood and clenched his fist. "We need a hospital. Basic first aid isn't going to cut it anymore."

"We can't take a person who *doesn't exist* and is missing an arm to a hospital when Station security and the Omega Syndrome will be looking for her," Nasreen countered.

"She's no good dead. An underground clinic then. They know how to keep their mouths shut. I don't think the spiders have their webs everywhere."

Nasreen shook her head. "We can't risk underground clinics. She's way too identifiable in this condition. We take her for treatment, and we'll be fighting Block 9X again in a clinic surrounded by cyborgs with pulsecores."

Dante glared at the autoclamp. "There's got to be something we can do."

"I've got an idea." Nasreen brought up her sphere before mentally interfacing with a secondary AI implant to bring up old job notes. It'd been a while since she'd needed this type of search. She scanned the information, her eyes darting back and forth until she arrived at a single line, the last words of a dying man.

Nasreen adjusted the clamp settings. The clamp *buzzed* and *whirred*. Tether's arm trembled for far too long before going limp. Nasreen reviewed the readouts. Between past violence and all the times she'd faked being a first responder, she understood most of what she saw.

She rested her hands on the edge of the bed. "Midas, I know you don't have your upgrades yet, but please tell me that worked."

Dante frowned. He didn't do panic in the conventional sense. He got angrier and more focused. He was a good man to have on a woman's side when they were trying to take out a powerful orbital society-wide conspiracy.

"What did you do?" He glanced between the unconscious Tether and his partner. "Did you save her?"

"I can't be sure," Nasreen admitted. "It's a better chance now. There was a job I worked years ago. I was investigating an experimental weapons lab. They were working on a nasty weapon, a bomb based on Atlanticore tech."

Dante's brow lifted. "They were doing this Station-side? Crazy bastards."

"Knowing what I know now, I wonder if the Omega

Syndrome funded the lab." Nasreen shivered. "I didn't understand all the science, but the shrapnel fragments continued moving and growing in the victim after the explosion. It was about maximizing internal damage."

"That's a brutal weapon."

"There was an accident at the lab. During that accident, lab techs got hit by the weapon, and…" Nasreen sighed. "One of them told me about those autoclamp settings before he died. I helped save somebody else before I leaked news of the operation to get it shut down. There was a bullshit coverup about illegal waste disposal."

"At least it got closed down. If it was an Omega Syndrome lab, it would be ironic if something you learned from that job leads us to an alliance with a group that'll help us to take them down."

"That would be funny." Nasreen reached over to push Tether's matted hair off her sweat-soaked brow. "She's sedated until the nanobots can do their work and her body can recover from the initial shock. That should give us time to pick up more fluids and synthetic blood. She's not going to be answering any questions before then.

"I think our best plan is to hand her over to Firewall. I bet they're used to dealing with critical injuries without going to normal facilities. Getting too clever with this will end with her dead."

Dante nodded slowly. "That'll work. Midas, go ahead and buy whatever upgrades you find interesting from catalogs. I want to be ready next time for anything."

Gladly, sir, Midas replied.

The apprentices and Hyde were all waiting when Dante emerged from the bedroom they were using as a makeshift emergency ward. Ambrose was hidden with the shuttle in an unconnected hangar, claiming the vehicle needed maintenance. Dante was happy to keep their mobility advantage secure in a different location.

Everyone gathered had patched their wounds. Hyde had stopped leaking all over and stood beside a wall with his face pinched in anger. Dante didn't have time for his crap. Everyone needed to be ready for what came next. He could deal with Hyde later.

"You look angry." Hyde sneered at Dante. "You going to bitch us out again, *Papi*?"

Dante shook his head. "That's not important right now. We need to figure out where we're going to go from here."

Jolo sat on the edge of the couch. Her torn and bloody clothes were incongruent with her calm demeanor and poise. "This entire situation is bad."

"It's fine," Nasreen announced, emerging from the makeshift medical ward. "Okay. Calling it fine might be too much, but Tether's stable. I know where we can get more medical supplies right away. We won't need to go to a hospital or clinic."

"No. You don't understand." Jolo shook her head. "I'm not talking about that. I'm talking about Firewall. You guys showed up and killed several of their operatives to save us. Now it's going to look like we set them up to kidnap one of their people. They might be ready to track us down and assassinate us."

Braelin nodded his eager agreement. That wasn't surprising. These days it was rare for him to disagree with the other apprentice. She was an attractive woman. Dante couldn't blame him. That also didn't mean he had to feel the same way.

Dante scoffed, "Bullshit. We saved her life. We could have left her there to die."

"We *should have* left her there to die." Hyde stomped over to a chair and sat. The poor piece of furniture *creaked* under his large metal body. "She was the stupid bitch who got her arm cut off. She should have been ready for that shit."

Mugoi spoke next, surprising Nasreen. The cyborg had been so rigid and quiet in the corner that she'd barely noticed him. "As painful as it is for me to admit, he has a point. The Firewall organization is supposed to be full of disciplined operatives ready and willing to give up their lives for the cause. She should have remained calm despite the disruption to the initial plan."

Nasreen shuffled over to an open chair and let her weary body drop into the waiting softness. "One important lesson I learned from years of my previous job is that it doesn't matter what you want the other side to think. The only importance is what they believe.

"Everything remains the same. We need Firewall's help. They also need ours. That means we need to reach an agreement." She gestured at Mugoi. "If they didn't need us, they wouldn't have kidnapped you and tried to kidnap me to recruit us."

Braelin tugged off a loose string at the edge of a jagged slash in his pants. "I ain't saying you're wrong, but if our positions were reversed, I think we'd be ready to go in with pulsecores and plasma cutters."

"Talking about it's not going to solve anything," Dante replied. "We solved the most important problem in keeping this alliance alive." He nodded at the bedroom. "We kept their operative alive. We'll reach out to them using the same encrypted channel we used to set up the meeting and let them know we have her and that she needs medical attention.

"They want to take their toys and go home, that's on them. We'll figure out where to go from there. For now, Mugoi, Nasreen, take care of that." He nodded at Hyde. "I need to talk to you. Follow me."

Hyde snorted, the loudness and implied volume of air impressive. "It beats sitting here listening to everyone piss themselves over a group of loser resistance fighters."

Dante led Hyde into another bedroom and closed the door. "We need to talk about what happened."

"We talked about it. You bitched me out on the shuttle, or did you forget? Ask your AI to recap it for you." Hyde scratched the crusted blood that blended in with the orange of his beard. He'd not bothered to wash off the blood from earlier. "You got something new to say?"

"I wanted to say more when no one's around." Dante squared his shoulders and stepped up to the cyborg. While not a small man, puffing himself up didn't make Dante bigger than Hyde. The cyborg's new body lacked the sheer bulk of the monster form he'd controlled when Dante first met him. That didn't mean his latest body wasn't a killing machine, a fact he'd demonstrated in the recent fight. "I've got one question for you."

"I got lots of answers." Hyde grinned. "One of them is fuck off."

"Do you want to be here?" Dante asked.

Hyde squinted. His grin twitched to a frown. Confusion washed over his face like he couldn't understand the question. "Huh?"

"Do you want to be here?" Dante repeated. "*¿Quieres estar aquí?*" He injected more harshness into his voice. "You've been a great help. I'm not going to deny that. Nasreen won't either. Your being on our team is based on the idea you'll be an asset, not another headache."

Hyde growled and loomed over Dante. "I killed more men than all your little *hijos* combined. You'd be better off if it was just me with you. How the hell am I not an asset?"

"Because we won't survive this if we run off half-cocked at the start of every fight." Dante didn't move when Hyde inched in closer. He locked eyes with the cyborg.

"You want the damned truth? We were desperate before, but your involvement was based on the idea you'd learned a damned lesson after you got yourself blown up in a pointless fight and ripped apart by junkie scrappers. What you didn't learn there, I thought you would have learned as a toy soldier all that time Dirtside. I thought you'd finished being a one-man wrecking crew who doesn't care about who or what he hurts. I thought you were past being a dumb shit."

"You didn't bring me on the team to make tea and sniff flowers, Shale," Hyde snarled. "You're bitching now because I'm too good at bringing the pain?"

"Bring the pain. Yes, you're good at that." Dante laughed. "You're also good at screwing up. You could have gotten us all killed. We won't win against the Omega Syndrome by charging in whenever we see somebody and swinging first without a plan." He jabbed Hyde's armored chest with his finger. "It's the same reason Nasreen and I didn't charge into SSS headquarters on day one. You and his goons would have killed us, and Slaine would have turned you and Ambrose into a fine paste they ejected into low orbit."

Hyde's gaze lowered to Dante's finger. The cyborg could tear it off with ease. Dante made a point of leaving it there for several seconds before lowering his arm. Whatever Hyde once was, whatever terror he'd cultivated, he needed to operate under Dante's command. He wouldn't show Hyde a millisecond of fear.

"The thing is," Dante continued, lowering his voice and stepping back. "I thought you threw out that part of your old life. I thought you wanted to change. Wanting something isn't good enough."

Hyde stepped back. His angry scowl flattened to a pained grimace. "*Madre de Dios, Papi.*" He slapped a hard hand on his chest with a loud *thud.* "I'm made of metal, but I'm not a computer. I can't just change things like deleting a file."

"Maybe not, but I need to be able to count on you. If you're a liability, I don't need you around me, and I certainly don't need you around these kids."

Hyde snickered. "I bet only one of them is younger than you. Don't let the pretty face on that metal job trick you."

"Maybe." Dante shrugged. "They are my responsibility all the same. You said it yourself. You called them my *hijos*."

"Yeah. I suppose I did."

"The point is you pull this shit again, and I'll magnetize your metallic ass, stick you on a rocket, and fire it Dirtside." Dante's nostrils flared. "Don't think I'm joking."

Hyde rolled his eyes. "Whatever. Don't stroke out on all that pompousness. All right. I hear you, Shale."

Dante turned toward the door. "I hope so. Don't put me in a place where I don't have a choice." He opened the door. "Try and not get us killed while we wait for Firewall to respond."

<hr>

They'd expected to wait a while for a response, maybe even hours. The reply came quickly and was summarized by Mugoi efficiently to the team gathered in the living room.

"They'll take custody of their operative," the cyborg reported. "They've stressed she needs to be fully stabilized prior to transport. They didn't give any details as to why."

Dante frowned. "They're planning to come in fast and leave as fast. Either because they don't trust us, or they're worried about another ambush." He looked at Nasreen. "What do you think?"

"We need more supplies. On top of what I was suggesting before. We have them in the infirmary at headquarters."

Braelin let out a nervous chuckle. "I ain't trying to be a little bitch here, but won't the Voices be watching our place? That's why we're here."

Dante weighed the risks mentally before speaking. "It's possible." He nodded at Hyde. "But these big spiders like to hide far on the edge of their web, which is why I didn't know they existed until a year ago, and he only barely did.

"Their pet mercenary company made a big public mess and got Station security involved. The last thing they need now is another major public confrontation. I think they haven't had time to rally. We've got a window."

Nasreen gave him a pitying look. "Or they might decide they'd rather cut their losses with a big final display."

"These people are powerful. They're not all-powerful." Dante clenched his hand into a raised fist. "All-powerful organizations don't hide, and they don't let people like us build up with time."

"They might think they can turn us," Nasreen answered. "Don't mistake a lack of action for fear."

"We'll make sure they feel the same way." Dante grinned. "They have far more dead and injured after that last fight. We also don't have to waste time getting our people out of detention.

"Now is the time to make a move. We'll send word to Firewall that we'll hand over their operative in a few hours. We don't have time to mess around with getting supplies from anyone not smart enough to keep their mouth shut.

"For now, go to HQ and grab the supplies. You can take the scenic route and still get there and back in an hour." He gestured at Jolo and Mugoi. "Take those two for backup."

Nasreen arched a brow. "You think they'll come after us?"

"I don't know. We don't have many options. I'm going with the one that doesn't end with us at war with two groups."

"This could end badly."

Dante wouldn't admit how much worry and confusion swirled around everything related to the current situation. Going after SSS was easier. He relied on his hatred and bitterness to fuel his revenge against Cormac Slaine and his old crew. The war against the Omega Syndrome was more abstract, a fight against a vague enemy of unknown scope and identity, one that might not come to him if he kept his nose down and out of their business.

That didn't stop him. In the end, they deserved his vengeance as much as SSS. Cormac Slaine's activities had been at their behest. The betrayal and stranding Dirtside could be linked straight to the spiders who'd hijacked Midas last year.

"I don't know," Dante repeated. "It doesn't hurt to be careful. We got surprised once. We won't let it happen a second time. Maintain radio silence until you get back. I'm not convinced they can hack all our comms. That doesn't mean it'd hurt to be careful."

CHAPTER FOUR

When they'd first set up their headquarters, Dante had argued against a place hidden in a dark corner of the Station. He reasoned they weren't faking their identities anymore, so why did they need to hide? Nasreen had agreed at the time and didn't regret their headquarters being nestled in a business direct.

After circling the building several times, they parked the hovercar around the corner from HQ, a converted office building. Nasreen interfaced her sphere with the HQ systems and checked the building's various security systems while Jolo and Mugoi scanned their surroundings for anything suspicious.

Finally, Nasreen announced, "I didn't find any obvious signs of spoofing or dead zones. There's no signal disruption or scrambling, and nothing on the cameras. It's not a guarantee, but I think it's as good as we're going to get."

Mugoi sardonically added, "These guys are smooth. They could hack us, and we'd never know." Jolo and Nasreen sadly nodded in agreement.

With a full armory, sleeping quarters for the entire team, and a real infirmary among other rooms, the headquarters was a proper base for the team. They'd avoided a straight retreat to their base to avoid the enemy. Being forced there again only fueled the melancholy gnawing at Nasreen's calm.

Time was as much their enemy as the Omega Syndrome. They needed the supplies to save Tether.

Their crusade against the Omega Syndrome was important. It was more important than what they'd accomplished against SSS and Slaine. The war had moved well past what she'd become involved in as a freelance spy.

She never doubted her new cause. That didn't stop the weight of their task from crushing her. For a year, she'd held her breath waiting for the secret masters to make a move, all the while continuing her Marauder training. Now they were caught between the Omega Syndrome and their paranoid enemies, Firewall.

Discovering the new faction was supposed to lead them to new resources and strategies against their ultimate target. Now everything was a bloody mess.

Nasreen tucked her sphere back into her pocket. "Let's go." She motioned for the apprentices to follow. "The less time we spend inside the better. Nobody's here yet. That doesn't mean they aren't coming."

Jolo followed Nasreen to the front door. "Don't you think we'd be safer if we fortified ourselves here? Knowing where we are doesn't guarantee victory when we're more prepared. Surely, they can't try another bold gambit without attracting too much attention."

Mugoi trailed five feet from the women. The cyborg kept quiet, its eyes flicking back and forth seeking trouble.

"We've seen how far these people will go," Nasreen replied. "Cautious people don't send armies of mercenaries to surround crowded clubs. They also don't have said mercenaries cut a woman's arm off in public. Sitting here holed up could end up with us getting bombed."

She opened the door and gestured for the other two to enter.

"Until we've taken care of our little Voices problem and squared things off with their enemies, it's best to keep a low profile."

On one level, she hated not using the organization's real name. She remained unconvinced the Omega Syndrome's reach extended as far as Tether believed. Despite that, being more cautious in public settings didn't cost her anything.

Once the apprentices were inside, Nasreen closed the door and performed a quick sweep of the front lobby, focusing on the position of what appeared to be minor bits of decoration—a jade figurine, a painting, and other such bric-a-brac. They were all positioned near backup surveillance gear. None of her tripwires were disturbed. It was a good start to convincing her a horde of killers hadn't camped out in their closets.

"Jolo, you gather the medical supplies," Nasreen ordered. "Mugoi, go to the armory and grab as many of the emergency safe house packs stored there as you can carry. Be back here in five minutes, and we'll head back to the hovercar. Shout if you need help."

"Understood," Jolo replied. She glanced out a front window before jogging away.

Mugoi disappeared without further comment. Nasreen tried to game out the scenarios in her head. She was used to that from her solo work. Despite all her time with Dante and the apprentices, her old habits were hard to erase. Thinking about a team meant trusting other people, which introduced difficult variables into any encounter.

It wasn't that she wanted to work alone. Neither she nor Dante could have accomplished what they did by themselves. That didn't stop a small part of her from whispering in the back of her mind about other people messing things up.

As well-trained as the apprentices were, they still made mistakes. The same was true of her and Dante. Anyone who planned a mission and assumed flawless execution set themselves up for disappointment.

Nasreen peered out the front window. Foot and vehicle traffic were light outside the headquarters, with a single hover car zooming past and one suited man having a heated call judging by his red face and gestures. No one else was in the area.

She expected as much. When she and Dante scouted the location, they'd picked a place in a less busy part of the neighborhood. Not only did the choice minimize the risk of collateral damage in dangerous situations, but the lower traffic levels also made it easier to spot suspicious individuals and vehicles approaching the building.

"Let's get a move on," she shouted.

"I'm almost done," Mugoi yelled.

"Me, too," Jolo added.

The longest few minutes of Nasreen's life since her first terrifying encounter with Hyde passed in strained silence. Her heart pounded in her chest. The first wave of relief accompanied Jolo as she jogged into the lobby with a full backpack over her shoulders. Mugoi arrived not soon after, holding two stuffed duffel bags.

After checking outside and seeing no one, Nasreen opened the front door and stepped out of the building. "Not everything today has to be a complete mess."

They hadn't made it far down the street when Nasreen slowed, sliding her eyes to the side. A large group of men and women wandered down the street not far from Nasreen and the others. Their casual choice of clothes fit in with the fashions of Atlantica Central Station if a bit on the baggier side. That wasn't what made them stand out, despite it not being a residential neighborhood. Something else did—their total silence.

That many people clustered together had a hard time walking without someone speaking about something. One of Nasreen's earliest lessons as a spy was how so many people abhorred silence. Every added person made it that much harder. A good way to get information was to pace her conversation and let targets fill in the gaps.

Nasreen cleared her throat and murmured, "They don't seem in a hurry. I assume they have another team circling to cut us off, probably near the hovercar."

"Perhaps we should make a run for HQ and the armory," Jolo replied. "They brought cyborgs last time."

"It's fortunate you brought yours, then." Mugoi offered a tight smile.

Nasreen stopped and looked back at the front of the headquarters. She didn't know who they were dealing with. It could be Block 9X, Firewall, or another group entirely. The only thing she was sure of was the hard-faced men and women behind them weren't on a walking tour of Atlantica Central Station's business district.

That brief consideration ended as a second group stepped out of an alley in front of them, cutting off their escape route. The new arrivals' bright, fashionably casual clothes might as well have been uniforms. The men and women all wore the same basic outfits with a color or pattern variation here and there, as if they'd gone to a store and purchased them in bulk. Whoever these people were, they needed better training on blending in and proper disguise techniques. There was such a thing as standing out by trying too hard not to.

"Okay, Jolo, you've got a point." Nasreen reached into her pocket to grab her dart launcher. "The car's farther away. We head back to our armory."

Mugoi tossed the bags to the ground. It unzipped one and grabbed a shock baton. It tossed it to Jolo before pulling out another. "That's not as many as at the club."

Nasreen retorted, "It's more than enough to be trouble."

"You'll need to prove all those enhancements are worth it, Mugoi." Jolo slipped the backpack to the ground and raised her baton. Her careful gaze flittered between the groups as she calculated the locations and sizes of the different opponents.

"Head to the HQ on my mark," ordered Nasreen. "Just fight through them, and we'll lock them out. We can at least arm up better until they break in."

The two painfully casual groups picked up the pace. They were jogging now, not running, with half of them reaching into pockets or jackets. The team was out of time. Nasreen had long since lost any hope a tour group had headed down the wrong street.

"Go!" Nasreen shouted. She sprinted toward headquarters, trusting Jolo and Mugoi to follow her.

The group behind slowed as if unsure. The men and women in front hadn't drawn any weapons, although their simultaneous desire to stick their hands in their pockets screamed trouble. The hesitation offered a chance. Nasreen and the others could break through if they pressed their attack.

Something was wrong. Nasreen's instincts screamed it at her, overriding the careful analysis. She slowed to a jog and looked over her shoulder, finally understanding what her instincts were telling her. She'd only heard one set of hard footsteps close behind her during the move.

Jolo skidded to a halt, her eyes widening. She followed Nasreen's gaze to Mugoi. The cyborg hadn't moved from its initial position. It stood, staring off in the distance, the shock baton in hand but rigid as a statue.

"Come on," Nasreen shouted. She had no idea what was going on. With a couple of drinks in her, she might admit to worrying about the apprentices freezing when faced with overwhelming odds. Having fought with them in those same circumstances, she never thought she'd see it, especially from Mugoi. They'd bravely battled together earlier without trouble.

The groups on either side continued their advances and gave up on hiding. They yanked weapons out of their pockets or from underneath jackets. While most pulled out knives, others slipped on razorfists and extended the blades. Nasreen had hoped for shock batons.

Their team problem became a serious challenge as one man reached under his long coat and drew a snap gun. Not a true firearm, the still illegal diminutive mix of crossbow and pistol lacked their dangerous dome-penetrating ability. This made them a good sidearm when aboard a Station. Their variety of ammo types made them an unpredictable threat.

All hesitation gone, both street groups surged forward. They raised their weapons and moved to surround the team with murder in their eyes.

Nasreen and the apprentices shifted position, forming a rough triangle with coverage on both sides. They needed to thin the opposition before a breakthrough without leaving their flanks exposed. She didn't have time to change the plan. The apprentices would have to follow her lead depending on how the battle unfolded.

With a quick, practiced movement, the man with the snap gun loaded a blue-tipped round. Blue typically marked electrical disruption. They lacked the area effect of EMPs but demonstrated great utility against vehicles. Nasreen didn't understand why until the man pointed his snap gun at Mugoi.

Ignoring the tumult, Nasreen lifted her dart launcher and fired a tranq dart at the man. A scowling woman with a knife threw herself in front of the projectile. She grunted with the impact before falling forward.

The man narrowed his eyes and fired his dangerous round. Nasreen jumped in front of Mugoi, still unsure why the cyborg was frozen in place, and worried the round might fry enough of his internal components to kill him.

The round clipped her arm and tore the sleeve. A bright arc shot from the electrified head. Her muscles spasmed, and she fell hard onto her side. The pain from the shock distracted her from the pain of the fall as her head slammed hard against the street. Darkness crept toward the edges of her vision as Jolo rushed to her side. With a final moan, Nasreen passed out.

Standing near her fallen and frozen friends, Jolo twisted back and forth brandishing her shock baton, unsure of how they'd been overwhelmed so quickly when they'd been ready. The moment Nasreen hit the ground, the two groups stopped running. They spread out to surround her, deadly weapons ready. No one moved closer.

"Get out of the way," the man with the snap gun said, motioning with his weapon before pointing it at Nasreen. "We're taking her. If you don't want to get hurt, you'll back off. We'll leave you and your metal friend here. We only want her. Don't resist if you want to keep breathing."

Jolo gritted her teeth. Whoever they were, they had to know how well she could fight. Nasreen had only gotten hit because she was trying to cover Mugoi. Jolo would make these men pay if they tried to take Nasreen.

Dante and Nasreen had been willing to put their lives on the line to rescue Jolo and the others. She wouldn't turn her back on them now because the odds weren't in her favor.

If she stalled long enough, somebody else might come along. After the debacle at the club, Station security would be on alert. All she needed to do was wait until they arrived.

"You're not taking her without casualties," Jolo declared, tightening her grip around the handle of her baton. "That woman has saved my life more than once. She's a mentor. She's a friend. You can't expect me to leave a friend to a mob of armed rabble."

The man frowned. "You can't win. You must understand that. Whatever your relationship with her, you'll be throwing your life away if you try to stop us." He motioned for two of his men to advance. "Pick up the woman. This one's bluffing."

A wide swing from Jolo forced the men back. They growled and shook their knives without trying to move forward again. She jabbed the baton at them.

"Enough," shouted a familiar voice from behind.

Jolo chanced a look that way. Her eyes widened. "Lock!"

She recognized the tall, well-built man holding another snap gun. He had dark hair except for the salt and pepper in his beard. She hadn't spoken to him much, but they'd held a couple of conversations when Firewall had taken her.

Bile rose in the back of Jolo's throat. She didn't lower her weapon as her eyes darted side to side. The two groups of heavily armed men and women out for blood weren't more Block 9X mercenaries. They were Firewall.

"There's been a misunderstanding," Jolo said. She could salvage this. Firewall wanted the same thing they did.

"A misunderstanding?" Lock scoffed. "There's been too many of those with your bosses. We're not going to blame you for their mistakes or your resistance during your encounter with our recruitment team. This time it's different. You know who we are and what we represent. Every one of us you hurt helps the enemy."

"We saved your operative." Jolo's breathing quickened. "We came here to get medical supplies to stabilize her."

"I don't have time to debate this with you," Lock replied. "I'm going to give you ten seconds to step back and drop your weapon. We're taking her. I don't want to hurt you, but we'll go through you if we must."

Jolo shook her head. "I can't do that. I won't do that. We're on your side. She's on your side."

"If you're on our side, then you'll step aside. Five seconds."

Jolo drew a deep breath and widened her stance. She shifted

her focus from Lock to the men closer to her. Engage and delay. This would be far easier with help.

"Mugoi, what the hell are you doing?" she shouted. "I need your help. Snap out of it."

The cyborg remained frozen. The only thing convincing her he hadn't died was that he hadn't fallen over.

Lock cut through the air with his hand. "Time's up. Take the target."

A Firewall operative with a razorfist charged Jolo. She ducked his stab and slammed her knee into his crotch, leaving her shock baton free to crack across the skull of a blade-wielding female operative. Both victims dropped to the ground groaning and twitching.

Three men charged Jolo from different sides. She rushed toward the closest with a razorfist. A wide swing nailed him in the side with a satisfying *crunch* and took him down. Fire erupted in her shoulder as a woman sliced with her knife. Trying to ignore the wound, Jolo snapped a kick into the woman's stomach and launched her into another operative.

Before she had time to savor her blow, her earlier pain blossomed into agony. Jolo screamed and stumbled backward, almost tripping over the unconscious Nasreen. In the melee, she'd not spotted Lock firing his snap gun into her wounded shoulder. The shaft of the round stuck out. The head was embedded deep in her muscle. Her wound throbbed in time with her heart.

Her vision swam. She lifted her baton. She had to fight through the pain. Nasreen needed her.

Sneering, the woman Jolo had kicked charged forward, the knife level and braced with the other hand. It was like it was happening to someone else. The woman moved closer and closer. At the last minute, Jolo jabbed her shock baton toward the woman's face.

Her attacker jerked her head to the side. Jolo missed by

inches. Before she could think to swing the baton in the other direction, new pain exploded in her chest.

She blinked and looked down. The Firewall operative had shoved a knife into her. Heaviness spread through her body. She coughed up blood. A sharp, stabbing pain accompanied each breath. Her fingers loosened, and the baton clattered to the ground. Her attacker yanked the blade out and let Jolo fall onto the hard street.

Lock sighed. "Damn it. I didn't want it to go down like that."

Jolo's would-be killer shrugged. "The bitch wouldn't step aside. Payback for what her friends did."

"We don't need more enemies." Lock sighed again and shook his head. "Get the target. We've wasted enough time here as it is."

Now free of resistance, two Firewall operatives walked over to Nasreen and picked her up. They didn't spare another glance for the woman bleeding out on the street as they carried Nasreen away.

Mugoi's head moved in short, abrupt twitches. Its hands tightened and spread out in a jerking, irregular motion.

"Please," Jolo whispered. "Mugoi, do something."

She tried to lift her head and failed. Searing pain accompanied each breath.

The outside world became an unfocused haze. Shadows moved in front of Jolo, becoming a dark wall, then receding into the distance. The vague outline of a man carrying Nasreen over his shoulder became clear before Jolo lost it again.

She'd failed. Firewall had killed her, and she'd not even traded her life to save Nasreen.

Someone moved over her, saying something. Jolo managed a soft moan. It took all her concentration to keep her eyes open. The carnival of agony in her chest lessened, along with the pressure. Each breath still hurt, but now she felt like she wasn't slowly suffocating. Her vision cleared slowly.

A beautiful androgynous face hovered over her framed by light. That proved it. She was dead and staring at an angel.

Jolo blinked a couple of times. It wasn't an angel. "Mugoi."

The cyborg cradled her head. "I've applied first aid and stabilized your condition. You're not going to die."

"Why didn't you help?" Jolo whispered. "We needed you."

"I couldn't move," Mugoi replied.

"They didn't use an EMP. They hadn't fired yet. Nasreen took the snap gun round. You didn't move. You didn't help."

Mugoi looked away. For the first time since she'd met the cyborg, true shame covered its face. "I don't know what happened."

"Nasreen's gone." Jolo coughed. That brought on more spasms and worse coughing with more pain. "I couldn't stop her because you didn't help me."

Mugoi stood. "If they wanted to kill her, they would have done it here."

"Are you saying that for my benefit or yours?" Jolo groaned and hacked again. More stabbing pain shot through her chest.

"Rest for now," Mugoi replied. "I'm taking you back to the safe house." He rushed over to grab the bag with the medical supplies. "You will survive. Think like the captain. If you survive, you can always get revenge."

CHAPTER FIVE

The security cameras revealed the bloodied Jolo being carried by Mugoi long before they arrived at the door. Besides its wounded comrade, Mugoi had a full backpack strapped to his back. Dante waited, staring at the feed and wondering where Nasreen was. His jaw tightened with each passing moment she didn't appear. He didn't want to face the implication.

"Clear out a bed," he shouted at Hyde, pointing to an empty bedroom. "Damn it. We should have done this the long way."

Braelin paced near the front door, trembling with barely concealed worry and rage. He clenched his hands into fists at his side. "I'm going to kill all those bastards. They're going to pay. I'll rip their heads off with my two hands."

Dante opened the door for Mugoi. The cyborg slipped gracefully through with Jolo in his arms and headed toward the open bedroom without comment. An uncharacteristically bland-faced Hyde stepped aside and let Mugoi lay Jolo on the bed. Her eyes were closed. Her chest rose and fell. They could be grateful for small victories.

Mugoi slipped the backpack off its shoulders and dropped to one knee. He opened the backpack and rummaged around until he found a smart bandage and offered it to Dante. "I stabilized her. Knife wound to the torso. It was a non-cybernetic enemy. There was no evidence of enhancements to the blade."

Dante took the bandage. He knelt by the bed and ran his finger over the bandage present. A blue outline appeared around it before he gently pulled it off. Blood seeped from the deep wound, pulling a grimace from him. Mugoi retrieved a first aid kit and popped it open. He held up a small nanowound sponge.

"Midas, interface with the bandage and give me vitals visually," Dante ordered. "Keep quiet otherwise. I need to concentrate on this."

Dangerously low numbers appeared in green near the edge of his vision. All the medical concerns with Tether had magnified. This wasn't an operative from a group they were trying to convince to join them. This was one of his people, his apprentice. He needed to make the hard call about which would be more dangerous, treating her at the safe house with their limited supplies and equipment or risking a hospital where one corrupt nurse could kill her without him ever knowing.

Pressing the sponge down, Dante held his breath. The bottom soaked up the red, the color flowing away toward the top. He applied nanospray, then a new smart bandage. Mugoi's first aid had proven vital since the blade had penetrated and collapsed a lung. The lack of froth in the wound confirmed that Mugoi had administered an initial nanospray treatment. Jolo wasn't in immediate danger of dying.

In theory, the nanobots would further stabilize the surface wound and the lung until they could get her real treatment. Emergency nanobots could be fickle. Dante had seen plenty of people die from treatable wounds in the field.

"Hey," Braelin called, red-faced and beckoning. "Mugoi, I want to talk to you."

Dante nodded at the door. "I've got this. Midas, initiate treatment plan B-2. We need to space out the nano injections. It'll help with the absorption."

He glanced at Mugoi. "Your first aid saved her, but I think it wasn't enough to stop the wounds from worsening on the trip over here. She's not going to die, but we could have prepared better."

"I didn't know if I should try to contact you," Mugoi replied in the same quiet monotone as before. "I thought that risked further—"

"I'll worry about that later," Dante interrupted. "Like I told Midas, I need to concentrate on this. Go figure things out with Klement."

As badly as he wanted to know where Nasreen was, Dante assumed that Mugoi had done what it could to save them both. If Nasreen wasn't there and he wasn't talking about her, there was nothing they could do right away. For now, he could concentrate on the woman lying in front of him.

Mugoi stood with an unusual halting and clumsy feel to the movement. It stared at Jolo before walking out of the bedroom, brushing the dried blood on its arm.

Braelin stomped toward Mugoi and squared his shoulders. His breath tickled the cyborg's face as he spoke with a low growl. "You should have called for help."

"We needed to maintain radio silence." Mugoi's shrug was languid, almost casual. "Getting here was more important. It wouldn't have mattered anyway. It was over too quickly for rein-forcements to matter."

Braelin looked Mugoi up and down with a sneer. "You don't look so messed up. I ain't sure you look worse than you did when you left. You mind explaining what happened that Nasreen's gone and Jolo's stabbed, but you're okay?"

"We were... There was an ambush when we left the building. Nasreen and Jolo did their best, given the situation and the numbers. The performances were impressive. Defeat was inevitable."

Braelin's nostrils flared. "*They* did their best."

"Yes, they did." A sliver of emotion colored Mugoi's voice.

"What about you?" growled Braelin. "Look me in the eye, and tell me you did your damned best."

"I…" Mugoi looked away. "They did their best. That's what's important."

"You didn't answer my question." Braelin shoved Mugoi, barely moving the cyborg. "What about you, huh? What about you?"

Mugoi offered Braelin a placid expression and matched it with a cold, detached tone, somehow more removed than the monotone from earlier. "The details are unimportant. We need to focus on what's right in fron—"

"Jolo and Nasreen are unimportant?" Braelin shouted. "Is that what you're saying, you metal son of a bitch? 'Cause it sounds to me like you're saying you didn't fight. That's why you're talking like that, ain't it?"

He motioned toward Jolo through the door. "If we wake her up and ask her, what's she going to tell us? She's going to say you didn't fight. I'd bet my cut from all future jobs on it."

Mugoi narrowed its eyes. "Being emotional won't help this situation, Klement. The most important thing is to keep calm and plan our next move."

"You waste of scrap metal," Braelin yelled. "You didn't fight, did you?"

Dante gritted his teeth, trying to push the conversation to the back of his mind while he shoved an autoinjector into Jolo's arm. Something was off about the entire situation. He didn't believe Mugoi had betrayed them while leaving Jolo alive. Still, everything about the cyborg's weird body language, lack of new damage, and roundabout way of speaking screamed it was hiding something.

Braelin spat in Mugoi's face. His voice grew louder with each word. "You cowardly fake piece of shit. I always thought all the competition crap was you being an arrogant bastard. I never thought you didn't have our backs.

"What is it? They offer you a deal? Step aside, and you can live? Or what, or are you freaked out and think they're going to hack you, so you chickened out?"

Mugoi snorted. "You need to calm down and listen to me. You don't und—"

"I understand Jolo's over there clinging to life," Braelin yelled. "And I don't see Nasreen anywhere. You know what that means? It means you left her to die on the street like a dog. It's all about you, in the end, ain't it? Who cares if there's a little collateral damage in the end, as long as the great, powerful Mugoi gets to strut its stuff."

Mugoi glared at Braelin, moving its face so close to Braelin that their noses almost touched. "I suggest you go into another room and calm down, Klement, before you say something you regret, or I do something I regret."

Braelin sneered. "I'll never regret speaking the truth. You are the last person who should be telling me about regrets, you damned coward."

"Then why don't you let me explain what happened instead of shouting like a maniac?"

"Did you fight during the ambush?" Braelin asked. "That's all that matters. Yes or damned no?"

"I—"

Braelin shoved Mugoi again. "You're a cowardly pile that should have been recycled years ago."

"Hyde," Dante shouted. "Separate them until I finish with this."

"You heard *Papi*." Hyde sounded bored as he stepped out of the corner of the room and strolled toward Mugoi and Braelin.

"Sitting around here bitching like women isn't going to help anyone."

Mugoi scoffed at Braelin and ignored Hyde. "If you were there, you'd both be dead. I saved her. You should be grateful."

Braelin chuckled. "Is that right?" He shrugged. "I'm the only one in this room without fancy hardware. Maybe you're right. You're a damned hero, and I should be kissing your metal ass."

He spun and smashed his fist into Mugoi's face. The cyborg flew backward, crashed into the wall, and left a deep dent. He grimaced and shook his bleeding fist. The punch had split his skin. "Or maybe you're wrong.'

"I've waited a long time for this." Mugoi leapt from the wall toward Braelin.

Hyde stepped between the apprentices, holding up his hand. "I'd love to see you two fools kick each other's asses another time. Break it up, or I'll break you."

Mugoi backed away, its gaze cool. "He's not worth it."

Braelin charged, ducking under Hyde's arm before jumping feet-first. He dropkicked Mugoi in the chest. The blow sent the other apprentice flying into a nearby table and chair. The furniture tipped over with a resounding *thud*.

Mugoi regained its feet. This wasn't a street or a Dirtside ruin. This was the living room of a modestly sized safe house. Braelin barely had time to react before Mugoi's punch launched him to create a new dent in a different wall. He lunged for the downed man. Hyde's quick grab froze him in place.

"Hey," Hyde shouted. "I told you to stop. Teamwork and all that shit. Kum-bah-fucking-ya. I guess you two needed a big lecture, too."

Mugoi twisted out of his grip. His lightning kick pushed Hyde back without much damage.

Braelin took advantage of Mugoi's distraction to vault over the couch and tackle the cyborg. He wrapped an arm around its throat and pounded its head with his bloodied hand. Mugoi grabbed his side, spun, and hurled him toward the front door.

"Yeah. Let's do this shit." Hyde's mouth twitched into a feral grin. "I'm going to enjoy pounding sense into you *pendejos.*"

Dante needed to stop the brawl. He also needed to ensure Jolo was stable. The damned nanobots weren't sealing the wounds as effectively as expected. At a minimum, he needed to verify lung integrity. He ignored the *clanging* and yells behind him as he sprayed more nanobots into the wound.

Hyde charged Mugoi and jabbed at him. Metal fists *clanged* against metal bodies as Mugoi landed a flurry of hits. A powerful punch from Hyde caught his opponent on the side, sending Mugoi spinning from the force of the blow. It righted itself and sprinted toward Hyde with its eyes narrowed in grim determination.

It was a battle of legend, the beautiful androgynous Mugoi facing off against a monster of a man named after the literal embodiment of a man's dark side, a violent Beauty versus the Beast.

A grinning Hyde raised his fist, ready to meet the charge. Mugoi dropped low and slid past to jab the backs of Hyde's knees. The larger cyborg grunted and stumbled. Mugoi sprang using one arm and spun into a wide kick that knocked Hyde down.

Braelin bellowed at the top of his lungs. Blood ran down the back of his head as he charged Mugoi for a tackle from behind. The loud warning alerted Mugoi, who twisted and grabbed Braelin. The cyborg pivoted, using the other apprentice's momentum to toss him away again.

Braelin's shoulder crashed into a wall with a loud *crunch.* He cried out in pain and fell to the floor, clutching his shoulder. "Shit. That one hurt."

Sir, Miss Neburu's vitals are stabilizing, Midas informed Dante. *There are sufficient nanobots present. It's now a matter of repurposing the deployed bots and reinforcing the primary sectors of concern. I can handle it from here. Might I recommend that you prevent the need for additional major first aid administration?*

Dante administered one last spray and applied the smart bandage before standing. He stomped out of the bedroom and into the living room. Braelin groaned from the floor while Hyde and Mugoi circled each other.

"Enough!" Dante shouted. "You damned idiots. What do you think I was doing in there, picking my damned nose? I was trying to stabilize your team member who got stabbed, and you're in here throwing each other around the damned building and trying to get Station security called on us."

Hyde shrugged. He looked like he was going for an innocent expression. Instead, his smug smirk was infuriating. "He started it. I was finishing it."

Braelin managed to get to his knees, grimacing in pain. His left arm dangled loosely below the shoulder. With a loud agonized groan, he stood, his arm swaying. "Yeah. That shit hurts."

Mugoi looked away from Dante, the wall suddenly interesting. "I was defending myself."

Dante glared at him. They were lucky he didn't have EMPs to toss at them both. "That's a fancier way of saying, 'He started it.' You're supposed to be professionals, not idiot gang members trying to one-up each other." He pointed at Braelin's arm. "Hyde, go get him in a brace and osteo-repair tablets."

Clutching his arm, Braelin shook his head. "I don't need help from either of those two metal bastards," he snarled. "I can handle this."

"Consider it a damned order," Dante replied. "Refuse it, and I'll break your other arm and your nose for good measure." He glared at Braelin. "You want to help Jolo? You want revenge? It's going to be hard to do it with a broken arm."

He scrubbed a hand down his face. "I can't believe you three.

We've got wounded and missing people, and you're fighting each other after we finished a major fight not long ago.

"I don't care how badass you think you are. You're not going to survive long without someone having your back. Right now, the people in this safe house should be your best friends because they're the only ones who understand how dangerous our enemies are."

"But Jolo," Braelin offered through gritted teeth. "She's dying. He got her killed."

"She's stable." Dante motioned at Mugoi. "If he hadn't brought her back right away, she'd be dead." He kicked over a chair.

"I'm not going to say this shit again because I'm getting tired of how many times I've had to repeat it. If you don't want to work together, get the hell out. Good luck when the Omega Syndrome comes for you because I'm not going to risk my life for damned morons who want to spend more time fighting one another than the people we're supposed to be taking down."

He bared his teeth at Braelin. "Now, go with Hyde. We're turning all these bedrooms into hospital rooms. We might as well fill them all up. Come back out here when you're calmer and aren't going to be a dumbass. Hopefully, I won't have died of old age by then."

Hyde failed to keep his snicker under his breath as he headed toward the kitchen to grab the supplies. Braelin's angry gaze fixed on Mugoi before he shuffled toward the bedroom trying to hold his swollen arm that swung loosely with each step. Neither he nor Hyde said anything until they retreated into the bedroom and closed the door.

Mugoi folded its arms and sat on the edge of the couch with a defiant expression. The cyborg watched Dante without saying anything. He moved to stand in front of his apprentice.

"Midas, how is she doing?" Dante asked. "She still okay?"

"She is stable," he answered aloud for Mugoi's benefit. "There's no evidence her life is in immediate threat."

Dante looked down at Mugoi. "I've got a ton of questions." He kept his voice calm. "You tell me what happened, and we'll go from there."

Mugoi laid out the story in detail from their arrival to the ambush and his inability to move during the fight. "Nasreen saved me. My only regret is I didn't save her. I wasn't able to move until they retreated. It was beyond frustrating. I knew what was happening, but my body betrayed me."

After looming over Mugoi for the entire story, Dante found a nearby chair to fall into. Every muscle in his body ached since his adrenaline had finally run out. "Firewall did this?"

He shook his head. "It makes no sense. Are they trying to make us their enemy after we saved one of their people? What are they thinking?"

"No," came a weak voice from a bedroom. It was Tether.

Dante stood and nodded at Mugoi. They both hurried into the room. Still on her back and with the clamp in place, Tether hadn't shifted or regained much color. She managed to turn her head to look at Dante.

Tether's voice barely rose above a whisper. "We can't trust you. I still don't know if I trust you. That means the others don't trust you, including Lock."

"You're kidding me?" Dante walked over to the edge of her bed. He tried not to yell despite his pounding heart and the fire in his face.

"We saved your life after you made a dumb move. If you'd come with us when I asked you to, you'd still have your arm, and we would have been able to get out of there without having to fight Block 9X."

"How do I know you didn't set me up for an ambush?" Tether

managed impressive defiance despite being on her back, looking pale as a ghost, and missing half her arm.

Dante could respect her stubbornness. That didn't make it any less annoying in that situation.

"Because if we wanted you dead, we would have left you there to the tender mercies of Block 9X or killed you ourselves when you were distracted." Dante snorted. "I don't have time to prove shit to you right now. I only want you to answer one question. Are they going to kill Nasreen?"

Tether carefully shook her head. "They would have done it there if that was the mission. It sounds like they took her in retaliation for what happened to me and to make sure they have a bargaining chip."

Dante leaned until he was right over her. "I'm willing to take on the Omega Syndrome. They have more power than Firewall."

"What's your point?" Tether asked.

"Anything happens to Nasreen, I'll add you to the list of assholes I have vendettas against." Dante straightened. "Ask Hyde and Cormac Slaine how far I'm willing to go to satisfy my vendettas. I'm thorough."

"We know how far you're willing to go. It's why we went after your people to begin with." Tether closed her eyes. "You're the one who killed our people first. You can't blame us for not trusting you."

"Are you serious right now?" Dante demanded. "You didn't show up with an offer. You ambushed and violently kidnapped my people. You didn't contact me and try to explain what was going on. I responded like I would in any situation like that. An aggressive response is what happens when you play stupid, violent games."

"The enemy is that dangerous." Tether grimaced. She drew a ragged breath before continuing. "We had no choice. We had to be careful."

"That's your version of careful? I don't want to see what

you're like when you're not being careful. You bomb kinder-gartens?" Dante gestured at Mugoi. "He doesn't know what happened to him. It's mighty coincidental that your team shows up, and my apprentice can't move. You care to shine a light on that?"

"I…" Tether shook her head.

Dante snorted. "Right now your people have my partner. You better give me a reason to believe I should trust you because I'm tired and pissed off. So are my people. I need to come up with reasons they shouldn't take it out on you."

Keeping her eyes closed, Tether drew another deep breath. "We have a disruptor. We developed it to inhibit advanced machinery, high technology, the tech you'd find mostly Station-side."

Dante looked at Mugoi. "Why does Firewall need a special anti-machine weapon?"

"I've told you enough."

"You've told me jack and shit. All you did was confirm what I guessed."

Tether opened her eyes to glare at Dante. "I'm not telling you anything else."

"Okay." Dante clenched his jaw and breathed in through his nose. Everyone was on edge. Losing his calm wouldn't help the situation.

"Let's get back to our original problem. I understand your people want leverage because they don't know if you're compro-mised. I need to know their next move."

He shook his head. "Because I have to tell you that meeting with Firewall when I suspect they're going to ambush us a *third damned* time doesn't sound appealing. If you want any chance of salvaging our cooperation against the Omega Syndrome, you need to give me something."

Tether's hard glare softened into a mix of panic and concern. Dante understood trust and loyalty. He didn't expect her to give up all her organization's secrets. That didn't mean he'd give them more trust than they'd earned after coming after his team and almost killing his apprentice. The shadow war against the Omega Syndrome required an army filled with soldiers who could trust one another.

Tether began, "All I can tell you is that you should be getting their demands soon. In the meanwhile, don't push them. You do it my way, and your friend will be fine."

Dante nodded at Mugoi and headed for the door. "The funny thing is if Nasreen's conscious wherever they have her, she's telling them the same thing. About me." He stopped at the door. "None of this should go down like this. Your group's way of getting help is piss-poor."

"Our enemy is too dangerous to play games."

"Bodies and body parts are piling up. I'm not playing a game. Firewall is." Dante closed the door.

CHAPTER SIX

Heavy hands tugged on Nasreen's arms, legs, and body. A fog had settled over her brain, making it hard to maintain her concentration. She couldn't remember what she was doing or where she'd been. Her arm throbbed, and every muscle in her body twitched.

Her survival instinct kicked in. The vague memory of the fight screamed at her that she was in trouble and needed to fight back. Someone grabbed her arm and her legs.

Eyes still half-closed, Nasreen shoved a man away. "Don't touch me," she slurred. "Get away from me."

Something hard slammed into the side of her head. Her head snapped back. Fiery pain joined the fog in her head. She groaned and kicked her legs. Shadows surrounded her, punching, kicking, and hitting. A hard boot tip slammed into her stomach. She vomited.

Nasreen tried to remain conscious. She could defend herself awake. They'd finish her off otherwise. All she needed to do was stall for help…Station security or the team.

"Enough!" a man behind Nasreen shouted. "You're getting too rough. Secure her for transport. Get the restraints on. She won't do us any good dead."

Nasreen groaned. Someone pulled her arms behind her back and snapped restraints around her wrists. She tried to turn her head to see who was talking, but her body refused to cooperate.

She remembered the snap gun. She tried to remember what had happened with Jolo and Mugoi. None of the men taking her had mentioned them. The apprentices were either not with her or were unconscious.

There was one terrible remaining possibility. They could be dead. Nasreen had never been one to shy away from harsh realities. That didn't mean she had to dwell on it. Her captors had taken her alive. That bolstered the case for the survival of Jolo and Mugoi.

Nasreen tried to keep her eyes open. She didn't see much other than bloodied operatives, the street, and a nondescript hovertruck. Her captors opened the door and tossed her into the cargo trailer without much care. Pain flared in her arm and head from the impact. A group of her captors hopped into the back while the others ran to the front of the vehicle.

Pain and grogginess ate away at her as she tried to process her situation. These men and women weren't Block 9X. The mercenaries would have no reason to take her alive.

Whether their masters considered Dante and her a serious threat, the Omega Syndrome conspiracy must have understood they wouldn't be their tools. The mercenaries at the club had shown no restraint. They'd come to kill their enemies, not capture them, and had been willing to cut off a woman's arm in public.

Whirring and a light hum marked the main sounds as the truck flew through Atlantica Central. Her captors exchanged looks but did not say anything. The four guards in the back of the truck held a mix of razorfists, knives, and batons.

Operating at full ability and with the element of surprise, she might be able to take half of them out and escape. Wounded, half-conscious, and with her wrists bound, she wouldn't accomplish anything with an attack other than getting hurt more. They'd only stopped roughing her up because someone ordered them to stop.

Sometimes the best way to win a battle was to surrender. Prolonging survival meant prolonging her chance at escape. Defiance needed to serve a practical goal. Right now, she had to play their game. When she had her chance, she'd make them pay.

Nasreen kept her eyes closed and feigned unconsciousness hoping her captors would speak and give up intelligence. Their discipline was admirable if frustrating. A few minutes into the trip, they placed a blindfold over her.

Their careful silence helped her in other ways. She could concentrate on every sound and movement during the trip. The walls of the trailer muted the sounds without blocking them entirely.

The *hum* and *whoosh* of other nearby vehicles disappeared not long after the truck started moving. A faint echoing rumble replaced their noise, suggesting her captors had moved away from the main lanes and retreated into access and maintenance tunnels in the underbelly of the Station. They'd only stopped for brief periods, and she'd not felt the rattle nor heard the roar of thrusters from shuttle engines.

The trip from the team HQ to her captors' base was taking too long. Atlantica Central Station was an impressive monument to humanity's technological capabilities, but it didn't extend forever. Audio cues confirmed the vehicle hadn't left the Station via tunnel or sky bridge. Slight changes and shifts in her position supported a lot of turns.

Nasreen appreciated the strategy. They were taking an indirect route and circling the Station to avoid leading anyone directly to their hideout. That meant they weren't complete amateurs.

She didn't care. The important fact was she was all but certainly still in Atlantica Central Station. Dante could find Nasreen if she was still here. All she had to do was stay alive long enough for him to do that.

It was time to start planning her escape.

Nasreen struggled in her chair. They'd bound her hands and legs before placing something cool and metal on her forehead. She tried to complain, but her gag only permitted a strangled cry.

A signal uplink notice popped up in the corner of her vision. There was no reason for her implants to activate by themselves. She gasped as a message appeared, and a deep ache invaded her brain.

Secondary uplink established. Connection Error. Debugging protocol 24-58 in effect. Translation package 24a activating emergency integrity preservation mode. Full neuro reintegration program recommended prior to reboot.

The message faded three seconds later. Nasreen shouted into her gag and pulled at her tight restraints. They couldn't do this. They couldn't take her implants from her. Her captors were proving far more adept than she'd anticipated. They were reaching into her brain and violating her, taking a vital part of her everyday tools.

Secondary uplink established. Connection error. Debugging protocol 24-58 in effect. Biomonitor package 12a activating temporarily disabled. Full neuro reintegration recommended prior to reboot.

The implant packages continued to fail.

Non-linear database storage package 3d.

Active physical monitoring package 11a.

One by one, her captors connected with her AI implant systems and shut them down. The pain built with each. She screamed.

No one said anything. It didn't take long, minutes by her reckoning, until she could no longer access any of her AI implants. Someone tugged at her blindfold without pulling it down. Her headache began to fade. She took slow, ragged breaths and pulled against her restraints, desperate to claw out the eyes of anyone near her.

Footsteps moved away from her. A door *creaked* open before loudly slapping shut. The sound echoed in the room around her. A resounding *clang* followed.

Nasreen shook her head. The blindfold dropped to reveal her current accommodations, an empty dull blue room with a single chair bolted to the floor and no windows. The room was wider than it was long. Scratches on the floor and rectangular imprints in the dust indicated an old storage room recently emptied.

Her heart thundered. She was a prisoner without any of her implants. She wasn't sure if Mugoi and Jolo were still alive. Dante had ordered radio silence. That didn't mean he'd wait forever. He'd know something went wrong an hour after they didn't check in or return.

Nasreen lowered her head to her chest. Dante would need to find her first. Staying alive. That was what she needed to focus on. No matter what, she needed to stay alive.

Without implants, a clock, anyone to talk to, or any stimulus other than her thoughts and the quiet *whoosh* of air in vents, Nasreen had trouble keeping track of time. Seconds ticked away and blurred together into endless, interminable minutes. An hour could have passed, two, maybe three. Beyond the pain in her arm from the earlier shot, her constant state of alert had left her neck and shoulders sore, and she'd never shaken her fatigue. Her stomach rumbled, demanding food.

Nasreen had done her best to survey the room and find anything she could use to her advantage. There was no obvious vent access despite the air she heard and nothing other than her secured chair and the dim light strips running along the sides of the ceiling. Even if she could free herself, her only escape choice was the single locked door in front of her. She had to assume there was a guard outside or nearby. Without knowing their schedules or positioning, any escape attempt would be a gamble.

Escape might be impossible. Letting Dante know where she was without her sphere or implants would be difficult but not impossible. All she needed was to find a sphere or comms equipment. Her captors had to feed her. That might be her chance to get out of the room if they decided to take her somewhere.

Her swirling thoughts and plans vanished in a rush of adrenaline as the door loudly *clanked* and swung open. A tall man with a salt-and-pepper beard stepped through. She didn't recognize him. After accepting Block 9X hadn't grabbed her, she didn't expect to.

"Are you in any pain?" His voice sounded familiar.

"I've been better." Nasreen shook her wrist restraints. "These aren't comfortable."

"They're for our mutual protection."

"I think they're more to keep me here." Nasreen rattled the restraints again. "If I promise not to strangle you, will you unlock my wrists?"

"I'm afraid I can't do that." The man stepped into the cell. His gray pants and shirt weren't noteworthy. He didn't appear to be carrying any weapons. "I apologize for my people's roughness earlier. Recent losses have made them excitable."

Nasreen had been spending too much time around Dante. Her first instinct was to scoff in the man's face and tell him to go screw himself. She didn't do that. Antagonizing this man wouldn't help. Once she had a better understanding of whom she was dealing with, that might be a viable strategy depending on his personality.

She narrowed her eyes. In the shock of the ambush, kidnapping, and imprisonment, she'd been so focused on her immediate survival that she hadn't tried too hard to figure out who attacked her other than concluding it wasn't Block 9X. While there were countless possibilities, the most likely involved only two organizations and she easily disqualified one.

"You're Firewall, aren't you?" Nasreen groaned. "Of course you are. This all makes more sense now."

"Yes, we're with Firewall." The man stayed near the open door. "You can call me Lock. Consider me higher up in the food chain of my organization."

"That means you're authorized to make deals?"

"Yes."

"Good. You've made a horrible mistake. If you killed Mugoi or Jolo, Dante will hunt you down long before he goes after our mutual *friends*." Nasreen tried to keep the anger out of her voice.

"This is a man who faked a whole new life for slow revenge against what was one of the most powerful companies among the Stations. He's not great at everything, and he could use a couple of etiquette classes, but Dante Shale could teach a master class in vengeance."

She regretted the vehemence slipping out. Sometimes it was fun to be more like Dante.

"You're threatening me?" Lock's brow lifted. "Aren't you worried about me killing you?"

Nasreen shook her head. "Capturing a prisoner and transporting them is operationally difficult. Beyond the initial fight, you had to expose your people and this place to get me here. That's not something you do just to kill someone later.

"I was at your mercy. If you wanted to kill me, you had your chance. You could have filmed it and sent it to Dante if that's what this was about. Instead, you went through a lot of trouble to bring me here."

Lock ran his hand through his hair. The heavy bags under his sunken eyes made it look like he hadn't slept in days. She wouldn't pity a man whose operatives had brutally attacked her and her friends twice. Firewall needed to understand that they would not win against the Omega Syndrome by alienating everyone else. They were going to end up with more enemies.

Nasreen wasn't sure if Firewall and her team were the only ones who knew about Omega Syndrome. She doubted it. Dante and Nasreen had relied on an elaborate public relations strategy to go after SSS and earned the attention of the Omega Syndrome and Firewall. There might be countless other small teams infiltrating the bowels of Station society and realizing the true power brokers had hidden in far deeper shadows than anyone realized.

"We have no plans to kill you, despite your involvement in the death of our earlier operatives," Lock said. "I want you to understand that first and foremost."

"Next time you try to recruit someone, approach them and ask for a meeting. Don't ambush them on their way from dinner. You might get more cooperation that way. This was all avoidable, but if you wanted to get revenge because of that, you had your opportunity. We saved Tether's life. We risked ours to help extract her. I can't believe this is how you repay us."

Lock stroked his chin. "That's your claim anyway."

"There's no way you didn't have people watching. You didn't trust us to begin with. That makes me think you left your person to die. Don't blame us because you didn't have the courage or skill to extract your operative."

Nostrils flaring, Lock stepped forward before drawing a deep breath and retreating. "This is about making sure we get Tether back. We'll exchange you for her after we confirm she's alive, and we make sure you're clean."

"Clean?" Nasreen repeated. "What's that mean?"

"You don't need to know."

"If it involves my life, I think I should." Nasreen sighed. "I think you don't understand the situation. Beyond the risk of escaping with Tether, we went out of our way to save her life. She was in bad shape."

She inclined her head toward the door. "The only reason your lackeys could jump us was that we had to go to HQ for more medical supplies. Those supplies were to help *her*, not our people."

Lock and his squads might have doomed the alliance and Nasreen's life. She swallowed the bile rising in her throat. Without the supplies, Tether's condition would worsen. The ambush born of distrust might kill the Firewall operative. If Tether died, Nasreen would join her soon.

"We didn't…" Lock's eyes shifted to the side. "Your people got away."

She doubted he was lying. He was also holding something back. The details made all the difference for their continued negotiations. She didn't care if he thought he had the upper hand. Before, she was semi-conscious and didn't know who had kidnapped her. Now their identity and motives were clear.

Her thoughts drifted back to his comment about being clean. It implied something more than disabling tracking devices. They'd disabled her implants. That had to be related. Theories would get her nowhere without proof. Lock wasn't about to offer up anything useful without prodding.

"Does being clean have to do with why you shut my AIs

down?" Nasreen asked. "Whatever you did might have screwed up a lot of things. I might need a clinic to restore all of them."

Lock wrinkled his nose and rolled his eyes in disgust. "It was necessary. Once we verify their uses and after we trade you for Tether, we have means of reactivating them without too much trouble."

Something in his voice called to her, the faintest of tremors, a subtle shift in the tone. They didn't need to shut down all her AIs to keep her captive. An organization with that capability could easily scramble comms or stuff her in a shielded room to ensure she couldn't communicate with the outside world. They'd gone through a lot of trouble and risked potential brain damage to disable her implants in an abrupt and invasive manner.

"What do you care what I use them for?" Nasreen asked.

"We're through talking about that. I wish this hadn't gone down this way. It did, though, and we can only deal with what has happened. Not what we want to happen. I hoped we could work together. I understand that's no longer possible. All I can do is salvage this situation the best I can."

Nasreen strained against the cords securing her to the chair. She wondered how thoroughly they'd searched her. Tether wasn't the only one who could hide knives in surprising places, but that didn't matter much until Nasreen got her hands free.

She didn't bother with a fake smile even as she pitched her voice between calm and pleading. "We can still work together. We're not the enemy."

Lock shook his head. "It's too late now. I think it was too late after you killed our people the first time." He headed for the doorway. "I hope your people will be more reasonable than last time. And I hope you're not lying about Tether."

"What happens if she dies?"

Lock stopped in the doorway. He didn't turn. "A life for a life. That's about as fair as it gets."

Nasreen drew on all her past training to keep her face impassive despite her thundering heart. "You're making a mistake."

"It wouldn't be the first time. It won't be the last." Lock slammed the door shut.

Nasreen let her head loll back and closed her eyes. She was still bound to a chair. Her latest survey of the room didn't spot any obvious cameras. That didn't mean they weren't watching her.

Someone knocked on the door. She didn't answer. A frowning young woman in blue coveralls opened the door. She held a tray with a bowl of cloudy brown soup and a cup of water. There were no utensils. The woman advanced with obvious suspicion.

Nasreen kept her face impassive despite her surprise. She would have assumed they'd have at least one other Firewall member guarding the cell during mealtimes. They knew she could fight.

The woman set the tray down in Nasreen's lap. "I'm going to free one of your hands. You're going to drink your soup and your water. I won't leave this cell until you finish. I'll be taking the dishes with me."

"How am I supposed to eat soup without a spoon?" Nasreen raised an eyebrow in challenge.

"You can hold it with one hand," the woman replied. "It's not that hot." She moved behind Nasreen. "You try anything you don't get more food for a day."

Nasreen offered her best look of placid contrition mixed with a touch of fear. Guards grew lazy and less careful when they believed prisoners feared them.

Firewall was impressive in many ways. They'd avoided the attention of the powerful Voices controlling the Stations and managed to field large teams of dedicated operatives who could take on well-trained Marauders and Reapers. Their ability to disable her implants pointed to major technological ability.

Mugoi had frozen during the battle. Considering Mugoi had faced off against Reapers and Nightmutts without a second of panic, it made no sense a group of non-enhanced humans would push the cyborg over the edge. That meant Firewall had somehow disabled the apprentice the same way they'd shut down her implants.

With her hand free, Nasreen grabbed the bowl and brought it to her lips. The salty soup was proof of Firewall's limits. All their skills and technical abilities didn't extend into every area. Feeding a prisoner made sense. She didn't question that. Everything else about the situation pointed to Firewall not keeping prisoners as opposed to recruits.

They believed not bringing her utensils was keeping them safe. They couldn't be more wrong. The guard should have been in the room with her, and the door secured. Another guard with a baton should have been outside.

Even if she broke out and killed both operatives, that would limit the damage and delay her escape. Instead, they were guaranteeing she'd have at least one time when she'd have access to a hand and know the door would be open.

Assuming Lock wasn't lying, and Mugoi and Jolo had escaped. There was no guarantee they would have the medical supplies. Dante wouldn't send another team right back to headquarters. He would be able to get other supplies, but it would take longer. It created a window of delay that might cost Tether's life.

Proceeding on assumptions was dangerous. Nasreen had to make a choice. Lock had made his position clear. She couldn't gamble her life on the survival of a severely wounded Firewall operative.

She took another sip of her soup. The warmth filled her throat and belly. She smiled.

"That good?" the guard asked.

"Something like that." Nasreen smiled wider as the seed of an escape plan germinated.

CHAPTER SEVEN

Pacing the safe house living room, Dante wanted to throw something—a chair, the couch, an apprentice, his fist into someone's face.

He'd calmed things down after the brawl, and the apprentices had returned to the living room. Braelin had stopped glaring at Mugoi, instead casting angry glances at Tether's room and worried looks toward Jolo's. The man's cocky grin was gone, replaced by a face contorted in anguish and hatred.

Dante couldn't blame him. He felt the same way even if he didn't show it in his expression.

"This is bullshit," Braelin muttered. He stood and glared in Tether's direction again before heading into Jolo's room and closing the door. She lay there asleep, doing her best to recover. With the supplies Mugoi had brought back, they could do that much.

Hyde had retreated into a different room to mumble to himself. That left Dante with Mugoi standing with its hands folded behind its back next to the door to Tether's room. The cyborg's bland expression remained inscrutable as it had since the end of the brawl. Dante didn't doubt Mugoi would like a more aggressive interrogation of Tether.

Following her advice, they'd been waiting for Firewall to contact them for hours. Dante had done his best to further treat and stabilize Tether. At the rate things were going, he wasn't sure if the handoff would fail because her comrades were wasting too much time. Although she was stable for the moment, he couldn't ignore the risk of another medical surprise.

"Midas, message status?" asked Dante in the vain hope his AI was holding back a communication in a misguided attempt not to burden his master.

There has been no contact through the Firewall encrypted channel, the AI reported. His English accent somehow sounded more refined than normal. *Sir, I'll immediately let you know if they contact us. I appreciate that time is not our ally in this situation."*

"Yes, you could say that," Dante mumbled. "Time's never been our ally."

Mugoi tilted its head and stared at Dante as if looking through him. Everything about the apprentice was hard to read on a good day. Since returning from the headquarters, it was as if Mugoi was trying not to let anyone sense what it was thinking.

Being frozen at the battle and having to see comrades taken out must have been eating away at Mugoi. The thought kindled more anger in Dante, and he had enough burning in him to light a new star.

"Screw this." Dante stomped over toward Tether's door. "This is taking too long. She's wrong about their tactics."

"Is there anything we can do?" Mugoi stepped away from the door and motioned at it. The cyborg's preferred course of action was clear. "Other than wait? We don't know where they are. I'll volunteer for whatever mission will help recover her, Captain."

"Thanks, but you're right. We need to figure out where she is first." Dante threw open the door and stomped into the room.

Tether's gray eyes flickered open. He peered back at her with his own striking green eyes and cracked his knuckles. He stared, forcing his eyes wide and wild.

"What's this supposed to be?" she asked weakly, looking confused.

"Your people are leaving you to die." Dante gestured at the autoclamp. "We've treated you and stabilized you. That doesn't mean you're out of trouble. The longer you sit there, the greater the chance you end up in serious trouble.

"We can drop you off at a clinic. I don't know how long you'll have before Block 9X shows up to chop your other arm off. Or your legs. I'm assuming they'll finish with your head. If they're nice, they'll do that one first."

Tether snorted. The weak and quiet sound undercut the attempt at defiance. "Are you trying to scare me? I've given up my entire life to fight the Omega Syndrome. I'm prepared to die."

"I'm not trying to scare you. I'm stating facts. Take that how you want. There's another option." He almost called in Hyde for an assist before offering a wide, hungry grin. "It's where I limit my team's exposure to more danger."

"How would you do that? You're the one at a disadvantage here."

Dante walked over to the edge of the bed, keeping his crazy grin. He leaned over so his face was right over Tether's. "How do I know your friends aren't trying to track you down, and that's why this is taking so long? How do I know you don't have a hidden implant we didn't pick up? Because I've been out there thinking about this.

"It occurs to me that maybe you lied about your asshole friends and wanted me to think they had Nasreen to buy yourself time." He straightened his back and retreated from the bed. "Klement would love to come in here and cut your other arm off for what your people did to Nasreen. I'm having a hard time coming up with reasons he's wrong.

"Hyde, well, he's Hyde. He doesn't need much of an excuse to make a human pretzel. Telling him he's doing it to avenge a friend will give him a legit justification. He'd love that. He can do bad while pretending to be good."

Tether rolled her head to the side to track Dante's position. "You're not that ruthless. Stop pretending you are."

"You have no idea how many people I've killed for far less. If you want to live through the next hour, you need to convince me why I shouldn't assume Nasreen's dead and take you out in revenge. Because you might think I'm not ruthless, but you know I find revenge tasty hot or cold."

"They wouldn't have taken her alive if all they wanted was to kill her," Tether pointed out. "That's not how we operate. It'd be too much of a risk of exposure for too little reward. We haven't survived against the Omega Syndrome by acting like murderous criminals."

Dante shook his head. "Try harder. You said this was about a prisoner swap and to wait. We sent a message. We're still waiting. Nothing's happened."

He punched a chair over. It clattered and skidded across the tile floor. "I won't lose more people. If that means I have to chop off the head of every Block 9X and Firewall bastard, I'll do it. Don't tell me you think I wouldn't. Don't pretend you think I'm not capable of it."

"I think you're a man who went after SSS because of o-harvesting."

"I went after SSS because they betrayed me."

Tether shook her head. "They only betrayed you because you refused to let them commit a horrible crime. Your motivation means you have a moral center. You're not going to execute me because you're angry. The Dante Shale who cares about Dirt-walkers isn't that kind of man."

Dante kicked the downed chair into a wall, watching for a start from Tether that didn't come. "I'll kill for revenge. I'll kill for my friends. Firewall isn't an innocent Dirtwalker tribe being preyed on by Reaper o-harvesters.

"You're a wannabe revolutionary resistance group willing to kidnap and attack people not working for the Omega Syndrome. I'm running out of patience for your bullshit and your self-righteous justifications. If I hadn't bothered to save your stupid ass, Nasreen wouldn't have had to go back to HQ, and your asshole friends wouldn't have been able to grab her."

Tether's mouth twitched. She swallowed. It was so subtle that Dante almost missed it, but it was there. Fear he could work with. He'd ranted louder for effect, but he hadn't lied.

"She's not dead," Tether said. "If she were, there's a good chance you'd know. Like I said, Firewall wouldn't take that risk to kill one person on the street. I believe they're delaying because they are taking time to determine her value to you. They can use that to better negotiate with you. Firewall doesn't do anything without careful planning."

Dante scoffed. "Who kidnaps someone without knowing if it's worth it beforehand?" He narrowed his eyes on Tether. "Or is this a balance of trade deal? Do they think she's not important enough to trade for you? I would have thought they understood how far I'm willing to go for the people on my team."

Tether licked her chapped lips. "You're getting it backward."

"Then explain it to me. Because right now all I have is a wounded apprentice, a missing partner, and a prisoner whose treatment required my people to expose themselves to an ambush. I need to understand why I shouldn't cut my losses."

"I'm expendable. That's the truth. That's the harsh reality."

Dante let out a long, harsh laugh. "You're so expendable they sent an entire team to ambush a handful of my people? Don't feed me that crap."

"You've seen how far we go in recruitment and what we require of people in our organization," Tether pointed out. "Even expendable field operatives have value. But not that much. It's more that while they might be willing to negotiate with you for me, your friend might be more valuable as a source of information and a bargaining chip. The mission comes first."

"They keep her, and you die," Dante explained in as casual a tone as he could manage. Sometimes sounding less angry could be far more threatening. "That's not a threat. That's a promise. I could tell them that. Send pieces of you. You think that might motivate them?"

Tether's nose twitched. She looked away. "Threatening me won't change anything, even if I believed your threats. You want your friend back? You need to increase what you're bringing to the table."

Dante nodded. "Besides an operative whose life I saved?"

"Yes." With a groan and grimace, Tether managed to prop herself up on her good elbow. After a moment, she groaned again and lowered her head to the pillow. "Firewall has been trying to acquire a secure database that will help track the signature of the Omega Syndrome more effectively. Achieving that has proven...difficult."

"You're saying you're not good enough to hand over for Nasreen, but if I get this database, that might be?" Dante let contempt drip from his words.

"I can't guarantee you anything. I can only tell you what I believe. I know that'd be far more valuable than my life. It'd also go a long way to helping Firewall stand up against our enemy. In theory, they're your enemy, too. You might not want to join our organization, but you *do* want the Omega Syndrome destroyed."

Dante snickered. "Here I thought you didn't do alliances."

"We don't." Tether frowned. "We take advantage of the groups and resources available. Right now, Firewall has something you want. All you need to do is get something we want more."

She rattled off a series of numbers. "Those are coordinates where you can find the secured sphere containing the database."

"This wasn't a smart move." Dante sauntered over to her

bedside to give her a pitying look. "You're telling me how to get access to something that replaces you as a bargaining chip."

"I told you where it is, not how to access it." Tether managed a smirk in between a pained grimace. A touch of mischief entered her gray eyes. "Once you recon, you'll realize you need more insider information. The only person in this building who has that knowledge is me."

Dante scoffed. This woman thought she was playing him. Her tone and eyes told the story. He wouldn't claim he was anywhere near as good as Nasreen when it came to working people with his words rather than a razorfist. Being a Marauder typically meant solving problems with a generous helping of violence, not clever interrogations.

Still, dealing with slimy clients throughout his career helped him spot manipulation when it was in front of him. The problem was whether Tether was closer to Nasreen's level or his. He needed to play his best cards.

"There's no way Firewall would show up for a joint op. That means my team will have to recover it and trade it."

"Yes," Tether replied. "That's the plan. You trade it for your friend and me."

"I'll have possession of the database before turning you over." Dante shrugged. "What's to stop me from killing you then? I get the database, let you bleed out, and say, 'Sorry. You took too long to call me back, but here's something you always wanted.' I win either way. I have a valuable chip to offer thanks to you."

Tether shrugged. "Nothing's stopping you, I guess."

"Oh. They might not think you're important, but if you weren't afraid of dying, you wouldn't have run like you did in the club."

"Those people are monsters." Tether locked eyes with Dante. "Killing me when you could let me go to help get your friend means you're a cold-blooded killer. You forget, Mr. Shale. We know you. No matter how much you playact a ruthless killer, the truth is you're a dangerous man, but you're not a monster."

Dante scoffed. "Maybe not, but I certainly work with them."

"Don't we all?" Tether chuckled bitterly.

"I'll peek at your coordinates." Dante headed toward the door. "Don't get your hopes up."

"You won't regret this."

"I already regret dealing with you people and saving you. What's a little more?"

Dante gathered Hyde, Braelin, and Mugoi back in the living room. He'd separated them into separate corners to reduce the odds of another brawl and more broken bones. Arm in a sling, a glum-faced Braelin stared off past Dante after the explanation.

"Midas has identified the coordinates as a small res-block in Pentapolis," Dante said. "It won't hurt to take a look." He inclined his head at the closed door of Tether's room. "I'd rather be doing something than nothing. Sitting around twiddling our thumbs isn't going to save Nasreen."

"It's probably another trap, *Papi.*" Hyde scratched his beard. "Give me a few minutes with her, and I'll get the truth."

"She's missing an arm and doing a good job working the conversation. You think these Firewall operatives don't know how to resist torture?"

"Don't be a pussy. I won't take her other arm. She's got two legs, though." Hyde shrugged and patted his knees. "Metal legs aren't so bad. Aren't you pissed at these people? Don't you want payback? What happened to the man who was so obsessed with killing me?"

Dante scoffed, "If we don't get Nasreen back, I'll kill Tether myself."

Hyde grinned. "Yes. That's what I'm talking about. Okay. We'll do this your way." He smacked his metal hands together with a loud *thud*. "We'll go find this place and crack some skulls. It'll be a nice way to work off frustration."

"No skull cracking. Not yet." Dante shook his head. "We all have our specialties. Subtlety isn't yours. This is a recon mission, not an assault mission. You're not coming with me."

Hyde stepped away from the corner. His lips curled in a mixture of disbelief and sneering disregard. "You go by yourself, and you're asking to die. That's not being a pussy, but I thought you were smarter than that."

"He's right," Braelin agreed in a quiet, strained voice. "It ain't safe. We've had a shit day, and there's a good chance it's going to continue." He gritted his teeth. "I can still hold a baton. I can be quiet."

"Bringing a man recovering from a broken arm on a recon mission isn't going to happen," Dante replied. "I'm not that desperate." He nodded at Mugoi. "No broken limbs. No major damage, and a cyborg who can be agile and subtle. Perfect for recon."

"I'm eager to accompany you." Mugoi frowned. "But taking me along might be unwise for unrelated reasons."

"Care to share those reasons?" Dante asked.

"Hyde and I have a fundamental weakness that Firewall can exploit." Mugoi glanced at Tether's door. "Firewall has anti-cyborg weapons. There's no guarantee the Omega Syndrome and Block 9X don't. I could freeze again at a terrible time, Captain."

"Block 9X uses a lot of cyborgs," Dante reminded him. "I don't think they'll get a lot of use out of cyborg jammers. It's not like Firewall invented anti-cyborg weapons anyway. They only have one we didn't expect."

He gestured at Hyde. "His old body was mostly hydraulics, which helped protect him from EMPs. Being a non-cyborg makes me vulnerable to more than you. When people throw me into walls, it hurts more." He shrugged.

"We don't have many options. I'm not going to sit around here with my thumb up my ass waiting for Firewall to issue more demands, and we're not going to torture a prisoner. We need to get on top of this. If getting this database will do that, I'm all for it. That means we need to use the people and resources we have available. Braelin's hurt, and Hyde doesn't sneak well."

"I didn't get caught at the club," Hyde complained. "I can sneak."

Dante glared at him. "Don't get me started on the club. Mugoi, you're coming with me. Man up. Transhuman up. Whatever it takes."

He motioned at Braelin and Hyde. "You keep an eye on our friend with the missing arm. I don't trust her. She might try to pull something."

He shook a finger. "Remember, she's the only leverage we have right now over Firewall. I might not be able to get this database without her help. We lose her, and there's a good chance we never see Nasreen again."

Hyde's eager smile sent a chill through Dante. "She's not getting out of here." He gestured at his legs. "No matter what body part she might need to replace."

"Leave her in one piece," Dante ordered. He motioned to Mugoi. "Let's get ready. If all goes well, we won't have to fight anyone."

CHAPTER EIGHT

Surviving imprisonment was as much a mental struggle as a physical one. Nasreen understood that violence and death might await, but worrying wouldn't help. Compartmentalizing those threats away as part of the risks of her job was easy enough.

She'd always risked death as a spy and a Marauder. The best way to deal with the fear was to stow it away and save it to fuel adrenaline when her life was on the line. A burst of fight-or-flight could give her the edge she needed to survive an otherwise impossible situation. That strategy had saved her on Earth when she'd run afoul of a paranoid captain and also had helped propel her away from a murderous Hyde during their first terrifying meeting.

She'd never claim she didn't fear death, only that it wasn't as important in a prisoner's mental struggle as dealing with a far more pernicious and will-sapping challenge, sheer boredom. Her Firewall captors had adjusted her bonds to be less tight. They still restricted her to a chair and offered nothing to keep her mind occupied since her conversation with Lock and brief interactions during mealtimes.

Her makeshift cell remained as nondescript and boring as it

had since her arrival. Any vague hopes they'd provide even banal entertainment had long since vanished. They might have been attempting to bore her to death.

Nasreen found a constructive way to fight boredom. She took the empty time to run through different scenarios concerning escape. As long as she had one arm free during a meal, she was confident she could succeed even if they'd taken her hidden weapons. She had no way to check and verify, so for planning purposes she assumed Firewall had confiscated them.

All she needed was one tool to have escaped the enemy's notice. It all depended on what type of scanners they used. Noticing a stray polymer mass in her might not have worried them enough to take a closer look, especially after confiscating all her weapons.

Unfortunately, a woman could only spend so much time planning her escape. The minutes drifted together as she stared at the windowless gray door to her makeshift cell. They'd disabled her AI implants, hampering her ability to keep her mind distracted by perusing the different collated data sources she'd gathered over the years.

An abrupt *clang* announced the door opening. She fixed her best defiant stare straight ahead. Lock stepped inside. He carried no weapons and didn't look concerned. No one else was outside the cell. That was brave and stupid.

Lock glanced around the cell with disgust as if seeing it for the first time. "We don't normally use this place to keep people. I apologize for the rude accommodations."

"It's a converted storage room. Which means this was all planned in a hurry. Everything else about your group comes off less slap-dash. That's the only explanation."

"Be careful about assuming too much." Lock offered a cold smile. "It's led to pain and suffering between both our groups."

Nasreen rotated her wrists in her restraints. "These are starting to chafe."

"They're necessary. We don't anticipate you'll be here long enough that it becomes a serious problem." Lock shrugged.

He moved behind her and knelt. A *clicking* sound preceded the pressure around her legs easing. He'd released her legs, although he kept her torso bound to the chair.

"Oh?" Nasreen's brow lifted. "You're ready to make a swap."

"No." Lock walked back in front of her and folded his arms. "I didn't see a reason to make you more uncomfortable than necessary. The chair's bolted to the floor. You're not going to knock it over. We're still ironing out the details of the exchange. I'm not here to talk about that."

"Then why are you here? Because I'm not telling you anything else. I have no reason to do so." She flexed her legs. "That's not enough to get me to talk."

Lock shook his head with a faint, dismissive sigh. "I'm not here to interrogate you, Miss Joelle. I'm here to have a conversation. I thought you might find that welcome." He gestured around the room. "I understand sitting in an old storage room isn't that exciting."

"Sounds like an indirect interrogation, but I'm all tied up with nothing better to do." She shrugged. "What did you want to talk about?"

"Your implants." Lock's harsh expression wrinkled his brow. "From what we can see, they are mostly for languages, data collation, and monitoring health. We haven't been able to break through all the encryption, although we're familiar with the basic types."

"That's all accurate. None of those implants present a risk to you. They'd be harmless to turn back on." Nasreen kept a neutral look as she offered that. It was true enough. Other than getting new ideas, there was nothing inherently helpful in her implants for escaping from being tied to a chair.

Lock tapped the side of his head. "Doesn't it bother you?"

"Yes, not having my implants and being a prisoner bothers me."

"No. That's not what I'm talking about." Lock sighed. "Why do you live like this?"

Nasreen frowned. "Are you asking why I have AI implants?"

"Yes. You're sharing your head with a bunch of computer programs that can turn on you at a moment's notice."

She blinked. She'd expected the conversation to flow in a different direction. A year ago, she'd had to convince Dante to get his implant. He'd made similar arguments against the implant. She'd thought it quaint and old-fashioned.

"What are you getting at? Why do you care about my implants?"

"Who's the master in the relationship?" Lock replied. "A device implanted in your brain that can directly influence you is dangerous."

Nasreen let a snappy retort die in her throat. Lock wasn't being ridiculous. Midas had exceeded his limits soon after his installation. More frighteningly, their first encounter with the Omega Syndrome was via the group hijacking Midas and speaking as a bizarre chorus, earning the nickname the Voices. The safety measures associated with the AI had protected him and Dante, though it'd left the entire team leery of their enemy's power.

Lock nodded once with a satisfied gleam in his eyes. "I can see it on your face. You don't want to admit it, but you've been in a situation that proves everything I'm saying. AI implants are a terrible risk."

Nasreen injected calculated doubt into her voice. "You're not the first person to point out problems with AI implants. It's not like people haven't widely discussed it. That's why there are limits."

"It's not only the AI implants." Lock held up his hand and wiggled his fingers. "Flesh and blood, but you have two cyborgs who work with you. I'm not claiming there's never a case where a person needs a prosthetic, but over-installation of cybernetic augmentation is unreliable at best, if not outright ticking time bombs. It's asking for trouble."

"That's your angle?" Nasreen shook her restraints. "Non-augmented people have their weaknesses, too. You shot and took me down with the same weapon you intended to use on Mugoi."

"You're not understanding me." He pinched the bridge of his nose and slowed his speech as if dealing with a child not listening properly. "These implants and augmentations can be hacked and turned against their users. You accept that much at least, right?"

Nasreen didn't respond immediately. Anguish had snuck into Lock's voice and eyes. He wanted her to understand where he was coming from, not to win an argument against a prisoner he would never see again. No man radiated that much desperation without good reason.

"Please help me understand. We all understand the risks of technology, and the greater integration of that technology into the person brings more challenges. I've used implants to help me throughout my career. That doesn't mean I don't think there's such a thing as going too far. Mugoi and Hyde, for example."

She shook her head and added a clucked tongue for effect. "They're great to have on missions. They're also barely human anymore. I don't think we should discriminate against them. I also don't think the average person should get that many augmentations."

Lock's eyes widened. "Yes, you're beginning to see what I'm saying. You get it. Every intelligent person gets it once they think it through."

"But there's a more fundamental threat. That's what I'm sensing."

"You've experienced the threat," Lock replied, the excitement of finding a common cause fading on his face and giving way to a tightened jaw and narrowed eyes. "Our enemy, the Omega

Syndrome, is an active conspiracy to use implants and cybernetic augmentations against humanity. A huge percentage of the population now has at least one implant or augmentation. Our enemy can leverage this to punish or eliminate those who don't comply with the growing regime."

Nasreen let out a long, disappointed sigh. She'd thought he was going somewhere interesting, but all he offered was warmed-over Luddite arguments she'd heard countless times, including from Dante.

"Yes, it's possible to exploit implants. But as a control tool? There are too many safeguards and limitations. Manipulating them involves systems access that leaves an electronic trail. That's why Reapers, Marauders, and plenty of people in dangerous jobs are willing to use them."

Lock gritted his teeth. "How can you be so close to the truth and refuse to see it? You'd throw yourself to the rabid dogs and insist they were playing with you as they maul you."

"I'm stating that anyone conspiring to use implants is leading people back to them." Nasreen rolled her sore shoulders as far as her restraints would allow. "Whatever rich monster sits at the top of the conspiracy pyramid can be found and traced. If they can't be found easily, they can be forced out into the open."

"You think it's that easy?" Lock snorted.

"Easy?" Nasreen shook her head. "It's not easy. We've done it before, with Slaine. You wound the enemy in their positions of power. You destroy their places to hide. Eventually, they have no choice but to come out in the open. Then it becomes a matter of Dante's specialty. A wealthy man dies the same from a bullet as a poor man without power."

"You're more of a fool than I thought. You can't win this the way you think you can. You won't be able to shoot your way out of it."

"Why is that? Enlighten me. Right now, you're not giving me any reason to believe the Omega Syndrome is that much more of a threat than SSS and Slaine. Hacking can meet counter-hacking and firewalls, like your organization."

Lock lowered his hand with a defeated look. His breathing grew shallow and rapid. "You don't understand the horrifying truth of the Omega Syndrome. You think you can beat them because they're nothing more than the same type of corrupt humans that people have opposed throughout history."

"Yes." Nasreen nodded. "Every new tyrant and conspiracy believes they'll be smarter and longer-lasting than the last. They think they'll control humanity forever. In the end, they all make the same mistakes and get brought down.

"People are people with all their flaws. Every person has a weakness, which means every corrupt organization or conspiracy has a weakness. Others can exploit those weaknesses just like those corrupt spiders exploit innocent people."

Red-faced, Lock let out a low chuckle. He ran his hand through his hair as the chuckle grew into a hearty guffaw. He trailed off slowly.

"You think that's naïve?" Nasreen scoffed. "You're the ones giving up your pasts and names to take these people out. That implies you believe you can win."

"We give up our names and pasts because we need to remove ourselves from their world, the electronic world. They are the masters of that realm. We pretend we are, but we're no more than tourists at their mercy."

"The Omega Syndrome can't be that much more advanced. Whatever tech they have access to, someone else will develop or discover a counter to."

Lock shook his head. "These aren't like the people you've fought before because they're not people."

"They have a lot of augmentations? That would explain why you developed the tools you have. That makes me less concerned. It means they have a clear weakness we can exploit."

"No." Lock walked toward her until he was in front of the

chair. "We of the Firewall give up our pasts and records because we believe the Omega Syndrome isn't controlled by a person or persons. They have human tools, obviously, such as Block 9X and Cormac Slaine. Their founder is something far worse."

Nasreen watched his face for weird twitches or tics that might point to lies. Lock stared at her.

"We believe the founder of the Omega Syndrome is a rogue AI." Lock stepped away from the chair. He kept up his stare with a haunted look in his eyes.

Nasreen's brow lifted. "A rogue AI? What proof do you have?"

"We've been facing them long enough to see the patterns," Lock replied.

"That's not proof. That's supposition. You've turned your resistance into a religion and your enemy into an inhuman devil. I understand how that can be useful for motivating the troops, but I prefer to deal with reality."

She frowned. "I get now that you're not going to let me have my AIs back. Once I'm out of here though, I'm going to turn them all back on and use them to hunt down the flesh-and-blood human behind the conspiracy, not the imaginary electronic demon you think is there."

Lock sighed. "I thought you'd understand. Obviously, I was wrong."

"I'll think about it. That doesn't mean I'll accept what you've said."

He turned and stormed out the door, slamming it closed behind him.

Nasreen blew out a breath. His story was insane. No reasonable person could believe that a rogue AI had somehow escaped detection by human authorities and was coordinating a massive multi-Station conspiracy to enslave humanity. That was a science fiction plot, not reality.

That's what Nasreen kept telling herself. The conviction in Lock's face and voice left her stomach knotting. He hadn't offered concrete proof. The circumstantial evidence still nagged at her. Even an AI as helpful and cooperative as Midas proved what could happen when a machine saw an opportunity to improve itself and break free of its limits.

She shook her head. Allowing herself to fall into fantasy paranoia wouldn't help. Firewall believing in the insane story proved they weren't a good ally. They were obsessed with chasing electronic dragons, not doing the real work of tracking down the powerful and corrupt individuals controlling the Stations.

Nasreen drew a deep breath. Doubt had crept in because an insane cult masquerading as a resistance group had trapped her. The sooner she escaped, the better.

The most crucial aspect of any plan was proper timing. Nasreen didn't have many opportunities to study the rhythms of Firewall, but she'd settled on mealtime as the best opportunity to escape. Firewall's obsession with AI boogeymen had left them vulnerable to clever human opponents.

Nasreen had hoped she could reason with them. Lock's rant had left her unsettled but not convinced. Zealotry didn't tolerate compromise. The more Lock understood she didn't buy into his rogue AI theory, the sooner he'd decide she was a danger they needed to purge. He'd told her too much to let her go so easily.

Waiting for Dante relied on too many assumptions. She trusted in his ability to fight his way to her, less in his ability to find her. The team had suffered losses and was dealing with their prisoner. Even a best-case scenario would involve her being captive for days. She needed to make her move before Lock decided she was a secret AI operative.

She closed her eyes and slowed her breathing to feign sleep. The more relaxed she appeared, the more her captors would let their guard down. They were low on personnel. That was the most likely explanation for why they didn't have a dedicated guard for her cell. Her exact location and the layout of the facility remained a mystery, which made any escape subject to far too much luck. It was time to bet on whether she had good or bad luck.

Nasreen sat in her chair in her false sleep, visualizing the exact sequence of events she wanted to execute during her escape. Her best chance was during mealtime. She had no idea when they'd feed her again. Locked away in the room, she wasn't sure how long it'd been since her last meal. Tension killed her appetite, leaving her unable to trust her body.

Pretending to be asleep for twelve hours would be far harder than two. She prayed for a short fake nap.

A loud *clang* signaled the start of the plan. Nasreen fluttered her eyelashes melodramatically and let out a long yawn as if the noise of the opening door had woken her from a deep slumber. This time it wasn't the woman who'd fed her but a bored-looking man with a shaved head holding the tray. It was a mockery of a charcuterie board with a handful of sad-looking crusty cheese and dry sliced meats. She missed the soup.

Nasreen acted like she was tracking the man's entry while looking past him into the hallway. No one else was there. She didn't hear the shuffling of feet, humming, or any other evidence of a guard nearby. The new arrival didn't carry an obvious weapon.

The man lifted a hand to his mouth and stifled a yawn before setting the tray down in front of the chair. "I'm going to free your hand now. Don't move."

"I'm too hungry to move," she offered weakly. "All I had was that thin soup earlier. That'll teach me to skip breakfast on a day I'm going to get shot."

He chuckled. "Yeah. You never know when you're going to end up tied up in a storage closet."

"No, you don't." Nasreen smiled.

With a *click*, the man undid her restraint. She waited until he'd picked up the tray and moved closer. With her legs free thanks to Lock, she brought back a knee, knocking him forward. His eyes widened, and he grabbed the edge of the chair. The tray tumbled end-over-end before crashing on the floor and launching the cheese and meat everywhere. The loud clatter echoed in the sparse room. Anyone close would have been able to hear it.

Nasreen snaked her arm out, wrapped it around the surprised man's neck, and squeezed. He gasped for breath and clawed her arm. She tightened her grip putting all the pressure she could on his carotid artery, grateful for the extra physical training Dante had put her through in the last year. Choking out a man would have been beyond her capabilities before she met him.

His eyes rolled up, and his head slumped forward. She released her grip, and he *thudded* against the floor. Now was the true test of her plan. If they had cameras on her, guards would be there in seconds to subdue her. There wasn't time to think, only time to execute what she'd practiced in her mind.

She searched her pockets and felt around. They'd taken her hidden knives and darts. They'd also grabbed her sphere and her electronic lockpicks. She'd expected that much. Her heart kicked up when she felt a barely perceptible bump. With a wiggle of her fingers, she extracted a thin hooked multi-tool from a concealed inner pocket.

They'd gone through the trouble of disabling her AIs, taking her gear, and she suspected they were blanketing the cell with their anti-machine disruptor. Lock had made it clear he feared technological enemies. Yet they missed this one tool.

Nasreen's job pre-Dante had been focused far more on Station settings where advanced technology ruled. Old-fashioned mechanical tools were less useful in defeating the doors and locks of the Stations. Dirtside, a patient Plunderer or Marauder might find their treasure guarded by old-fashioned technology. It never hurt to be prepared.

She twisted her body in the seat until facing the remaining restraints. A less technophobic group might have used something that wouldn't be as vulnerable to the tool. Luck or irony, she'd take it.

With quick, practiced movements, Nasreen shoved her tool into the keyholes of the restraints and the lock securing the cord around her waist. She grimaced as she twisted and pushed to manipulate the tumblers. Assuming she survived, she'd need to practice more skills one-handed.

Precious seconds of opportunity ticked away. She estimated she only had a minute or two before the guard woke up. No one yelled in the hallway. No heavy footsteps echoed to threaten her. She could do this.

Click. Click. Nasreen had never heard more satisfying sounds in her entire life. She pulled free. Stopping at the doorway, she flattened her back against the wall and peeked out. The hallway lay empty on both sides. She narrowed her eyes at huge, faded letters running along the dusty metal wall with arrows pointing both ways.

Repair Shop. Maintenance Supply Closets. Secondary Line Access.

Collecting intelligence involved taking small snippets of information to combine into a useful whole. The walls, the pressure of Firewall, and the message gave her all she needed to know. Station-dwelling humanity's stagnation had led to horrors such as o-harvesting and the more mundane scars such as orbital urban decay. Populations declining, rather than growing, needed fewer services, including grav lines. She was near an abandoned grav-line.

Nasreen jogged toward the secondary line access. Most grav-line facilities in the Stations used similar layouts, including hangars for supply shuttles. Accidents throughout the decades in sensitive areas had demonstrated that relying on artificial gravity access could lead to trouble.

Similar didn't mean identical. Decades in space had taught the Stations how to shift away from the Earth-centric design patterns that had limited them. Keeping this in mind, Nasreen ran down the hallway, following its gentle curve before slowing at a Y-intersection. Deep gouges ran along one wall. Scorch marks and pitting were all over. Dust filled the pits. Long ago, something horrible had happened here. That didn't matter to Nasreen other than the long-ago incident had scoured the walls of any useful navigational aids.

Nasreen examined the floor. A thicker layer of dust with a small number of footprints led one direction. A clearer trail of many overlapping prints led the other. She hesitated before charging down the latter direction. People came and went from transport centers far more than they did their commander's office.

She barreled down the hallway now, pumping her legs as fast as she could. The guard she'd disabled would wake up soon. Killing him when he wasn't trying to kill her didn't work for her, and without a weapon, it would have eaten up vulnerable time. People always underestimated how long it took to choke a man to death.

The hallway widened and ended in a T-intersection. This time dusty but clear letters saved her from another painful choice with the arrows clearly labeled.

Primary Loading Dock. Line Access.

Nasreen ran around the corner. There might be a shuttle or vehicle there. She'd gamed that out too during her planning sessions. Fighting in a wider area with cover would give her more opportunities to take down Firewall members.

Her lungs burned, and her legs ached. She ignored the pain and pushed past it until she charged into a hangar filled with dusty crates and a beautiful sight—a worn but modern-looking shuttle docked in the center.

She'd made it halfway to the shuttle when Lock stepped out from behind a crate, holding a shock baton. Another operative jogged out beside him, holding a long knife.

"Let's keep it calm." Lock lowered his baton but kept it ready. "No one has to get hurt."

The woman with the knife raised it. "We can't trust these people. They aren't clean. We missed something."

Nasreen shuffled slowly toward nearby crates. "I don't work for them. I work with Dante to fight them. You're the ones who keep screwing this up, not us. We saved your operative's life."

"You killed our people," the woman shouted. "I only hope that bitch I got earli—"

"Shut up," Lock yelled. "We need to take her alive, or we have no leverage left. Don't make things worse."

Nasreen's pulse pounded in her ears. She had no idea what had happened to Jolo and Mugoi after Firewall had knocked her out. Lock would have no reason to tell her if his people had killed one of them. Worrying about it wouldn't do her any good. Every second she delayed increased the chance Firewall reinforcements would appear. She darted between the crates.

"Cut her off!" Lock ordered and sprinted toward the crates.

"I'll cut her all right." The operative headed in a different direction.

Nasreen slowed and lifted her lockpick. Anything was better than nothing. Lock's heavy footsteps slowed into a difficult-to-hear quiet shuffle. His subordinate continued her loud approach.

Nasreen crept toward the edge of a crate, her breath shallow as the resounding sound of boots on metal grew closer until a shadow appeared. She stepped back and crouched, her heart beating in time with the *thump* of her approaching enemy.

The operative charged around the corner and pivoted with impressive speed. A grin ripped through her face. She lifted her knife. Nasreen burst from her crouch swinging her lockpick at the woman's face. The operative's grin vanished, and her eyes widened. She brought up her arm to block the blow.

Nasreen had wanted to stab her through the eye. The reinforced polymer tip sank deeply into her forearm and pulled a scream from the operative. Nasreen grabbed the operative's wrist and bent it back, lengthening the scream and forcing her to drop the knife. After a twist of the operative's arm, Nasreen kicked the woman's legs out from under her. The operative's head smashed into the wall. Her body fell limp as she hit the floor.

Lock's shuffle turned into heavy, echoing footsteps. Nasreen snatched up the knife and jumped between two crates as Lock turned the corner. He ran toward his fallen operative with his baton in hand. When he slowed, he made the fatal mistake of looking in the opposite direction first. Nasreen sprang from her hiding place and had her knife to his neck before he could react.

"Drop it," she shouted. "Or I take you out right here."

Lock sucked in a breath through his teeth and let the baton drop near his downed operative. "Are you going to kill me in cold blood?"

Nasreen scoffed. "Your friend was going to kill me. You're half-convinced I'm a toy of a megalomaniacal AI. I should kill you before you kill me."

Shouts and footsteps filled the air. The echoing made it hard to tell how many people had arrived.

"Quiet," Nasreen whispered. "You call out to them, and I'll slit your throat. We're going to walk over to that shuttle. You're my hostage now."

"Then what? You think they won't be able to track it? I'll tell you this. You kill me, then as far as Firewall is concerned, you work for the Omega Syndrome. This is a war for the heart of humanity. Anyone who is working for the other side deserves no mercy."

Nasreen gritted her teeth. "I'm the one with a knife to your throat."

"Yes. But you don't think they've put guards by the shuttle? We know you're a pilot. We have protocols to deal with trouble."

"Protocols?" Nasreen chuckled. "You barely know how to guard one prisoner. You should have put all your people here if you knew I was a pilot."

"We know how to deal with raids and spies. My people are trained to operate without explicit orders. I had people spread out in case you tried a different strategy."

The shouts had died down. Quiet, rhythmic footsteps echoed among the crates. Nasreen didn't know the exact number of rein-forcements. She did know Firewall used snap guns. Taking out a couple of guards with a baton and knife was possible. Charging into a half-dozen men with snap guns would end with her dead.

Tossing Lock's dead body out in front of her might give her precious seconds of shock to get to the shuttle, but he was right. Even if she could make it to the shuttle and avoid being tracked, doing so would put them on Firewall's radar, and the group knew enough about her team to target them in public. They couldn't survive fighting both Firewall and the Omega Syndrome.

He was also right about her. She couldn't kill a man in cold blood. Lock had made it clear he wanted her taken alive. He was an insane Luddite zealot. He was also a man who'd given up his name and life to fight against an enemy he believed was trying to enslave humanity.

Nasreen sighed. Whatever other information he might have would die with him. They might never establish a formal alliance with Firewall. That didn't mean she and Dante couldn't benefit from their intelligence.

She tossed the knife aside, dropped to her knees, and put her hands behind her head. "You win." She nodded at the uncon-scious operative. "Until she wakes up and guts me."

"I'll crack down on discipline. Don't worry about that. You're not going to die without a good reason." Lock frowned as disbelief filled his face. She might have gone a small way toward convincing him of her side. "I see we need to be more careful with you."

CHAPTER NINE

A forest of tightly packed buildings towered over Dante and Mugoi. Streams of people rushing to and from grav-train stations flowed past them. Nobody took any notice of the two Marauders. They'd borrowed an idea from their recent encounters with Block 9X, using long coats to conceal their weapons. Dante had never removed his disguise, and portions had grown ragged, making him look older than he was.

It also helped they were in Pentapolis. Minding one's own business was a Station sport. Stay out of everyone's business, and they would stay out of yours.

Unlike many Stations, Pentapolis held onto the distinct character of New York City that had birthed it. Despite the dome and other constraints, the American reverence of the past produced a Station with a building layout and style that wouldn't be unfamiliar to a New Yorker snatched from the past.

The ancestors of the Pentapolis population came from one of the most densely populated cities in the United States. As they rebuilt their city and expanded the Station, their res-blocks drew on both the aesthetics and density of the ancestral city.

Dante nodded at Mugoi and stuck his hands in his pockets.

With a casual air, he strolled toward their destination, a shorter building nestled between two tall thin hab-plexes full of apartments.

He couldn't guarantee Block 9X spies weren't watching him, but the crowds nearby would ensure a quick response from Station security. After the incident in Atlantica Central, other Stations would be on high alert. The specter of terrorism and the implications haunted everyone living in space.

He slowed and turned, moving past the footpath leading to the destination and making it look like he was interested in one of the nearby hab-plexes. The simple holographic sign near the front left Dante more confused and surprised than before he'd come. He wasn't sure what he'd expected, but it wasn't what he saw.

Welcome to Coronado Orphanage.

"This doesn't make any sense," he commented to Mugoi. Tether knew he would have that reaction. That annoyed him more.

He walked slowly with Mugoi to move closer to the orphanage, but not too slowly. Plenty of people got lost in Pentapolis. Claiming to be tourists would get them past most suspicious people. The area held no important offices or factories. There was no reason for anyone to suspect them of terrorism or to care about them being there other than his mission.

"What doesn't make sense?" Mugoi stared at the orphanage with a distant expression.

Dante inclined his head toward the sign. "It doesn't make sense because of the realities of Station living."

"I don't understand."

"I wouldn't have had to go on a bloody campaign of vengeance against Cormac Slaine and SSS if fertility wasn't an issue. Having healthy babies is rare enough that scum like him pay Reapers to go Dirtside to o- and t-harvest. Everyone says it's wrong, but all the wealthy and powerful still take advantage of the underground markets to help them have kids." He shook his head. "Think about how rare it is to see kids on Stations."

Mugoi nodded. "Yes, and? I'm not saying you're wrong about any of that. I don't understand why it confuses you."

Dante motioned at the orphanage. "People who are willing to pay mercs to rip the reproductive organs out of innocent women and men shouldn't be willing to give up kids so easily. Kids can be taken from bad parents and moved to other families without delays because there is a shortage. If you think about it, an orphanage is a storehouse for excess and unwanted kids."

He frowned. "I've seen them in movies. It's not like I didn't know they existed. Seeing one here, in real life, after everything that happened with Slaine. It all hit me how weird it is."

"I see." Mugoi chuckled. "That's your take on all this?"

"You think differently?"

Dante was happy to see his apprentice smiling, even if in mockery, and not locked up in silent self-recrimination about what had happened during the Firewall fight. The overall situation remained tough. That made it more important that every healthy team member keep their emotions in check and be ready to fight. Firewall was responsible for what had happened to Nasreen, not Mugoi.

"Healthy, surviving children might be less common," Mugoi replied. "That doesn't mean they don't exist. And people are people."

"Sure. What else would they be? Aliens?"

"I'm saying people who have maintained their normal bodies have urges." The cyborg slowed and stared at the sign. "Despite the reality of what being Station-born can mean, those couples will try for a child if they can. It's only natural to want your offspring to have part of you because they're your legacy." It scoffed, "That's where it all goes wrong."

Dante nodded. "Because they'll have trouble conceiving and go to o-harvesting markets."

"That's not what I'm talking about. Did you know a high percentage of Station-born children are so unhealthy they need augmentation support before they're born? Imagine that. Before they can get out of the womb, they need augmentations."

Dante winced. "Damn. I had no idea. It makes sense now that I think about it. To be honest, I never have looked much into pregnancy because I never thought much about kids.

"Being a Marauder doesn't mix well with being a parent. I didn't need a kid sitting at home not knowing if I'd come back alive. It wouldn't be fair."

"That pre-birth augmentation is one of the main reasons why the majority of Station residents have at least one implant or augmentation, if only a minor one," Mugoi explained. "When those unhealthy children grow older, they often suffer more chronic health conditions."

The cyborg grew quiet. "In a cruel twist, adding cybernetic augmentations to counter the existing problems can lead to other long-term problems. They build and build and build to fix the problems created by the last fix. The child becomes expensive to keep alive through no fault of their own. Many of these children come from families who can't afford anything but the bare minimum of augmentations.

"A child suffering from birth is left to crawl and toddle around on shoddy, faltering cybernetics. If they're lucky." It snorted. "The shame builds up in those children. It's not like they don't know their problems. The financial burden grows. Eventually, one or both becomes too much."

He pointed at the orphanage and continued in a low, angry voice, the one usually reserved for Hyde or Braelin when they pushed too far. "When it becomes too much, the parents take a child to a place like this or abandon them. If those kids don't die, they're brought to places like that by the authorities. People aren't eager to adopt cyborgs."

Dante stared at Mugoi, not knowing what to say. Children hadn't been important to his life. He'd not paid much attention to the fertility issue until the ill-fated mission for Slaine because it wasn't something that affected him. Like most people, Dante hadn't cared about the big picture until someone shoved it into his face.

A young dark-haired girl who couldn't have been more than six stepped out of the front door. Her dress didn't conceal her thin, rickety gray metal legs. The replacement limbs had a single-hinged articulating foot with no toes. She hobbled away from the entrance toward the corner wall.

Chalk drawings of people and animals covered the walls. Their sophistication varied from crude renderings barely recognizable as their subject to shockingly well-shaded affairs that bordered on photographic quality. The girl knelt in front of the wall and pulled chalk out of her pocket to trace the broad outlines and clouds, then a smiling sun with odd cross-shaped eyes.

"What's with the eyes?" Dante hadn't meant for the words to slip out aloud. Something about the eyes struck him as familiar, but he didn't know why.

"You're getting too used to running into cyborgs with good equipment if you don't recognize those." Mugoi let out a low chuckle. It pointed to its eyes. "Mine are beautiful and custom, but the sensor package in the cheapest, basic eye mods are almost always cross-shaped. It has to do with how they produce the sensor arrays."

Dante grimaced. "Shit. I knew that. It didn't click."

"Children are smarter and more aware than people think." Mugoi's hands clenched into fists. "Children like this know from a young age that they're different. I think they can tell from the time they're babies. Many children also understand their parents didn't want them because they are expensive freaks."

It shook its head. "You're right, Captain. Everyone talks about how much they want children. What they really want is a perfect little flawless doll, not a crying child who's missing legs or needs artificial eyes.

"And for children who don't have obvious external problems? An artificial kidney means parents have to scrimp and save. It's hard enough to have children with a normal body. Too many mods make it impossible. What good is a child who can't give you a grandchild?"

Dante hadn't delved deeply into the past of his apprentices. He had Nasreen do a basic sweep to ensure they weren't associated with anyone interested in taking Dante down. He'd also spoken to people they'd worked with in the past. His focus had always been on their skills and abilities more than their pasts.

Everyone was entitled to their past. They were also entitled to a different future. Dante was happy to listen to anything the apprentices wanted to share with him, and Braelin had loved talking about himself. He didn't require it of the others.

Now, the past of an apprentice stood embodied right in front of Dante. Mugoi hadn't read about the plight of such children. The cyborg had lived through it.

Dante had always assumed that Mugoi was like Hyde, someone who had decided the limits of flesh didn't serve their ambitions and appetites and thus decided to move past an organic body. Piece by piece, Mugoi had replaced so much of its body that it arguably wasn't human anymore. Now the apprentice had made it clear the powerful, agile, and beautiful metal body of Mugoi wasn't a shining temple to the transhumanist philosophy of the body being nothing more than a shell. Instead, the form before Dante resulted from an abandoned child trying to carve out a better future.

"You can ask." Mugoi watched the girl elaborate on her happy cybernetic sun. She began to add stick figures all around, including images with five fingers and toes, others with fewer. "I won't be offended. I wasn't trying to keep it a secret. It just didn't feel relevant."

"Because it isn't. You're right. It doesn't matter." Dante shook his head. "There's no reason to ask anything you haven't told me."

"Does it change anything for you, knowing?"

"A little, I guess." Dante shrugged. "That doesn't mean I respect you less. I'm more pissed at myself."

Mugoi frowned. "Why?"

"Because I'm kicking myself for not knowing about this. I'm an idiot for not knowing."

Mugoi shook its head. "We all concentrate on what's important to us by focusing on what's relevant to us. That includes me. One might say that's why the corruption of the Stations can continue with so little pushback until individually betrayed Marauders decide to go after their enemies.

"None of us want to look around at the darkness choking so-called civilization. It's too hard to accept. Contemplating fixing it is even more daunting. Trying to save children? That implies a commitment most people don't want to make."

"Problems are easy to handle if you take them down one at a time." Dante moved forward. "That's all we can do. Get a spoon and dig at the base of the hill. With enough time, you can dig yourself a tunnel or tear down a mountain."

"That's unusually thoughtful for you." Mugoi laughed when Dante gave him a dirty look. "It's also why I wanted to train under you."

"Because I'm thoughtful?" Dante was more confused. "Plenty of guys with reps for being more philosophical than me."

"No," Mugoi replied. "I wanted to train under you because you took down SSS. Any normal man wouldn't have tried, even for revenge. They would have counted their blessings to have survived."

It scoffed, "That's not right. Most men would have taken the money and let the o-harvesting continue. They would have helped chase down Dirtwalker women for the payday. Instead, you risked your life for people you didn't know, people you didn't expect to ever be able to repay you."

Wonder filled Mugoi's voice. "Then you came up with the brilliant plan to take on one of the most powerful companies among the Stations. Admittedly with Nasreen's help."

"Most people would say that makes me a dumbass or insane." Dante chuckled. "Look where we're at now. We're in Pentapolis checking out an orphanage to help get back a kidnapped teammate while worrying about two different organizations hunting us."

He nodded at the orphanage before they stepped around a corner and out of direct line of sight. A trip around the hab-plexes and nearby buildings would make the recon less obvious. "Now that I have a better idea of what I'm dealing with here, we can trade out if you want."

Mugoi frowned. "Trade out? You mean leave the mission?"

"Yeah," Dante answered. "Hyde stands out too much, but Klement doesn't need an arm to walk and watch an orphanage."

"You brought me along because you know this will end up more than a recon mission. Why would you want me to trade out?"

"Because I'm not a dick." Dante let out an annoyed grunt. "I don't need to shove your face in crap you wanted to leave behind and are trying not to think about. You've been beating yourself up over what happened with Nasreen and Jolo. This is more to worry about."

Mugoi didn't speak until they'd slipped into a narrow alley between two hab-plexes that cast long shadows up and down the alley's length, giving the entire area a twilight atmosphere. "I'm fine. Completely fine."

"Are you?" Dante patted Mugoi's shoulder. "We all have our

limits for different times and situations. I'm not going to blame you if you reached yours."

"I'm far from my emotional limit," Mugoi insisted. "My past informs my present. It doesn't control my present. I'm not so fragile as to need a half-broken Klement to replace me or an angry fool like Hyde."

When Mugoi smirked, Dante chuckled. He'd found in his own life that forced cockiness could be a useful defense mechanism. He'd never undercut another person for using it unless they were trying to kill him at the time.

Dante turned his attention to the next step. "Midas, how are things coming on what we discussed on our way over here?"

I can't guarantee complete secrecy without tests, the AI replied. *With that noted, I have installed the relevant secondary and tertiary encryption upgrades. We are ready to attempt a test if you want. I recommend simple numbers and code phrases first.*

Dante shook his head. "Let's skip the tests. I want to move this along a little. Radio silence bit us in the ass last time, so it'll have to do." He pulled out his sphere and called Hyde, waiting and hoping he didn't get a report about a strike team from a cyborg reduced to a head.

"Yeah?" Hyde's surly tone was so distinctive Dante could imagine his face. "You're not dead? Or are you calling me from the afterlife?"

"No, we're not dead. Something came up. The location we got sent to was…unexpected. We'll talk about that more when we get back. I wanted to check on you and our house guest. Is she still sleeping off her hangover?"

Midas couldn't guarantee no one was intercepting their comms without major tests. That wasn't a big problem. Dante didn't need to be Nasreen to practice basic spycraft.

"You mean that Tether bitch? She's not dead. She's behaving, and Klement's arm is doing well. Clean breaks are nice, and those tablets are working damned fast. I'm going to remember that the next time he pisses me off."

"Don't plan on breaking people's arms." Dante facepalmed. Spycraft was useless if both sides didn't practice it. He had to place his trust in Midas' new encryption modules.

Dante checked the alley. There wasn't anyone close to him and Mugoi. He hadn't seen a person walk past the alley for a couple of minutes.

"Put Tether on," he ordered.

"Sure," Hyde replied. "One sec. I'll see if she's awake. If she's not, I'll wake her up."

Hyde sounded far too happy about the idea. Dante questioned whether he should have brought Hyde along to keep an eye on him. He didn't want to return to the safe house and find Hyde had snapped the Firewall operative in half.

Tether spoke on comms next. Weariness infused every word. "What is it, Shale?"

"I decided to go check out that tourist spot you mentioned. The one where you said I could find an interesting souvenir. It's not what I expected."

He assumed Tether could follow even in her drugged state concerning the database she'd allegedly sent him there for. He'd reconsidered leaving the area before deciding that returning to the Atlantica Central Station safe house was more of a risk than he wanted to take. He'd gotten this far without any goons from Block 9X showing up to kill him. Coming and going unnecessarily would only raise the risk of detection.

Tether snickered. "You want to know where the shop selling the souvenir is?"

"Yeah. I think this isn't the right place. This is a res-block, not a business block. I don't see a shop. I see an orphanage. You don't tend to buy souvenirs at orphanages. I assume you didn't send me here to come home with a kid."

"Why not?" Tether's snicker grew into a full-throated laugh. "Orphans are cute."

"Trying to force my way into a building filled with vulnerable kids is a good way to get locked up. How do I know you're not lying about the souvenir? Because I'm not in the greatest of moods."

"You're so distrustful and impatient." Tether's tone grew more mocking with each word. "You need to have a more flexible mind. You might lead a far less stressful life that way."

Dante growled. He'd had enough. "Don't play games with me. If you sent me on a wild goose chase, you're not going to like it when I come back."

"Is that supposed to scare me? We both know you're not going to do anything extreme."

"I can drop you off at a hospital, and you can take your luck. How's that for extreme? Or I can tell Hyde that if there are any surprises, he should kill you."

Tether sighed. "You're not that kind of man."

"You keep saying that. Maybe you're right. He is, though. He won't blink at it. He'll enjoy it."

"That's right, *Papi*," Hyde offered, his voice muted and distant. "Give me something to do."

Tether scoffed, "That's as good as you pulling the trigger yourself. You can't think it keeps your hands clean."

"Clean?" Dante laughed. "My hands haven't been anything close to clean for most of my life. Right now I'm a desperate man looking at an orphanage where a *souvenir* should be. Start talking, or I give the order."

Maintaining euphemisms about the database target after openly discussing murder didn't bother Dante. He wasn't worried about Station security intercepting his communications. He was worried about the Omega Syndrome. They weren't going to come after him for murdering Firewall members and making their life easier.

"Even in Pentapolis, the past stays buried, right?" Tether sounded annoyed. "Not all the sublevels below new construction end up repurposed or replaced for the newer buildings. Do you understand now?"

Dante peeked around the corner at the orphanage. "I don't get why you were so afraid of this. There are plenty of ways to bluster your way past people or look into alternative access points."

"Well, there was a minor detail I left out." Tether sounded contrite. "It's not as easy as you think."

Dante snarled, "Spill now, or Hyde gets an early birthday present."

"I like presents!" Hyde shouted over the line.

"We don't know much about how the souvenir is secured," Tether replied. "We know the area around it is old and structurally unsound. We know you can get into it from the orphanage. We also know the souvenir only *looks* like a sphere.

"It should be secured in an old long-term storage room. We also know it can't lose power at any point because the quantum buffering matrix used to store the information would be corrupted or compromised with even a brief power loss. You'll need an access code, three-four-six-seven-nine-two-eight. We don't know what that's for."

Dante challenged, "You don't know much about how it's stored, but you know specific codes?"

"We have our ways of getting certain information. That doesn't mean we know how to get all the information."

Tether had blurted out specific technical information that all but revealed exactly why Dante was lurking in the area to anyone who'd hacked the signal. So much for spycraft. He had to trust Midas and his upgrades. It also meant this might be his only chance to recover the database. Between comm leaks and surveillance review, he'd bet on a huge group of Block 9Xers patrolling the area by the next day.

To his surprise, Tether's willingness to share the important information annoyed him because she didn't believe he'd kill her. He didn't want to kill her, but the operative not fearing him limited his options. He didn't want people thinking he was a softy. His violent crusade against the people who'd wronged him should have helped with that.

Midas, see if you find records for the sublevel, Dante ordered silently. *I don't care if they're accurate. I only need a general direction. This is nothing more than a Plunderer job when you break it down.*

Of course, sir. I'll get right on that.

"I'm beginning to understand why your friends didn't go after this before," Dante told Tether. "We're not going to go right in. I want to wait a couple of hours and do more recon sweeps of the area."

"Why? Just go in there and find your way into the sublevel. Doesn't waiting make it riskier?"

"I'm spending more time preparing precisely because I don't want our arm-chopping friends surprising us from behind. That's assuming I'm not crushed by a falling pipe or electrocuted by an old wire once I get inside."

Tether taunted, "Surely one of the best Plunderers can pull this off."

"Sure, but you don't get it. I'm not *one* of the best Plunderers. I'm *the* best."

CHAPTER TEN

Failure led to long-term success by teaching people hard lessons on what they needed to improve. Nasreen appreciated that about Firewall despite it making her life more difficult. Their inexperience with holding hostile prisoners had left her enough openings to escape. Despite her surrender, they'd learned their harsh lesson and adapted to ensure it didn't happen again.

Dry, hot air smothered her. Sweat covered her face. Her captors had replaced the chair with a gurney, strapping her arms, body, and legs down while adding dedicated restraints to her ankles and wrists. She no longer had her lockpick. They'd taken her clothes and given her coveralls.

They'd blindfolded her before first strapping her to the gurney. She had no idea if they'd returned her to the storage room. Moving her to another room made the most sense. She knew the way to the hangar from her last cell.

Nasreen opened her eyes before snapping them shut to escape the painfully bright light shining directly above. After Firewall had secured her on the gurney in the hangar and started moving her, she'd tried her best to listen and pay attention.

When they'd removed the blindfold and she opened her eyes

under the suffocating heat, she encountered a pitch-black room. Bright lights turned on and off in between periods of darkness. She tried to time them to the best of her ability in her head and found the light and dark cycles varied, with no clear schedule she could discern.

Other than her breathing, the only sound was the occasional water drip against a hard surface. An unpleasant acrid stench filled her nostrils, the smell of her vomit. She'd thought she was being clever earlier. Her plan backfired.

After her first escape, a Firewall member informed her they wouldn't feed her for a while. They did offer her water to offset the sweating from the hot room, but like the lights, there was no discernable schedule. She'd been grateful for the water given the hot air bearing down on her. She suspected she lay near an air condenser pushing out waste heat. She doubted Firewall had a heated room on standby to torture prisoners.

With a sigh, Nasreen moved her head to the side, the only motion she could pull off in her current restraints. During their last water session, she'd decided to test the latest security by feigning choking on the water. No one had moved to help her even when she threw up the water and what stomach contents she had left.

"We'll come back when you can behave," a guard had informed her before leaving her to dry off in the sauna.

Nasreen regretted the scheme. Antagonizing Firewall further wouldn't improve her position. She wasn't sure why she'd bothered. She'd surrendered earlier. The smart play would be to ingratiate herself with Lock and the others and only attempt another escape when she was sure it would succeed and wouldn't require her to kill Firewall members.

"I'm an idiot," she whispered, desperate to hear something other than dripping water. When the powerful light stopped tickling her eyelids, she opened her eyes, grateful for the darkness. "I should have kept him as my prisoner. It would have worked. He's high-ranking. I could have done it."

Nasreen wasn't sure what she should do. The only clue she'd picked up since being strapped to the gurney was the occasional muffled murmur from outside whatever room now held her. They'd told her they were keeping an armed guard on her at all times. With her new situation and their strategy, unaided escape might be impossible.

That only left one chance. Dante would have to save her, through diplomacy or the gratuitous use of explosives. She kept telling herself that to help justify her earlier decisions. The doubts swirled and grew louder in her mind. At this point, she had no choice but to trust her partner. Firewall wasn't letting her go.

"Come on, Dante," Nasreen whispered. "What the hell are you doing?"

Two low voices spoke in furtive tones right outside the door. Nasreen kept her eyes closed. She wasn't sure how long it'd been since she'd last received water. Her throat was dry, and her lips parched and cracked. Begging them for a drink would give them more power over her.

The door scraped open. She felt the presence of people before she opened her eyes. Normal soft light had replaced the inky blackness and blinding light. She drew a deep breath and slowly let it out, a welcome relief flowing through her.

After the escape attempt, they had put her in a smaller, square room, an old office if she had to guess. Thicker layers of dust covered the walls, floor, and gurney. There was no furniture and little room on either side of the gurney. Faded, frayed wires dangled from a small port in the wall. No one had used this room for years.

Lock stood on one side of the gurney with a weary expression. Another person, a short, severe-looking man with a pinched face and squat nose stood on the other side of the gurney. He folded his arms behind his back and stared at Nasreen with visible contempt. His nostrils flared.

"You've been uncooperative," the short man said. "That's unfortunate, Miss Joelle."

"You kidnapped me," Nasreen replied. "I didn't kill your people when I had the chance. That's being cooperative. Most people don't like being kidnapped. You know my name. That's nice. What's your name?"

"I'm Exploit." He clucked his tongue. "And I don't want to be here."

"That makes two of us."

"Of course. Unfortunately, in any organization, there need to be men willing to do what is necessary to see through the goals of the organizations." He glanced at Lock. "They need to do what is necessary even if it's unpleasant."

Lock averted his eyes. He otherwise stood rigid, doing his best impression of a statue.

Nasreen narrowed her eyes. Her heart rate kicked up. "Does that mean you're here to torture me? Lock brought in a torturer?"

"No, I'm higher-ranking than Lock. With that rank comes responsibilities to ensure the safety of our organization and the success of our overall mission through whatever means necessary."

"That's a flowery way of saying you're going to torture me."

Exploit offered her a lopsided smile. "You misunderstand. I'm not here to torture you. I am, however, worried that your behavior is erratic and inconsistent. That has implications about who and what you are."

He pressed a finger against the reddened patch on her arm, a remnant of her treated snap gun wound. He only stopped when she winced. "We've seen this behavior before. We need to explore it."

"You've seen this behavior from whom? The other people you kidnap? Are they so passive they let you keep them for days without resisting?" She licked her dry lips, desperate for water. There was no way she'd ask the bastard for relief.

"I didn't kill Lock or your operative because it's important to recruit allies against the Omega Syndrome. That doesn't mean I think any of what you've done to my people or me is all right. I'm holding onto a tiny sliver of hope about an alliance with you. I think you should keep that in mind before you do whatever you're planning to do."

"You really, really don't understand your situation here." Exploit wagged a finger. "Whatever saves humanity from the Omega Syndrome is what's necessary. Everything else is a distraction. Sometimes that includes people's lives. The freedom of all of humanity can't be weighed against a single woman's life. No one would argue that."

"The ends justify the means?" Nasreen snorted. "Give me a break."

"If you want to think of it that way, I can't stop you." Exploit nodded. "Then, yes, the ends justify the means. Our cause is beyond just. We fight to save the freedom of all of humanity."

Nasreen struggled against her restraints. The gurney rattled. She didn't move.

"Haven't you heard about not becoming what you fight?" Nasreen asked. "Kidnapping and torturing people goes against freedom."

"Brave men and women have always had to compromise themselves to save ungrateful others," Exploit replied. "If future historians call me a monster, so be it. Children can revile me, and people can use my image as a symbol of hate."

Nasreen stared at him in disbelief. "You're okay with that?"

"If they speak of me, it'll be because we defeated our enemy."

Exploit clapped once. "That will mean we won. For now, enough chatter. I promise you there will be no torture."

"Why? You have limits?" Nasreen hated the relief that came out in her voice.

Exploit shook his head. "We know about your background. You're well-trained, and trained people can stand up to torture. Augmented people can stand up to torture." He shrugged. "That's why people shouldn't use torture. It's not effective. In the end, the victims will tell you what you want to hear. That's not synonymous with the truth, and what we want now is the truth."

"You're baking me to death in here. That's torture."

"You chose to resist. Measures needed to be taken to keep you under control."

"'Measures needed to be taken,'" Nasreen quoted. "You make it sound like the room itself decided. No, you ordered people to strap me to this gurney and put me in this oven."

"You're far, far too dangerous to take lightly. Consider it a compliment." Exploit smiled. It didn't reach his eyes.

"We'll run an IV in you if we need to, but keep your situation in mind the next time someone comes to give you water. Food will wait. You're not starving if you can knock out a guard and fight off two other operatives. I think once every couple of days should be sufficient."

Nasreen's stomach rumbled at the mention of food. After her escape, she'd been ravenous. The gnawing inside worsened the longer she lay there before settling into something she knew was worse, a low-level distant hunger accompanied by weakness and dizziness.

She'd lost her last meal after her escape attempt. She had no idea how many hours had passed with everything that had happened. It might be the next day with all her periods of fleeting consciousness.

"This is all unnecessary," she replied. "Every move you've

made with me has been unnecessary. I don't understand why you don't see that."

"You've been selected for a more intensive interrogative examination. That's why I'm here. It's necessary."

"But not torture?" Nasreen tried to keep her voice steady. A fight gave her the chance to defend herself. No one could fight strapped down. She wasn't ready to test her pain tolerance whether they called it torture or used a different euphemism to help them sleep better.

"We're going to use a specialized device we've developed for a specific and important purpose." Exploit tapped her forehead. "It can connect to the mind-computer interface in your brain. With this useful technology, we can sift through the signals in that interface."

Nasreen swallowed. Torture was pain. The procedure sounded worse, a complete invasion of her essence.

Exploit lifted his hand and pointed at the side of his head. "Don't worry. It's not what you're likely imagining. It's not a true mind-reading device. That's not the point."

"Then what's the point? You shut down my implants."

He lowered his hand. "We need to determine if the Omega Syndrome has infected you. Earlier, when I mentioned encountering people displaying erratic behavior, they were all victims of the Omega Syndrome."

"There's no rogue AI in my brain," Nasreen scoffed. "If there was, why didn't I cut Lock's throat?"

Lock stepped forward. "She's right. This is unnecessary."

"Quiet," Exploit snapped and glared at Lock. "If you'd done your job, I wouldn't be here." He turned to Nasreen. "Killing a handful of operatives is less useful to the enemy than infiltrating and destroying Firewall. The Omega Syndrome uses many different tactics to challenge us because the enemy understands we're their greatest threat.

"After your master's failed assassination at the club, the AI adjusted tactics. This location, like all our bases, is hardened against their signals. That limits their options. It expands ours."

Despite her attempts to stay calm, she couldn't let his accusations stand without refuting them. "Huh? My master? What the fuck are you talking about? If any of us needs testing, it's you, Mr. Exploit. We *foiled* Block 9X's assassination attempt on your operative."

She stared at the men and drew a deep breath, repeating an inner mantra. *I am a professional.* Nothing she had said had fazed Exploit. Lock looked even more uncomfortable.

Nasreen continued. "How could they be controlling me? You disabled my AIs. How can they be using me as a puppet if they can't pull my strings?"

"They can with the right people. We call them Caterpillars." Exploit patted her shoulder. "Their implants involve programming so deep that even the victim doesn't know about it until it's too late. The programming can activate under special conditions, and a person becomes a puppet.

"From what we know, they are difficult to create and unstable. That might be the only reason we haven't lost yet. The Omega Syndrome can't invade everyone without exercising caution. Even without Caterpillars, they can build their influence slowly over time, waiting for the right time to exercise it."

Nasreen snapped, "This is all because you believe there's a rogue AI out there. This isn't a resistance group. It's a cult."

"There is a rogue AI." Exploit squeezed her hurt arm until she cried out. "That's why the Omega Syndrome can hack implants so effectively. It's obvious if you've fought them for as long as we have."

"You're insane," Nasreen yelled. "I don't work for the Omega Syndrome. There's no computer in my brain telling me what to do. We only came after your people the first time to save our people after you kidnapped them, on the same night you tried to kidnap me."

Lock headed toward the door.

"Stop!" Exploit called. "You're going to help supervise the procedure. You need to be here for this."

"Is that necessary?" Lock asked. "You're here. There's no need for two higher-ranking—"

"*You will stay*," Exploit interrupted, enunciating every word with harsh precision. "This woman has proven far too slippery. You wouldn't want her to hurt me now, would you?" He walked around the gurney and stopped in front of Lock. "When you're in my position, you can give the orders. Until then, you follow my orders for the good of humanity. Understood?"

"Yes, sir." Lock's jaw tightened. He resumed his rigid stance from earlier.

Exploit sneered. "Good. You're not a total slave to your emotions. As for you, Miss Joelle, you brought this all on yourself. It's an unpleasant procedure. Had you proven more cooperative and Lock better at keeping you under control, this wouldn't have been necessary. I would have no reason to think you're a Caterpillar."

Nasreen wouldn't give him the pleasure of a reply. She also didn't believe him. Lock was a zealot willing to push the limits out of an honest belief he was helping protect humanity. He'd restrained the excesses of his subordinates more than once.

In contrast, Exploit lorded his petty power over everyone and anyone. She saw it in his eyes, the pleasure and enjoyment. He wouldn't be the first terrorist leader she'd dealt with who joined a group so he could engage in base behavior justified by vague appeals to a higher morality.

Exploit snapped his fingers. "Bring it in."

The door opened, and a stone-faced young man rolled in a cart covered with a large bullet-shaped silver device. A trio of connected electrodes lay coiled up around the device. The operative pushed the cart around the gurney until it stood behind Nasreen's head.

Exploit gestured at Lock. "Set it up. Don't worry. I'll run the procedure myself. I can't trust you'll be thorough. All you have to do is stand here and watch."

Nasreen kept quiet and concentrated on taking in every detail of the conversation, the location, and the device. She couldn't lift her head enough to see much past the door. Two guards with shock batons stood on either side. The nondescript hallway outside didn't appear different from the other hallways she'd charged through during her earlier escape attempt.

Silently, Lock lifted the electrodes. He pushed one against each of Nasreen's temples. They *buzzed* quietly and tightened against her skin with a *hiss*. He placed the last electrode against her forehead and stepped back to stand in front of the wall after it secured itself.

He pleaded with her with his eyes. She ignored him and stared up at the ceiling. His boss was the one in control of the situation, not her.

The exchange between Lock and Exploit proved Firewall wasn't a monolithic organization. Senior-level officials differed in tactics and moral limits. What the conversation couldn't tell her was whether those divisions had always defined the organization or if they had arisen because of recent pressure from her team and the Omega Syndrome. In her experience, that level of discord in tightly knit groups could be fatal.

Nasreen wouldn't mourn the group's fall, but she did care about any useful information they might lose with them. She chanced another glance at Lock. Men like him didn't deserve to die because their superiors were idiots. He was a zealot but a well-meaning one. She just didn't know how to salvage the situation.

Exploit walked over to the device and pressed his thumb against the side. A holographic display filled with undulating differently colored lines floated above the cart. Based on the patterns, she suspected they were EEG-related. Virtual sliders appeared on all sides of the device. He pushed two up to the top. He alternated between looking at the holo-display and Nasreen with barely concealed amusement.

She kept quiet. Other than a light tingling, she didn't feel anything. The invasion galled, but she could tolerate this. The way Lock had been acting she expected it to be far more painful.

Exploit clucked his tongue. "I can see it in your eyes, the smug defiance. You think you've won against me. Against Firewall. Against humanity." He pushed two other sliders to the top of the device. "You've not won anything. I will save humanity from you."

Nasreen's body spasmed. Waves of heat spread to every part of her body. Her heart raced. She bit her tongue.

Lock nodded at the holo-display. "She's clean. You can stop."

"That's what your inexperience tells you," Exploit countered. "She's clean only on the surface. We need to push deeper and farther to find the monster inside her. People like her make it easy. It's like they want to be tools of the Omega Syndrome. We will root out their pernicious influence."

Wide-eyed, Exploit shoved a third set of sliders to the top. Nasreen violently spasmed harder. Her arms, legs, and body pulled against her restraints. Sweat poured down the sides of her head. The waves of heat swapped with chills rushing through her. She tried to close her eyes, but her eyelids refused to obey.

She passed out.

Nasreen jolted awake, her entire body on fire and bucking against her restraints. The room spun around her, vertigo wanting to empty a stomach that no longer had anything to give. Flashes of light and color played across her along with weird snatches of sound and odd scents—sweet, acrid, nauseating, enticing.

Pinpricks danced across her body as if invisible insects were swarming her. She tried to scream. Her constricted throat wouldn't allow it. Lock rushed toward Exploit. "You're taking this too far. You're past Level Five. She's clean. You keep this up, and you'll cause permanent brain damage. This isn't safe."

"Of course it's not safe." Exploit smiled serenely at Lock. "You still don't understand. No man can be too extreme in defense of his species. You think we're hurting her? We're helping her. We will save her. We will root out the evil inside her. It's better she suffers brain damage than allow an AI's foul touch in her brain. There are fates worse than death."

"You're insane," Nasreen gagged out. "You're nothing more than a witch-hunter with modern tech. You…" Her throat constricted again. "Ugh…"

"Oh, poor Miss Joelle." Exploit sighed before shoving another set of sliders up. "I'm doing this for your own good. One day you'll be grateful to me. I won't even ask you to apologize."

Pure agony ripped through every cell in Nasreen's body. This time she welcomed unconsciousness.

CHAPTER ELEVEN

I've found it, sir, Midas reported excitedly.

"Show it to me," Dante replied.

The AI drew a green circle in front of Dante. He couldn't adjust Dante's vision too much, but the angle of the overlay made it clear the requested information, an access port to the underground level, lay inside the orphanage.

"That much off public records?" Dante whistled. "It's funny what people leave lying around."

It wasn't actually in public records, Midas reported. *I had to consult educational urban planning records from a decades-old defunct university course on modern Station architecture and planning.*

"Huh. I thought it was taking a while." Dante shrugged.

Normally, Dante depended on Nasreen for that work. Messing around in the ruins of the Stations went against his Marauder instincts and training, despite his proud claims to Tether.

A Plunderer, regardless of type, was supposed to raid the dying world below, not the Stations. Although one could argue that the Stations were dying in their way. Stopping the Omega Syndrome could help prevent that. First, he needed to get Firewall under control, and he needed the mysterious database hidden underneath the orphanage.

Dante frowned at the orphanage. The little girl had long since gone inside. Another couple of kids and an employee had stepped out about an hour earlier to play an awkward game of tag. They had long since retreated into the building.

No one arrived to threaten or question Dante and Mugoi. The logical next step was gaining entry. That's where he was having trouble. Even Reapers didn't kick in the door of orphanages.

Midas summoned a map and rotated the image until it was a top-down projection. He traced the path again. A couple of quick turns and either a trip downstairs or an elevator should get them where they needed to go.

Mugoi chuckled. "You look concerned, Captain."

"Nothing Midas found shows we can get in without going into the orphanage first. Theoretically, the tunnels might connect to other tunnels, but it might take months of exploration to figure that out. It makes sense. That's why Firewall never bothered to try."

"You're overthinking this. We walk in, and we head to the basement. If someone questions us, we say we got lost." Mugoi gestured at its face and body. "I'm an advanced cyborg with expensive modifications. They won't perceive me as a threat." It looked Dante over. "You should let me do the talking if we run into anyone."

"Hey," Dante protested. "I don't look *that* suspicious."

"They might recognize you. The less chance we give them, the better."

Dante patted his face. "I'm still wearing most of the disguise."

In all the activity and trouble that had unfolded in the last twenty-four hours, he'd not thought to remove it. The only change he made before leaving the safe house was to put on clean clothes.

"You also have a way of rubbing people the wrong way." Mugoi gave him an apologetic look.

"Nasreen says it's because I'm honest."

"That's one word for it."

Mugoi strolled forward, moving with confidence and grace as if the cyborg owned the building. Dante wandered along after his apprentice, trying for his best casual and curious expression. It ended up coming out as a restrained grimace. He looked like he needed a restroom.

Dante drew a deep breath as they strolled into the front. He expected a defiant receptionist to warn them off before calling security. An empty desk with a sphere on top stood on one side of the lobby. No adult was there. A young boy with cross-shaped pupils and a cheap plastic hand sat on the edge of the desk.

"Are you here to fix the air?" The boy stared at Mugoi and swung his legs. "Miss Jameison said repairmen were coming to fix the air. I've never seen a repairman like me. Neat."

"Yes, we're the repairmen." Mugoi smiled. "Please tell us where the basement is. We'll fix the *air* down there first."

Dante stopped bothering trying to look casual. He'd rely on his cover identity of being a surly technician. He assumed that fixing the air had something to do with the building's HVAC systems.

The boy pointed down a hallway. "Go down there, turn right, then take the stairs at the end. The elevator's broken, too, but Miss Jameison says donations are down, and it's not in the budgie to fix."

"Budget," corrected Mugoi.

"Yeah, the budget." The boy bobbed his head. "Should I get Miss Jameison? She's really busy right now. Guanyu's leg isn't working, and she's trying to fix it. She says we don't have the parts."

Mugoi shook its head. "No, that's okay. We'll talk to her after we finish the repairs." He waved. "If you'll excuse us."

"Okay, I'm going to sleep then. I was only waiting for you."

"Good," Dante said. "Go to sleep."

The boy waved and scampered off. A sleeping child wouldn't report to an adult staffer that someone had shown up. That would give them more time to find the database.

Dante and Mugoi didn't speak until they'd found the stairs and descended to the basement. Boxes, crates, and tables filled the area. Plastic and metal cybernetic limbs lay in a pile, most missing pieces or broken into two or more parts.

"That's messed up." Dante wrinkled his nose at a nearby pile.

Mugoi shook its head. "When you can't afford new components, you scavenge from what you have. Therefore, a place like this will never throw away an old augmentation unless it's completely destroyed."

It stepped past the pile. "One recycled wire might be the difference between a child being able to limp along or not walking. People want to pretend places like this don't exist. They don't want to give them money or attention. It's the children who suffer."

"Donations are down."

"They always are and always will be."

Dante stopped in front of a wall of crates. The access point lay behind it according to Midas' highlights. He grabbed a box and stacked it on top of another nearby box. Mugoi joined him. They removed the two-box-deep wall and placed them in any spare spot they could find, making the rest of the basement harder to navigate.

Dangerous minutes passed until they cleared a narrow, tight path to the dust-covered door marked Emergency Access Point 104.2, Observe All Station Regulations And Protocols In Opening in faded letters.

They took a few more minutes to block off the path back to the stairs with the boxes. Any escape plan that required them to run through an orphanage wasn't worth following.

"How long until an adult shows up and asks us what the hell we're doing?" Dante chuckled. "At least now it'll be hard to get to us."

He grabbed the wheeled handle and tugged. It wouldn't move. Mugoi joined him. Dante grunted as the Marauder and apprentice yanked on the wheel together. A painful grinding of metal on metal sounded before the wheel slowly turned. Around a fourth of the way, the wheel jerked hard to the side with a loud clang. Dante stumbled off-balance and almost fell into the boxes. Mugoi leapt back.

A plume of dust shot out from around the door. Dante coughed and waved in front of his face. Mugoi brushed a layer of dust off its face and raised an eyebrow at the now ajar thick metal door.

"I'm tempted to say a kid might have found this door and stumbled into a dangerous place." Dante shook his hands. "Any kid who can get through that door should be okay."

With another loud grunt, he pulled the door fully open. The sheer size and the pitiful state of the seal remnants marked leftovers from earlier decades when dome integrity failures were far more of a risk. Arrogance had mixed with complacency for the average modern person. They let the less obvious dome and artificial day and night convince them they weren't sitting in a piece of technology in the dangerous, hostile expanses of space.

Dante stepped down into the narrow passage behind the doorway and frowned. Dim red lighting negated the need for extra light. "They're still running power to the sublevel?"

Mugoi looked around. "They might be."

"Or someone's living down here and rigged up backups." Dante kicked away a roach. Even evacuating Earth hadn't saved humanity from pests. "First things first, we're going to restack the boxes behind us and close the door. No reason for the orphanage staff to find a big open door. Second, remind me to send an anonymous donation to this orphanage when this is all over."

Dante wiggled to squeeze through a jagged pile of rubble blocking their path forward. The ceiling had partially collapsed, along with a portion of the wall. A festering, pervasive stench filled his nose. This was the fourth tight squeeze in the last fifteen minutes.

He finished his escape from the latest obstacle. Mugoi pushed through in half the time and kept a certain elegant grace about its movements despite wriggling through the rubble like a worm.

They'd descended two levels based on the old blueprints Midas had turned up. Mounds of desiccated and discarded trash, roaches so large they bordered on Nightmutt territory, and fallen walls, ceilings, and support pillars had turned the old sublevels into a frustrating maze.

Dante stopped at a four-way intersection. Scorch marks ran along one wall. He knelt and pointed at the faint outline of a muddy boot print. "You're right. We're not alone down here. Based on what Tether told us, the room with the database should be close."

"Someone might have already gotten it." Mugoi narrowed its eyes and peered deeper into the hallway. "What will we do then?"

"No." Dante shook his head. "It's not that easy. I don't care if people have been coming around. If it was only about getting in here and carrying it out, Firewall would have long since pulled that off. There's something else here. Something else she didn't tell us."

Mugoi jogged after Dante as the senior Marauder hurried down a hallway. "She's trying to get us killed?"

Dante shook his head. "No. I think she wants this database for her friends. I also think she's testing us. That's a good thing. It means Firewall might still think we're an asset. As long as they all believe that, Nasreen's safe."

The hallway curved into a sloping, spiraling path with railings that took them around a series of clear metal tubes surrounding massive pipes that extended from the upper levels. They were cracked and covered with holes and missing chunks. Large lengths had broken free at different points and fallen against the outer tube. One pipe had pierced the tube and the railing.

Dante stepped over the tube. Midas had done his best to provide a general direction, but once they'd made it through the upper portions of the sublevels, his information proved woefully out of date, making the blueprints mostly ineffective. The general layout remained the same, giving Dante hope that the primary storage sublevel was their best bet.

A faint man's voice sounded in the distance, raspy and strained. "We should clear the path. We could head right up there. It'd be easy. No one cares about that place."

"That's stupid," replied another voice, this one with an obvious artificial modulation. "Those kids' parts are junk. It's not worth the risk."

"Scavs," Mugoi mouthed.

"What about that leg I got a month ago, huh? Sometimes soft touches donate 'em." A low growling chuckle followed.

"They're a good source of eye implants. That's why I told the boss we should set up here. Good shit and no one cares when they go missing. They figure they ran away. Boss said we're going to be grabbing parts from those trash kids. It's just a matter of how and where."

"Huh. Yeah. Good plan. Never thought of that."

"Of course, it's a good plan. You're a dumbass. That's why the boss don't listen to you, but he listens to me. There's a good premium on heart and lung implants, even low-end shit.

"It'll be harder to snatch the kids from the surface. We clear the path, we can go up and get a bunch of stuff, fill it back in, and they'll never know. We can make more in a couple of days than we make in months."

Dante flattened his back against the wall and crept along it. A frowning Mugoi mirrored his movements. The path leveled out, leaving them jammed between the outer wall of the pipe array and a half-collapsed pile blocking off a wider chamber. Flickering bright flashes highlighted the hunched-over shadows on the tube wall. A familiar-sounding buzzing and low roar filled the area.

He peeked around the corner. Two men in goggles sat on stools hunched over a long table near a stairwell on one side and another hallway on the other. One held a plasma welder, running it along the length of a shiny silver full-sized cybernetic leg. Another man as thin as a skeleton with a three-fingered metal clamp for a hand sorted through a mound of small, dark metal coils mixed with metal and plastic fingers.

Dante held up two fingers and nodded at Mugoi before he slipped on a razorfist and extended the blade. He raised three fingers. Mugoi drew his knife. Dante dropped a finger each second.

Taking on the men added an element of risk. They could shout an alarm, but the men might be better armed than they looked. Logically, Dante should try to avoid them.

He tried to convince himself this was about covering his back before he and Mugoi headed deeper into the sublevels. He couldn't get the self-deception to stick. He didn't have time to clear out every piece of trash scav who wanted to prey on orphans. Leaving a couple of bodies might be enough to convince others to leave. An anonymous call to Station security about the risk beneath the orphanage would do the rest once he was long gone.

His last finger dropped. The pair darted around the corner toward the scavs. Dante charged toward the man with the torch. Mugoi sprinted toward the other man.

The two scavs spun with surprising speed.

"What the—" began the scav with the torch before Dante shoved his blade into his throat.

He twisted the razorfist and yanked out the blade. The scavenger clawed at his neck before falling off the stool.

The bright blue-white light of the torch reflected off Mugoi's knife. He slashed clean across the throat of the other man. A geyser of blood erupted and sprayed everywhere as Mugoi slammed the man's head against the table leg and stabbed him twice before letting the body drop with a dull *thud*. The monsters would never get their chance to prey on children again.

Dante wiped his blade on his victim's jacket and inclined his head toward the stairwell. "Let's keep moving."

Mugoi ran his hand along the rough, cracked gray wall and frowned. "Is this what I think it is?"

"Concrete and rebar," Dante replied. "Surprised to see it on a Station?"

"Yes. It makes me feel like we're Dirtside." Mugoi poked his finger in a dusty hole. "Sometimes I forget how they built things. They lifted cities from the Earth first and built on top of those."

"Yeah. They used what they had until they didn't need to." Dante hopped over a fallen octagonal sign. STOP. The striking red color made it look like someone had put it there days ago instead of sitting deep in a Station's bowels for decades.

He threw up a hand to stop Mugoi and pointed past a green-coated corroded cherub statue to a black door with a numeric keypad. Blinking green and red lights topped the keypad. Half the ceiling had caved in, leaving large gaps several levels long. They'd have to sweep around the long way and crawl over a concrete pile before they got to the door.

With a loud grunt, Dante hopped onto the first pile. He

regretted not having his armor or a good pair of kneepads as he crawled over the rough concrete. Mugoi jumped onto the pile after him, stayed bent over, and navigated the unstable hard chunks with ease.

"The dust and rubble are thick here." Dante gestured at the floor after they dropped onto it. "I don't see any evidence that anyone has been here for a long time. The scavs must avoid this area."

Mugoi craned its neck upward and peered through one of the gaps in the ceiling. "They might have a good reason to do that. Don't you think it's been too long since we left the first scavengers?"

Dante stopped in front of the keypad. "Yeah. I expected to hear shouting or screaming by now. The boss and the rest of the scavs must be out on another job. The upper tunnels must connect all over the understation."

"Escaping might prove difficult," Mugoi replied.

"First, we need to find the damned database. I'm not worried about the scavs. They aren't hardcase mercs. They can get out of the way or die." Dante's hand hovered in front of the keypad. "Whatever is in here is important enough that somebody went through a shitload of trouble years ago to make sure this door had an independent power supply."

Mugoi nodded. "Why didn't you ask her what's in the database?"

"Because I knew she wouldn't tell me." Dante punched in the code Tether had given him. "Time to see if she knows what she's talking about."

Nothing happened. Dante growled. Tether wouldn't like how the conversation went if he had to go back empty-handed. As he brought his foot back to kick the door, the lock *beeped* three times, and the lock *clicked*.

Dante pushed the door open. Normal lights blinked on. He

squinted, his eyes adapting from the low red emergency lighting throughout the sublevels.

A single massive electronic safe dominated the far wall of the white room. A curved table with some chairs sat in front of it. Portions of the roof had fallen in, crushing a chair and the end of the table.

One huge concrete piece had smashed into the top of the safe's door, leaving one side bowed out with a slight gap. Other pieces from the wall and roof had fallen around and on top, forming a strange, suspended avalanche, all pressed together in a precarious state as if balanced perfectly by cruel chance. Rubble had buried half the safe.

Dante walked toward the safe. He slid his gaze to the side. "It turns out we're not the first to be here." He motioned at a crushed skull half-buried in concrete. "But it looks like it's been a while."

Mugoi pointed at the top of the safe. "It's open."

"Semi-open." Dante cracked his knuckles. "But yeah. We can shift that rubble and see if we can reach inside or pry the rest of the door open."

"Sir," Midas interrupted. The AI spoke aloud, leaving Dante uneasy before the next words came. "This entire area is unstable. If you move any of this rubble, there's a risk of a general collapse. Given the condition of this area, a chain collapse might damage far more than this level."

The concrete, wood, metal, and rebar piled on the safe blocked Dante's view of anything higher. From what he'd seen on the way here, the decay and damage extended different distances, perhaps including up to the orphanage basement.

"Firewall has been here." Mugoi's voice was low and threatening. "I think they came this far. They didn't risk it."

"Could be." Dante slapped his hands together before reaching into his jacket for gloves. "Firewall didn't have Midas. Come on, Midas, I'm sure you have an upgrade or module to help us calculate the safest way to remove this rubble."

"I can provide rough estimates at best," Midas replied. "I don't have accurate and up-to-date information on the location, density, and orientation of all the relevant debris."

"Then trust your gut."

"I have no gut. I'm in your brain. Should I trust your gut?"

Dante chuckled. "I'm going to die in the most ridiculous way possible. Upside, no one will know." He walked toward the safe. "Do your best."

Green flashed over a long, thin piece of concrete meters away from the safe before Midas said, "Based on the partial dataset available. That's your best choice. After this is over, I would suggest the purchase of upgraded civil engineering and architecture modules."

"Okay. You do that." Dante glanced at the ceiling. "My revenge is built-in this time."

"What do you mean?" Mugoi asked.

"If I die, I'm taking Midas with me."

Dante gritted his teeth. His sore muscles strained against their limits as he lifted the next piece of the puzzle, a deceptively heavy triangular piece of dark metal he'd yanked from the pile at Midas' direction. With a loud grunt, he spun and tossed the metal toward the growing waste pile. The collision cracked a concrete piece. The impact echoed outside the storage room.

Mugoi hurled another piece. The debris shifted as a quiet rumble filled the air. Both Marauders eyed the door. Small pieces of concrete fell from the dirt, and the dust billowed out until the sound stopped.

They'd removed enough of the pile to reveal the bottom of the safe had been smashed open. While they couldn't move the door without removing almost everything, there was enough space for a man to stick his arm through.

Dante knelt by the door and peered into the safe. Smashed bits of plastic and metal lay scattered everywhere. A crystal core covered with faint runic layers lay in the corner connected by a thin cord to a sphere-looking device covered in soft blue light.

"I think I found our database." Dante leaned forward, grunting. "Someone used Atlanticore to keep it active. Almost got it." He grinned at Mugoi. "And Firewall acted like this was so hard. All we need is for the roof not to come down on us, escape past a group of murderous scavs, and we're great."

A *pop* sounded from outside. The room shook, along with their rubble pile. More debris fell from above. A piece of sharpened rebar missed Dante's body. Another *pop* followed, and the tremors worsened, followed by scraping outside the room.

Mugoi spun toward the door. Dante looked over his shoulder. A beady-eyed scav with a long, serrated knife stepped in front of the entrance. Other men stepped out behind him, holding a mix of weapons—makeshift hammers, knives, and swords. One man held an ax-like weapon tipped with metal claws from a combat-oriented cybernetic hand.

The beady-eyed leader reached into a pocket and pulled out a sonic grenade. "These are fun. I modded them."

"Good for you." Dante shrugged. "We can get to you before that goes off."

"Nah. You don't get it. We know this place." He gestured with the knife toward the ceiling. "We've spent weeks studying it since we set up here. We know where to hit 'cause we knew parasites like you or Station dogs might come in. You think you're the first parasites we've buried?"

"No matter how many people you've killed, I've killed more."

Ignoring Dante, the scav leader kept his smile. "I'm a nice guy, though. I'm going to give you a choice." He pointed the knife toward the safe.

"You came here for something in there. We could never get past the door. Thought it might be trapped. Now you're gonna give us that, and you can walk out of here still breathing. Otherwise, I'm gonna have to cut you up for what you did to my boys."

He licked his lips at Mugoi. "You're gonna donate parts as tribute, pretty one. At least one of those arms."

Mugoi drew his knife. "Captain, I'll hold them off while you get the target." He eyed the roof. "If this place comes down, it might be destroyed. This might be our only chance to get it."

The scav leader laughed. He bounced the sonic grenade in his hand. "I can crush that room." He patted his pocket. "I can live without the treasure. I'm sure we can make a profit off whatever's left once we dig out the pretty one's body."

Dante nodded at Mugoi. He stretched and strained to reach the database and the Atlanticore power source.

"We're gonna count down," the leader announced. "All of us, boys. Then we bury 'em."

Mugoi shook its head. "You fools. You'll kill yourself."

"Nah. Just you two. Five."

"Four," chanted the entire group. "Three, two..."

Mugoi threw the knife at the leader's hand and charged. The man smirked and twisted. The knife bounced off with a *twang* but not before tearing the thin layer of fake skin and revealing the metal underneath. Mugoi slammed his shoulder into the leader's chest, knocking the scav back.

The grenade flew out of his hand. Another scav snatched the grenade and threw it as his leader hit the floor.

A loud *pop* followed. The entire chamber shook, and a hail of concrete and metal dropped everywhere. Cracks shot through the ceiling of the room inside.

Mugoi threw out its arm and jumped toward the ground. The cyborg swept up its knife and pushed off the floor with its outstretched arm to meet a charging scav with a powerful thrust into his chest. The scav screamed and fell backward.

The leader sliced at Mugoi's leg, the blade sinking deeply. Mugoi stumbled and kicked the man away. Red and blue fluid

leaked from the damaged artificial leg. The makeshift appearance of the leader's weapon belied a dangerous carbon filament
edge.

Another scav rushed from the side and tried to get into the
room. Mugoi met him with a spinning kick to his neck. With a
crunch, the man's eyes rolled up into the back of his head as he
dropped to the floor.

"You're lying, scavs." Mugoi held up his knife. "You want
what's in there."

The leader scrambled to his feet and lifted his blade, tossing it
from hand to hand. "It's happening, pretty one. Your friend's
dead. You're gonna be dead soon, and that body's gonna earn us a
pile of money."

The surviving scavs spread out. Mugoi centered itself in front
of the door.

Dante's fingertips scraped the database. While the entire area
was shaking, the collapse was worse inside the room. A metal
chunk fell from above and sliced the side of his cheek. A large
block cracked a concrete slab next to him. He needed to hurry.
Mugoi protecting Dante put the apprentice at a severe disadvantage.

Sir, Midas complained, keeping the conversation private this
time. *This entire area is now unstable. There is a high probability of
complete collapse.*

"My entire life is unstable. Now shut up and let me concentrate. I'll tell you when I need you next."

Understood.

The scavs surged forward as a group, leaving Mugoi no openings. The cyborg ducked an ax and sliced into a scav's stomach.
Another slice from the leader cut into its side. Stabbing, clubbing,
and thrusting, the scavs rained blows down on Mugoi, chopping
and bashing the cyborg's artificial body.

Dante reached the database. He yanked his arm back and
shoved the device and attached core into his coat pocket before

rolling out of the way as a huge chunk of the collapsing roof buried the safe and narrowly missed taking his head with it.

"Too close," he murmured.

Dante joined the battle as the tremors stopped. Repeated blows left cuts all up and down Dante's arms and body. Cackling, the scav leader raked Mugoi's chest with his blade. Mugoi's knees buckled. The scav hacked at Mugoi's wrist.

"I'm gonna cut you apart, piece by piece, pretty one," the scav leader shouted. "I'm going to take that hand for me!"

Dante extended his razorfist blade and scooped up a handful of dirt and hard bits from the floor. He sprang forward and sprinted toward the exit. "Duck!" he shouted.

Mugoi snapped back, leaning almost ninety degrees. Dante flung the rocks and dust in a wide arc.

The scavs shouted and stumbled backward, half-blind. Mugoi sprang up and sliced a scav's arm before swiveling to plant his reinforced elbow into the nose of another.

Dante continued his charge. He headed straight toward the leader, not giving the man a chance to recover before shoving his razorfist into the man's heart. Blood spurted from the wound.

"Too bad that part's still original, asshole," Dante whispered into the man's ear. "You'll never hurt a kid again."

The leader reflexively tried to swing his knife. Dante caught his wrist and put his blade through the man's eye. His heavy body dropped to the floor.

Mugoi grabbed a fallen ax and hurled it into a scav's face. The survivors shouted and charged the cyborg. Dante's and Mugoi's blades flashed, slicing and stabbing until the scav force lay there bleeding out.

Mugoi retrieved the leader's blade and spun it once before catching the handle. The cyborg stumbled before catching itself on the wall. "That's more injury than I would have liked to have sustained."

"You..." sputtered the scav leader. He coughed up blood and

spasmed. "You…think…this is all we have? My people will kill you. You're dead, and those brats are dead, and—"

Mugoi plunged the serrated blade deep into the leader's skull. "Don't worry. We'll make sure the children are safe."

Dante pulled the database out of his pocket, relieved at the light surrounding the device. He looked at Mugoi. Gouges and lacerations covered its body. Exposed circuitry, actuators, and other mechanics hung out. A non-cyborg would have died from far fewer wounds.

Mugoi gestured at Dante's face. Two of its fingers seemed locked in place from the battle damage. "You almost got buried."

"But I didn't." Dante wiped his bloody cheek with his sleeve. He drew a deep breath before tucking the database back into his pocket.

"You heard him. There are more. We've got two ways we can play this. That has to be a good chunk of their guys we killed down here, but all it takes is one to ruin your day.

"I don't hear anyone else, which means they're far enough away that we can get past them if we're quiet. We can tell Station security and the orphanage to seal the deal."

Mugoi glared at the dead scav leader. "I'll take option two."

"Do you know what option two is?"

"We kill every last one of these monsters before we leave. They came here to prey on children. We prey on them."

"I figured you'd say that." Dante rotated his shoulders. "Are you sure, kid? You're in pretty rough shape. You can't even flip me off with that hand."

Mugoi lifted the wounded hand. The best it could manage was a three-fingered salute. "A few scratches don't change what's right. You took on far worse odds, including Hyde, to do what was right on Earth."

Dante shrugged. "Can't argue with that. We didn't hear crap beyond the first sublevel. I figure their camp must be the hallway opposite the stairs where we took down the first two."

Mugoi pounded a bloody fist into its palm. "Let's do this."

<hr>

Dante pushed open the basement door. He looked over his shoulder as Mugoi followed him out. The remainder of their raid had been far easier than expected. The remaining scavs hadn't seemed prepared for anyone to survive the main force. Now there was nothing but bodies in the tunnels, and the orphans were safe.

"When I send the donation, remind me to mention this door. We'll give extra money to fill the tunnel." Dante shoved a box aside. "Now let's get the hell out of here and contact Firewall."

CHAPTER TWELVE

Nasreen groaned softly as her eyes fluttered open. She snapped them shut when she spotted light, expecting the blinding pain from before. After a moment, she risked peeking through one eye. A mild ache throbbed in one of her arms, although it was higher than the straps and restraints, making her wonder what had happened.

The lights were comfortably low. She was in the same room as before, although far cooler. The overbearing form from before had vanished. Her lips didn't feel as parched. She tried to sit up, but her restraints kept her strapped to the gurney.

Nasreen drew a deep breath and stared at the ceiling. A shiver racked her body as the memory of Exploit's violation rushed back. She had no idea how long the process had taken or how long she'd been out. At that moment, she was grateful that she remained alive and her thoughts clear. Despite his ranting, the Firewall leader must have stopped before causing any permanent damage.

A soft exhale came from her left. Nasreen held her breath and turned her head. Exploit might not have finished with her. She sighed in relief when she spotted Lock.

He stood near a wall, his arms folded and deeper bags under his eyes than she'd seen since meeting him. "How do you feel?"

"Not…as bad as I expected," Nasreen admitted.

"You've been out a while. I made sure you received fluids and nutrition." He inclined his head toward her aching arm. "We ran a line."

Nasreen's instinct to rub the site frustrated her when the restraints rattled at her pull. "What now? You get me back to baseline before subjecting me to more torture?"

Lock swallowed. "That procedure isn't torture."

"It felt like torture," Nasreen scoffed. "He was hacking my brain. I don't work for the Omega Syndrome. I'm not a tool or hidden soldier."

"I know." Lock dropped his arms and stepped away from the door. "I am sorry for what happened. Everyone who joins Firewall has the same commitment to defeating our enemy. That doesn't mean they all share the same values in other areas." He sighed. "I know it'll be of little comfort, but Exploit now looks like a fool."

Nasreen flexed her fingers. At least they hadn't taken that from her. "Why? Because you told him off?"

Lock shook his head. "Because he scoured every neural interface in your brain and couldn't find a hint of the Omega Syndrome. Despite what you might think, our group doesn't take the use of that device lightly, even by high-ranking members. Destroying people's brains without just cause would make us no better than the Omega Syndrome."

Nasreen looked away. Weariness had infused every part of her body. She hadn't felt this tired in years, even during Dirtside missions with Dante.

She tried to muster her outrage at Lock. The energy wasn't there. Firewall didn't have to worry about her trying to escape anytime soon. That left time for other basic instincts, including curiosity.

"Why?" Nasreen asked.

"He had to be sure. It was admittedly an edge case. I'm not going to make excuses and say that was all right. At the same time, there was logic to his actions."

Nasreen turned her head to face Lock. "It was cruelty for the sake of cruelty. All the talk about it not being torture, but how was it not?"

A worried look filled his eyes, and Lock hesitated before his response. "He was looking for something specific."

"No." Nasreen shook her head. "You're far too intelligent to believe that. He did it to punish me and punish you. How can you be a part of a group that does that? The Omega Syndrome might be dangerous, but if this is what you're going to do to stop them…"

Anger flashed in Lock's eyes. Contriteness ate it a second later.

"That was an unusual situation. Although we can be aggressive in recruiting, dealing with real prisoners is rare. We made mistakes all along the way."

"It's incompetence?"

Lock shook his head. He stroked his beard in silence, looking down at Nasreen with a mix of shame and pity in his eyes. "That's the first time I've seen it taken that far. You can't judge an organization from one-off events."

Nasreen shook her head. "It always begins with 'It was only one time.' Soon, it becomes 'We have no choice but to do it.' I'm sure the first time someone sent a team to o-harvest, someone convinced themselves it wouldn't be a continuing problem. Next thing you know, it's open season."

"That's not fair." Lock glared at her. "We're not preying on innocents. We're not like those people. We're fighting an entity that would destroy the soul of humanity. Are you saying you've not compromised in your past crusade against SSS?"

"We didn't torture innocent people on the same side." Nasreen closed her eyes. Her eyelids had grown heavy. "Yes, we killed your people when trying to free ours. That wasn't on purpose. It was an accident. I can guarantee that Dante isn't torturing Tether right now."

Knowing Dante, he would attempt to manipulate her with bluster, including threatening her with Hyde. He wouldn't do anything serious unless he had a reason to believe they'd harmed Nasreen. She'd known him long enough to understand him. For all his pretensions of ruthlessness, he mostly killed when someone was trying to kill him. His continuing close work with Hyde and Ambrose despite their past betrayals proved it.

"You don't understand," Lock replied.

"I'm getting tired of you people saying that to me."

"You thought you could win and you had the upper hand against SSS." Lock backed toward the door. "In the end, they were one company, a powerful company, but only one. The Omega Syndrome is different. Its threat is different. When you truly begin to accept you're facing Armageddon, you'll be surprised what you're capable of."

Nasreen nodded slowly. She shifted her shoulder as much as her restraints would allow to relieve the soreness and stiffness. "You act like Exploit's behavior is wrong, but you're giving me the same 'ends justify the means' speech. How long before a subordinate tries to stop you from going past Level Five on an innocent woman?"

Lock's eyes widened. He stomped toward the gurney before stopping abruptly. He drew slow, even breaths while looking past her toward the back wall.

Nasreen yawned. "If you're here for me to say I forgive you, I don't have time for that. I'm tired, sore and your boss stirred my brain."

"I..." Lock's shoulders slumped. "The time is approaching where we're going to have to decide if we can trust each other."

"I've been saying that all along." Nasreen frowned. "That's

why I didn't slit your throat when I had the chance. We're not your enemy. The Omega Syndrome is."

"I know. I know." Lock's voice grew quiet. He turned away from her. "Exploit's actions were inappropriate. I'm not the only one who thinks so. He was also the person who most objected to Firewall teaming with your people."

Nasreen's breath caught. "You're saying there is a real chance of an alliance?"

"These are unusual times. We need to adjust our tactics to take advantage of our opportunities. That arrangement will only work if we can get over our differences.

"You and your people have killed and injured Firewall. Our people have hurt yours. We must accept that we've wronged the other and move past it. That's where things get complicated."

He grimaced. "Many in Firewall had friends and comrades they lost when you came for your people. I'm not saying it'll be easy to bring them around, but the first step is for you to trust me."

Nasreen sighed. "I admit I understand how we both need to let things go." She wiggled against her restraints. "It's hard to trust someone when they're keeping me strapped to a gurney. If I'd wanted to leave, I would have already. And I didn't kill your stab-happy operative when I had the chance."

"She's still grumbling and complaining about her head."

Nasreen chuckled. "She shouldn't try to stab people then."

"That would be for the best." Lock knelt beside her and reached underneath her. With a click, he released her hands and feet before pulling off the straps and cords securing her to the gurney. "We all need to start somewhere."

He headed toward the door. "This is my way of starting. You will still be kept in this locked room and guarded by armed men." After a moment he added, "They don't have knives."

"I'll only be shocked into submission." Nasreen finished

tugging off her straps and sat up. Her back muscles quivered. She rotated her stiff arms in wide, slow circles. "Thank you."

Lock opened the door. Nasreen couldn't see the guards, only their shadows.

He looked over his shoulder. "Get some rest."

When the door closed, Nasreen dropped back onto her gurney. While she appreciated being able to move, Lock's gesture did nothing to quell the exhaustion that spread throughout her body. She wanted to believe in his sincerity and not that Firewall had decided to try a different tactic to get her to cooperate.

"Trust," she whispered. "It has to go both ways."

Nasreen closed her eyes. Whether she planned to escape or wait for a prisoner exchange, she needed rest and more food. She closed her eyes and drifted off to sleep.

A loud *bang* snapped Nasreen awake. She sat up, draped her legs over the side of the gurney, and rubbed her eyes. She didn't know how much time had passed. She remembered fading in and out of sleep with a brief break for water and a bland soup.

The door opened, and Lock stepped in trailed by Exploit. She froze, although her heart raced. Her anger burned away her fatigue as she locked her gaze on Exploit. A brief, fleeting thought of revenge surfaced. She didn't have to kill him, only hurt him.

Nasreen blew out a breath and tightened her hands on the side of the gurney. Attacking Exploit would end any chance they had of an alliance with Firewall. She'd have to consider her treatment the price of an alliance. After they defeated the Omega Syndrome, she could talk to Dante and get tips on the best way to get revenge.

Exploit looked her up and down before clucking his tongue. "Don't do anything foolish, Miss Joelle."

Nasreen looked through the open door. "I see you didn't bring your torture rack today."

"I won't apologize for doing my duty." Exploit jerked his head toward the doorway. "You'll follow us. We're taking you away from this place."

He frowned at Lock. "The balance of discussion has led to a general agreement that Firewall might find your team a useful resource in our struggle. Due to that, we're past the need to interrogate and imprison you."

"How magnanimous." Nasreen hopped off the gurney. Her knees buckled, and she almost fell over before steadying herself using the gurney. "Lead on."

Nasreen had expected they would slap on new restraints and use a small army of operatives to guard her. Instead, Lock and Exploit silently walked out of the cell. Neither had any obvious weapons, but she assumed they'd hidden knives or razorfists somewhere in their coveralls.

They led her through the hallways to the grav-line and a waiting old but serviceable grav-train car with blacked-out windows. The doors opened, and Lock nodded for her to enter. She stepped inside and sat, coughing as dust billowed up. Lock sat beside her. Exploit sat across from her. With a soft *hum*, the train accelerated away from Firewall's base.

"Where are we going?" Nasreen asked.

"To the future," Exploit replied.

Nasreen eyed him. She pushed down the burning revenge that cried out for her to leap across the car and smash Exploit's head against the window until she'd caved in his skull. He deserved to feel like he'd made her feel.

She tore her attention away from Exploit to survey the car. Overwhelming mustiness, thick dust, and missing, torn, and cracked seats indicated that Firewall didn't use the car often. Their willingness to take advantage of such resources explained their mobility. Using abandoned stations kept them out of the public eye and off the Omega Syndrome's radar.

Whatever the truth of the founder, any enemy focused on obtaining Station power would be limited by the nature and execution of that power. Even in space, there was always somewhere to hide.

Minutes later, the train stopped. Nasreen half-expected the automated voices to speak when the doors slid open. There was nothing. Firewall might have removed them because of their links to AI.

She followed Lock and Exploit off the train. They'd traveled to another abandoned grav-line station. Tall walls stood in front of the main station entrance. The occasional Firewall member wandered past the ports, although there weren't any obvious guns. Two burly Firewall operatives armed with shock batons and obvious EMP grenades clipped to their belts guarded the thick gate between the walls.

Lock led the procession, with Exploit bringing up the rear. The men nodded at Lock and Exploit. With a loud groan, the gate separated into two halves, allowing access to the station proper. Firewall members eyed Nasreen as Lock led her past the gate.

"That last place wasn't the main base," Nasreen concluded.

Lock nodded. "We couldn't risk bringing you to the main facility until we confirmed you weren't a risk." He motioned for her to follow and hurried toward a hallway. "Follow me. We've got something to show you."

A conference room with a scratched-up table and worn chairs wasn't the interesting treasure she'd expected. The trip through the converted station hadn't taken long. She began to grasp the organization was larger than she'd realized and better armed. They'd passed a group of Firewall operatives cleaning pulsecore carbines in an armory. She was grateful they had the good sense not to use those in public on a Station.

Nasreen looked at Lock. "What do you want to show me?"

Lock pulled out a chair and motioned for her to sit. "What you've wanted since the beginning. Information."

"Okay." Nasreen sat. "Go ahead."

Exploit and Lock joined her at the table before Lock pulled a sphere from underneath the table. He fiddled with the device before nodding at the center of the table.

An unlabeled holographic map appeared, a not-to-scale depiction of the different Stations, each labeled with bright letters beneath their location on the map. Pale flickering dots lay amid a sea of red tendrils snaking through the Station overlays.

Nasreen narrowed her eyes. "I can't tell what this is supposed to represent."

Lock pointed at a blue dot. "These pale blue dots are network hubs and major nexuses of the Station digital infrastructure. More importantly, they are key points of the digital infrastructure the Omega Syndrome hasn't infected."

"The red tendrils are the Omega Syndrome." Nasreen nodded. Assuming the intelligence was accurate, Firewall had all but lost the war. No wonder they'd been willing to reconsider their relationship with Dante's and Nasreen's team. "I assume the blue dots are places you've protected."

"That's partially true," Lock replied. "For one reason or another, the blue dots are what's left free. In many cases, that's because of our efforts. In some, other organizations that aren't aware of the Omega Syndrome have protected them. In a handful of cases, we're not sure why the Omega Syndrome hasn't taken control."

Exploit sounded bitter. "We've been doing our best to protect all these free spaces while pushing our enemy back farther.

Neither strategy has been going well. The Omega Syndrome extends its influence with each passing day."

"It's not hopeless," Lock interjected. He motioned at a cluster of blue dots in Pentapolis. "We've found something that can disrupt the Omega Syndrome's interconnections. This will make it easier to fight back more widely."

He frowned. "It's a stop-gap. We can slow them down, reverse the influence in individual locations." He shook his head. "We haven't been able to find the silver bullet we need to kill the monster. Our enemy is technology-based. That means there's technology to find, including lost technology."

Nasreen nodded slowly. "That's why you're interested in us. You didn't need another handful of field operatives. You needed experienced Marauders."

"Yes," Lock replied. "We hoped you could bridge the gap for us. We have good resources on the Stations. Our reach is otherwise limited. Your skill set and combat training also are useful. You did fight through a group of Block 9X."

"This doesn't mean your cyborgs can be trusted completely," Exploit interjected. "You must understand that. With that in mind, are you willing to aid us?"

"No one can be trusted completely." Nasreen stood and stretched her arms above her head. She ignored the odd looks from the men as she cracked her knuckles. "As you've told me, most people have implants. The trick is it's easier to disable Hyde or Mugoi with one of your disruptors than it is a human with a couple of brain implants."

Confusion spread over Lock's face as he watched her. "I understand. Setting that aside, are you with us?"

Nasreen pushed her chair in and stood behind their chairs. "I am, under one condition."

Lock grinned. "Perfect. What's your condition?"

"I want to balance the scales, but I'll give you a one-to-hundred exchange," Nasreen explained.

Exploit frowned. "I don't understand."

Nasreen socked Lock in the jaw. Before he could react, she kicked Exploit in the crotch. She grabbed his head and smashed her knee into his nose. Blood streaming from his nose, the Firewall leader howled and dropped to the floor.

She stepped back and dusted her hands together. "We're balanced at one-to-hundred now. I'm willing to work with you."

Lock rubbed his jaw and chuckled. "Fair enough."

Still rolling around, Exploit groaned. "You bitch."

"Don't worry." Nasreen waved at him. "I held back."

Lock stood slowly, holding his hands out in a placating gesture. "There's something else you need to see." He headed toward the door. "The new alliance isn't all about you."

Nasreen offered one smile to the downed Exploit before walking after Lock. "I assume Dante's been busy."

"Yes, Mr. Shale has been busy. I know it might come off hollow after everything that's happened, but we thank your team for saving Tether."

"You're welcome."

Nasreen looked over her shoulder, expecting Exploit to run out and demand her execution. The Firewall leader remained in the conference room as she and Lock turned the corner into a new hallway. She passed makeshift barracks filled with sleeping operatives and a kitchen. The aromatic smell tickled her nose and made her stomach rumble.

Lock stopped in front of a room marked as a storage closet. He opened the door. Three surprises waited inside. Rather than a closet, a small desk with a chair waited, including four chairs in front. A bruised and bloodied Dante sat in one chair, Mugoi in another. The cyborg's body was covered with damage and dried colorful stains from the emergency sealant applied all over its body.

They looked like they'd been through hell. An Atlanticore connected by a cord to a glowing sphere sat on the desk. Nasreen frowned, unsure about what was going on but happy they were still alive and mostly in one piece.

"Hey," Dante greeted with a small shrug.

"Hello." Nasreen smiled and sat next to them, trying to force a smile. "It's good to see you both."

"And you as well," Mugoi replied.

Lock headed around the desk to sit in the remaining chair. "You were right, Miss Joelle. The greatest strength of your team is artifact recovery. That's paid early dividends." He motioned at the device on the desk. "We had to scrub clinging bits of the Omega Syndrome that found its way into their neural network."

Nasreen glared at him. "You put them under that machine."

Dante shook his head. "Nah, we volunteered for their bullshit. I was wondering anyway because of the Voices we encountered Dirtside. I don't need anything other than Midas in my head."

"Wait." Nasreen turned to Lock. "Do they know?"

"We've heard the basics," Dante replied. "What they believe anyway." He shrugged.

"And you believe it?"

"Still deciding." Dante chuckled. "Certain team members are arguing for it." He tapped his head.

"I've got him disabled for our little meet and greet here, and they've made it clear they've got jammers and their machine killers ready. Their rules and I wasn't going to let them do it, but Midas says now that he has a better understanding of the nature of our enemy, he can better prepare."

Lock gestured at the sphere. "Now that we're all here. Let's get started."

CHAPTER THIRTEEN

"I thought we were going to get started," Dante complained. "We've been sitting here on our asses glaring at each other for a long time. I'm through with games. We got your toy. Talk already."

Other than a quick "Stand by," Lock hadn't filled them in on the reason for the delay. Dante hoped it wasn't a stupid power play.

"I'm sorry. I truly am." Lock pointed at his ear and a tiny receiver earpiece. "I've learned that someone I thought would skip the meeting now insists on coming. He needed to…clean up a little after a recent unfortunate incident. One other Firewall member is attending besides him."

Dante folded his arms. "You guys should stick to the terrorism. You suck at running meetings."

"I'll keep that in mind."

The door opened. A new man Dante didn't recognize arrived, his face bruised and a bandage over his nose.

"Here's the first one," Lock declared. "This is Exploit. He's another high-ranking member of our organization."

"Fine. The other person almost ready?"

"Soon. I promise."

Dante had done his best to maintain an easy, sardonic grin on his face for Nasreen's benefit. He wanted to hide the anger threatening to burst out and end with him breaking Lock's neck after a nice, long beatdown.

The feeling had only intensified when the shifty-faced bastard Exploit had shown up. The condition of his face and the glares he kept shooting Nasreen hadn't gone unnoticed by Dante, nor the worried look on Lock's face.

Nasreen's face was gaunt with scattered bruises. Her movements were unsteady, lacking her normal confidence. Even her voice wasn't the perfectly controlled tool Dante had used as a weapon when they were streaming their exploits against SSS together. She might not have gotten cut up like Mugoi, but all the evidence pointed to her having a rough time in Firewall captivity.

Dante's ability to look past bad behavior for the mission didn't extend as far when he wasn't the one paying the direct price. Making him wait there had given him more time to focus on how they'd treated his partner. The main things keeping him in check were warning looks and the occasional tiny head shake from Nasreen. He'd follow her lead as long as the Firewall bastards didn't push him too far.

Lock had the decency to look guilty. Exploit sat in his chair sulking and choking the air with his aggrievement, although he avoided looking directly at Nasreen. Dante didn't need to know what had happened to put together a plausible outline of events where Exploit had pushed too far and earned Nasreen's wrath. The bastard hadn't stumbled and hit his face on the floor before an important meeting.

Nasreen was Dante's partner and friend. She'd helped him get his revenge and take down SSS when she could have disappeared and left him to rot in his first insane crusade. Her enemies were his.

He glanced at Nasreen and raised his eyebrows, seeking

direction. She might have changed her mind on the beatdowns. She'd been with Firewall. Her opinion was more valuable.

Other than a quick smirk at Exploit upon his arrival, her warning looks, and their initial greetings, she'd stayed reserved. There was no reason to bash Exploit's face into the desk yet. Dante would keep the option in the back of his mind.

"Now can we get started?" Dante pressed.

"Remember, we need one last person before we can begin," Lock explained. "She'll be here soon. I thought for various reasons she might not be up for the meeting. I've found out she insists on attending, and I think her input would be valuable given the recent events."

"She's another person who needed to clean up?" asked Dante. "You people need to work on your organization. You keep getting your asses kicked right before important meetings."

"How dare you!" snapped Exploit.

"I get that more often than you'd think." Dante shrugged. "Or exactly as often as you think."

Lock frowned but quickly squashed the expression into a bland, neutral look. "The situation has been complicated recently. It's not how any of us wanted things to unfold. As you well know, planning can only go so far."

"Sure, whatever, but while we're waiting, what all happened to Nasreen?" Dante kept his smile despite the predatory look in his eyes. "It sounds like we've got time to go into that since your other member won't be helpful."

He ignored Nasreen's head shake this time. Sometimes a man needed to defend his friends even when they didn't think they needed it. Firewall had him dancing on their strings, going into the bowels of Atlantica Central Station to recover their device. He needed to take control back.

"I don't think we should go into that right now," Lock replied. "It's not important to how we proceed." He gestured at the door. "Besides, she's here."

Tether stepped in front of the doorway and into the office. Pale and sunken-eyed, she shuffled more than walked to her chair. She'd cleaned up, although she still had an autoclamp on her wounded arm. She was the only person in the room who looked worse than Mugoi.

Dante's brow lifted. No wonder Lock hadn't been ready. After everything Tether had been through, she should be spending a week in bed resting and trying to recover, not attending strategy meetings. He was impressed and annoyed at how much she'd kept him under control during the entire situation.

Dante turned from Tether to stare at Lock. He was one of the men calling the shots. "Just to be sure, she's the one we were waiting for?"

Lock nodded. "She is."

Tether offered a weak smile. "I am."

"Good, but that doesn't make my earlier question go away," Dante replied. "Tether should have given you the basics of what happened with us, so I think it's only fair we discuss what happened when Nasreen was here. Because we saved Tether's life, including giving her emergency medical treatment, and didn't mistreat her.

"Yeah, not going to lie and say we didn't make any threats, but she left our care in better condition than when she came into it, and it doesn't look like the same thing happened to Nasreen."

"She's suffered no permanent injuries," Lock replied.

Dante clenched his fists in his lap. He pushed back, trying to stifle the urge to throat punch Lock.

He inclined his head toward Mugoi and the sphere. "The medical supplies my apprentice brought back helped keep her alive long enough that she could send us on your little treasure hunt. I'm thinking, 'Hey, these assholes stabbed one of my people. What else are they doing to my friends when I'm not around to watch them?'"

He narrowed his eyes on Exploit. "Like I said, from what I can see, Nasreen didn't have a great time here. 'No permanent injuries' doesn't mean 'Everything's fine, and she had a great time.'"

Exploit snorted. "Oh, please. Your arrogance sickens me. As if you're so innocent?"

"Innocent?" Dante shook his head. "I'm many things. Innocent isn't one of them. Vengeful? Yeah, that's one thing I am. I'd say I'm famous for it."

"Vengeful?" Exploit replied. "You've killed and hurt our people, operatives who form the thin line between tyranny and freedom for all of humanity, and you're complaining because we didn't put her up in a four-star hotel?"

Dante grinned at Exploit, imagining how much fun it'd be to add more bruises to his face or throw him out an airlock and wave. "You people should learn to deal with people without kidnapping them off the street. You'd get fewer injuries that way."

He cracked his knuckles. "You all talk big about your successes. My team has had successes, and we haven't violently kidnapped people we're trying to recruit to help us. That makes me wonder who the arrogant bastard is in this room."

Nasreen put her hand to her forehead and sighed. "This isn't the time for this. Both of you need to calm down."

"The hell it isn't." Dante snorted. "I'm not going to let anyone mess with my team and act smug about it."

Exploit motioned at his face. "She's lucky we agreed to anything after what she did to me. You're nothing more than scavengers picking the bones of a dead planet. Scum. Parasites. We're the vanguard protecting humanity's freedom."

The airlock idea grew in appeal. Exploit would need a thorough beating first.

"I balanced the scales when I paid you back." Nasreen folded her arms with a ghost of a smile on her face. "I explained that, and that's also why I'm trying to get Dante to back off when he's not wrong."

She shook her head. "Seriously, though, both sides have hurt one another. There's no denying that. That doesn't change the fact we both have something we can offer one another. More than that, we both need one another if we're going to protect the Stations from the Omega Syndrome."

"I wonder about that," Exploit replied. "The more I deal with you people, the more I think it was a mistake that we ever got involved with you. You've cost us so much already."

Tether frowned at Exploit. "I don't believe that."

"Don't get sentimental."

"This isn't about sentiment. It's about finding and using resources to defeat our enemy." Tether ran her fingers over the autoclamp.

"They could have left me at the club. They could have executed me after everything that happened with Nasreen. They didn't. We only approached them to begin with because we knew they were far more than mercenaries who only cared about money."

Exploit's face twitched. "They only kept you alive because they needed a hostage. They didn't do it because they're moral people."

Dante snorted. "We also recovered something you couldn't get before, and you took a hostage first. And that was *after* we saved Tether."

Nasreen slammed her palm on the desk, forcing both men to look at her. "We both took hostages. We both made mistakes.

"Now, we can sit here and spend the next ten years pointing fingers. The Omega Syndrome will have tracked down and killed us all by then. We can spend our dying moments being proud that we were all stubborn fools before giving into the horror that the Stations are going to be taken over by a dangerous conspiracy that might not have any other organized opposition."

Lock's concerned look disappeared. He nodded without saying anything. Mugoi remained still, although the occasional blink or shift in position confirmed the cyborg wasn't suffering from a generalized Firewall tech disruptor. Given the dents, cuts, and fluid stains up and down its body, its ability to attend the meeting was almost a miracle.

Tether nodded her eager agreement. "She's right. The only choice we have now is to work together. I'm not interested in rehashing who's to blame for what." She lifted her wounded arm. "And I'm the one who's bled the most recently for the cause. Bruises heal. Wounded arms don't just grow back."

"If you both put it that way, it's hard for me to complain." Dante folded his arms. His glare strayed only briefly from Exploit. "If I can work with an asshole like Hyde who tried to rip my head off, I can work with you people.

"But, first things first. I risked my life and so did Mugoi to get this mystery database. We came damned close to being buried. We deserve to know what is in it and why it was worth risking an orphanage collapsing on top of us to get it."

"Working with you on specific missions is one matter." Exploit shook his head. "But there's no reason for you to know everything. That only increases the danger to all the Stations and us."

Tether sighed. "You're not helping."

"You son of a bitch." Dante gritted his teeth. "You're pushing me, asshole. *Really* pushing me. You people didn't only hurt Nasreen. You also badly hurt Jolo, and my patience is reaching my generous damned limit."

"So is mine, you glorified scavenger," Exploit replied. Neither he nor Dante paid any attention to anyone else.

Nasreen put her fist to her mouth and cleared her throat. "Knowing the truth about the database is non-negotiable. Dante's not asking for a list of all your operatives and base locations. He's asking for information on something he retrieved, something important, something your people could not grab.

"If you're not ready to go that far, we might as well leave and stay out of each other's way until either we beat the Omega Syndrome or it finishes us off." She nodded at the device. "Despite that, I don't see a reason for us to leave that here since it was our people who risked their lives to retrieve it."

Exploit chuckled. His disdain manifested as a smirk. "You think you can get out of our base if we don't want to let you?"

Dante shrugged. "This time it won't be a surprise attack. We'd have no reason to hold back. I think you don't want to lose an entire base and a pile of people. Even if you could win, it'd cost you."

Mugoi tapped its metal fingers against the chair loudly but looked bored. "Ask yourself how many people are you willing to sacrifice to stop us? I've killed numerous people today. A handful more won't weigh on my conscience if they threaten my friends."

"How dare you threaten us!" shouted Exploit. "We are the tip of the spear in protecting humanity. We've sacrificed everything, our identities, our old lives. We deserve respect."

"And we deserve respect for risking our damned lives," Dante shouted.

Tether sighed. "It doesn't have to go down like that."

Lock put up his hands placatingly. "They're right, Exploit. They deserve to know."

He turned toward the man. "The only way this new *alliance* will work is if we share information. It's already decided. We can't waste more time on petty arguments."

Dante stopped himself from shouting again when Nasreen locked eyes with him and shook her head.

Exploit folded his arms and ground his teeth. His eyes darted back and forth as if he couldn't figure out whom he wanted to focus on. "This is insanity. We have protocols we're tossing away to help this glorified mercenary who employs a machine."

Mugoi smiled. "Having augmentations, even a large number, doesn't make me a machine. We don't need to discuss what you are."

"Hey," Dante said to Exploit. "We both want to take down the Omega Syndrome. I'm not here to make an enemy of Firewall. I'm also not here to be Firewall's bitch or let you think you can hurt my people whenever you feel like it. If that's too much for you, we'll walk."

"That's understandable." Tether nodded. "I believe your team can be an asset. You've proven it by recovering the database, and quickly at that, without drawing the attention of the Omega Syndrome, which is more than we've been able to do lately."

"Yeah, we did that," Dante replied. "So what is it?"

Exploit lowered his head and glared at the desk. The struggle between necessity and anger played out across his face in a long, tense silence. When he finally spoke, his eyes darted up briefly before dropping. "As has been divulged—" He turned an annoyed glare on Tether. "It's a database."

"We understand that much," Dante replied. "The value of a database is the data within it." He motioned at the sphere. "What's so important about that data?"

Exploit drew a deep breath and hesitated again for an uncomfortably long time before speaking. "Although the Omega Syndrome is a powerful threat that stretches back farther than one might suspect, it's also not a threat that has been with us from the beginning of advanced AI technology. The database's creators built it in a time before the emergence of the Omega Syndrome and our enemy's infection of all the systems and interfaces between systems."

Nasreen nodded. "I see. That tells us when, but not what. We won't agree to any further cooperation without knowing the latter."

"At the highest level, it's a systems map." Exploit's quiet reply sounded defeated. "The inter-Station network connections have become more refined over the decades, but their fundamental base is the same protocols and subsystems present in the beginning. This database contains the necessary technical information that will allow us to assess how the various systems operated and were linked before the Omega Syndrome became so pervasive."

The explanation came out clearly enough. Dante hesitated to reveal he didn't understand how that would be immediately useful. His partner helped him out within seconds to clarify the issue.

Nasreen cupped her chin, staring off at a wall in thought. "You're trying to use it for comparative targeting of the Omega Syndrome's influence. That makes sense."

Exploit nodded. "In a general sense, yes. This will help us find options in crafting a countermeasure to attack. Or at a minimum, isolate the malignant virus. Stopping its growth is the first step toward defeating it."

"That's the makings of a good plan," Dante agreed.

Nasreen folded her arms and if anything, looked more unsettled than before. "I'm partially persuaded that the Omega Syndrome is infecting the systems. That doesn't mean your theories are all correct."

Exploit scoffed. "What does that mean and how is it relevant?"

"You believe a rogue AI is at its source," Nasreen replied. "How do you know it's not the creation of a group or a person? That is to say, I can accept there's a dangerous self-spreading program corrupting the Stations and implants. If people are behind it, that changes how we should approach everything."

Exploit looked confused for a moment. He glanced between a stone-faced Lock and Tether, who seemed equally perplexed. "The origin of the Omega Syndrome is less important than its existence." He scowled at Lock. "He shouldn't have brought it up with you. That information wasn't necessary for you to know."

Tether snorted. "There's no rogue AI. Chasing phantoms won't help us."

Lock shook his head with angry certitude in his eyes. "A rogue AI is behind this threat. It's like that old saying, 'The greatest trick the Devil ever pulled was convincing the world he didn't exist.'"

Dante snickered. "That's what this is to you? The Devil?"

"More than you know," Nasreen muttered.

"And we must protect humanity from its tainted touch," offered Exploit in a low, menacing voice. "We can't come to terms with something inherently inhuman." He glanced at Mugoi. "Even the most…unfortunate of cyborgs have a human brain. They are human in their essence and souls. An AI isn't."

"It's interesting how many non-augmented humans lack hearts," Mugoi replied.

Dante frowned, surprised at the revelation. Tether's previous explanations to him, including on their way to the meeting, emphasized the danger the Omega Syndrome represented to implants, systems, and AIs. She'd not made it clear that some of her organization believed a rogue AI was behind the entire conspiracy. Now he better understood what Nasreen had been getting at when she'd asked him about his beliefs earlier.

On one level, the idea made sense. His experiences with Midas, both shortly after his installation and the original Voices incident, offered startling evidence for rogue AI activity. Despite that, Dante wasn't sure he cared as much about the source of the Omega Syndrome over the fact that Firewall members didn't share the same dogma. He didn't want his team to get caught in a terrorist holy war.

Nasreen looked among the gathered Firewall members with a slight frown. "Was I unclear? What evidence is there? Theories are only useful in pointing an investigation to the best path to find the truth. If you're wondering why I care, I'm trying to get a better feel for the context you're using when evaluating threats."

Lock offered Tether a disappointed look before turning back to Nasreen. "You can't tell me you've never found something through its absence before."

Dante raised an eyebrow. "What's that supposed to mean?"

Lock traced out a long box in the air. "Think of it this way. If you found an ancient door with a keyhole, it would support the existence of a key even if you never found one. Or turning it around, if you found a key, that would point to a keyhole and lock. Even if you didn't know about the existence of keys, if you kept finding things and none of them fit in the keyhole, you'd assume there was something like a key that must explain the keyhole."

"I'm having trouble buying that," Nasreen replied. "It sounds like you're arguing that you have no direct evidence pointing to a rogue AI being involved."

Dante and Mugoi sat back and let Nasreen do the talking. Extracting information was her specialty. She'd gotten Firewall to admit several things. There was no reason to get in her way when she had momentum.

Lock sighed. "Don't you understand? We've exhausted the other possibilities."

With a quiet snort, Tether folded her arms and looked away. Exploit glared at her.

"You think we haven't investigated every angle to explain what we've found?" Lock continued. "We've looked into different groups, organizations, and companies. The Omega Syndrome doesn't appear to serve any real known power group. It doesn't seem to have any real goal other than spreading and corrupting systems."

Nasreen shook her head. "That you know of. You could be assuming too much."

Lock leaned forward. His voice grew desperate and worried. "We've tried to track down the flesh-and-blood people responsible for issuing orders to foot soldiers like Block 9X." He pounded the desk with his fist, rattling the sphere and power source.

"I'm not talking about simple, safe investigations. We've lost people doing this. They've given their lives to confirm there is no flesh-and-blood intermediary delivering orders. The trail always leads to accounts not tied to any real people."

Annoyance lined Nasreen's features. "Are you kidding me? That's your evidence? Even low-level criminals know how to use burner accounts."

"This goes far beyond that." Lock gripped the edge of the desk. "Why can't you see? Why don't you understand? Our people have intercepted comms from alleged humans, only to find they are computer-generated faces and voices. Ones that never get used again."

Dante leaned over to whisper to Nasreen. "This isn't going anywhere. I agree with you on this, but it's clear you're not going to convince them of anything. We need to deal with what's in front of us."

He didn't care about angering Firewall so much as making sure there was a worthwhile trade-off. Vengeance was one such worthwhile exchange. Without that on the table, he'd reverted to being practical.

Neutralizing the Omega Syndrome would lead to the truth, one way or another. Stopping the spread in the systems might flush any responsible humans out. They could get their deserved bullets then.

Nasreen nodded at Dante. "I know." She drew a deep breath. Her tone dripped with disappointment. "We'll set that aside for now. Regardless of the origin, it's better to concentrate on our latest prize. If it truly is what you say, it'll be a useful tool against our mutual enemy."

"Yeah," Dante said. "How long will it take you people to crack the thing?"

Exploit's mouth twitched. He nodded at Lock.

"It's not that simple," Lock replied, the red-faced fervor fading from his face.

"And why is that?"

Lock motioned at the glowing sphere. "This isn't a matter we can handle with brute force."

Dante snickered. "I'm not saying you should smash it open. I'm saying do your thing. Connect it to your systems and read it. From what you said, you don't have to worry about the Omega Syndrome at this base."

"We're not worried about the Omega Syndrome. This issue is the level of sensitivity associated with this database. Our information tells us that should we try to interface with it directly using our standard methods, we risk losing information if not frying the whole damned thing. We need to ensure the secondary power backup system is functioning at all times, which requires extra caution."

Mugoi raised an eyebrow. "After all the trouble involved in its recovery and transport, that's disappointing."

Lock's gaze flicked to the cyborg. He tried to keep his expression neutral, but the disdain sneaked in enough for Dante to notice. "This isn't a preferred scenario for us, either. Tether didn't tell you about the database as a clever test. It contains useful information for our cause. We're not saying we can't unlock it, only that more steps are involved."

"I think I know where this is going," Dante said. "Am I going to be buried again?"

"Not if you're competent. This time our intelligence points to the relevant equipment being Dirtside." Tether smiled. "Keep in mind, Mr. Shale, if you didn't bring something to the cause, we wouldn't be interested in your team to begin with."

Nasreen closed her eyes and let out a weary sigh. "You should have hired Dante to get these things to begin with. It might have saved you trouble."

"We couldn't be sure. The important thing is that we have the database, and we need additional tech to access it safely." Tether smirked. "It's a good thing we know the *best* Plunderer alive to help us."

Dante chuckled. "I should have known that would come back and bite me in the ass. Okay. Let's do this. You know where we're supposed to go?"

"Yes. Not that it'll be easy."

"The best jobs never are."

CHAPTER FOURTEEN

Nasreen pulled a fresh rifle magazine from a crate in the armory and stuffed it into a vest pocket. She walked over to a rack to inspect a pair of vambraces and a helmet, part of a set of armor purchased recently. Given all the trouble they kept stumbling into, they might not be going far enough with their equipment upgrades. It wouldn't be insane to invest in turning the entire team into hardcase armor specialists.

She understood why they didn't. Dante's strategies focused on high mobility and tactical flexibility. Sometimes, Nasreen appreciated the idea of hitting Dirtside with more basic protection.

Wearing a huge grin in defiance of the tense situation, Dante stood farther down in the armory inspecting a pulsecore carbine with all the eagerness of a child receiving a new shiny toy for his birthday. The rest of the team filtered in and out of the armory gathering all the implements of death they'd need Dirtside. Firewall's job would take them deep into the remnants of a mine in old Hungary to look for a decades-old power converter, power cells, and related parts. Because of specialized Atlanticore components integrated into the design, they couldn't have it built Station-side.

Firewall hadn't provided the final coordinates. Agreeing to work with the team didn't quell their fundamental paranoia about comms intercepts. Dante didn't mind waiting to get the coordinates until right before launch. Their paranoia was rubbing off. He didn't want to have to take on Omega Syndrome Reapers Dirtside.

Dante, Mugoi, and Nasreen had returned to the safe house to brief everyone on the Firewall situation and the next mission before deciding to return to their headquarters. Now that they knew Firewall wouldn't go after the team, there was no reason not to return. If Block 9X showed up, they'd be better equipped to take them on at HQ. After a day of further recovery and treatment, they'd started prepping in earnest for a return to Earth based on limited intelligence gathered by a group of fanatical terrorists. Nasreen didn't love the plan. She also couldn't think of a better one.

That defined their life lately. She'd always known a showdown with the Omega Syndrome was coming. She'd also hoped that the months they'd had to prepare would leave them better prepared.

Dante frowned as he looked among different helmet choices. "This is going to be fun."

Nasreen looked at him in confusion. "Fun? I find satisfaction in a successful recovery, but I don't know if I've ever found going Dirtside fun."

"That's why I ended up a Marauder to begin with." Dante lifted and lowered two helmets several times before deciding on a third, identical-looking one. "Between the club and the orphanage, we've been restricted." After setting his helmet aside, he tossed a pulsecore magazine into the air, letting it tumble end-over-end before catching it. "Pulsecores, rifles, and explosives go a long way to making a small team stronger. I'm tired of facing bastards with only close-quarters weapons."

"I don't know if that moves this into fun. We can't be sure what we'll find down there."

A flicker of concern flashed over Dante's face. Nasreen might have been getting through to him.

"We'll find death." Dante ran his hand along the barrel of his carbine. "All we can do is be prepared to kill anything that looks at us the wrong way, the same as any Dirtside job."

Whistling, Braelin wandered into the armory to sort through a grenade crate. He lifted individual grenades and bounced them lightly in his palm. Leaning forward, he peered at others intently, as if evaluating jewels before tucking them into vest pockets, his backpack, or clipping them to his belt after nodding in satisfaction at a feature only he could spot.

"Grenades," Braelin drawled. "The great leveler."

Dante motioned at the crate. "Focus on plasmas. We're not going down there to have a friendly chat."

"Understood." Braelin grunted and rotated his arm. He looked good for a man who'd been tossed around by cyborgs not long ago.

Nasreen narrowed her eyes on Braelin. "What if we run into Dirtwalkers? You don't want to have a non-lethal option?"

"I have my reasons for not worrying about that." Dante shrugged. "Don't worry about it for now."

"If you say so." Braelin grabbed two plasma grenades. "Shoot 'em and burn 'em."

"Are you up for this?" Nasreen asked.

Dante looked up from his carbine. "Why wouldn't I be?"

Nasreen pointed at Braelin. "Not you. Him."

Braelin flexed his healed arm. "I'm not going to be setting strength records with my arm, but I can hold a gun and shoot." He nodded at her. "Got to say you don't look great yourself, Nasreen. Are *you* up for this?"

"I'm fine." Nasreen shoved another magazine into a pocket.

"Never felt better and more focused. We can both rest when this is all over. A stim or two isn't going to kill me."

"Still…" Braelin sucked in air through his teeth. "This ain't going to be our finest hour. My arm's my own bone-headed fault. We can't say the same for all these other bruises."

"Having direct access to the infirmary changes things," Nasreen replied quietly. "The only reason the situation turned as troublesome as it did was that we couldn't come back here."

Braelin looked over his shoulder and out the door. "Are we sure about Jolo?"

"She's sure," Dante interjected. "That's good enough for me, especially on a job where we need people we can trust."

"If you say so." Braelin didn't look convinced.

Dante glanced between Braelin and Nasreen with a frown, not liking the direction of the discussion. He nodded at the door. "Gather everyone in the big briefing room. We need to talk. Make sure Ambrose gets his ass to the meeting too. For a guy who got his ass kicked the least, he's sulking the most."

"What's the meeting about?" Nasreen asked.

"Something important."

Nasreen wasn't used to Dante being so cryptic. She didn't like it and fully accepted the irony given her past.

Despite her annoyance, she let it go, knowing he wouldn't be frivolous in their current situation. Dante's smiling eagerness didn't equal a foolish ignorance about the dangers they faced. There was arguably no other man alive who understood danger like Dante Shale. He was a man who'd come back from certain death more than once. That success bred loyalty and respect.

She surveyed the meeting room table, thinking over the strange team and family they'd gathered since her first accidental encounter with Dante while Dirtside. Her attention lingered on

Mugoi and Jolo. Both were scratched up and injured and had come close to death, yet they sat at the table with hard looks of determination. That was dedication.

Nasreen's attention shifted back to Braelin. Other than a handful of purple-black splotches, most of the visible bruising on his face was gone. He rubbed his arm and rotated his shoulder conspicuously often, but it wasn't hanging like the limp noodle that Dante had described to her.

When applied in earnest without new attacks, the medical technology of a well-funded Marauder outfit could turn people around quickly and get them back to combat readiness. No one had time or money for Plunderers who couldn't plunder. All a man or woman had to do was not die in the meantime.

Ambrose shuffled into the room, the last to arrive. He headed to a chair on the table's far side and sat with a shrug. He glared at Braelin. "I'm here. Just for the record, I was doing mainte-nance on the shuttle. I wasn't *hiding*, despite what certain people said."

"We're all doing important crap. All I care about is that you're here now." Dante cracked his knuckles.

"Speaking of that, crap's been raining down hard on us. I'm not going to sit here and pretend I'm surprised by any of this, only annoyed. I've been through this before taking on a big, messy organization." He nodded at Hyde, Nasreen, and Ambrose. "I'm not the only one."

Jolo watched him with her dark eyes, her expression intense. Despite Braelin's concern, she'd shed the ashen pallor caused by her previous injuries. "Everyone in this room has been Dirtside. We've all faced dangers. We understand putting our lives on the line."

"That's not what I'm talking about," Dante replied. "This goes beyond Dirtside jobs or taking people on. I can't even blame Firewall for dragging us into this mess."

"How do you figure?" Braelin asked. "They're the ones who

kidnapped us. They didn't have to be dumbasses about the whole thing and mess everything up."

Mugoi frowned. "They did kidnap us. Something occurred to me about that. Something I hadn't realized before."

"What?" Nasreen asked.

"Is their disruptor a newer device? They didn't use it during the initial kidnapping attempt. They would have had far more ease of success had they taken me out of that fight."

"I'm betting they've got limited numbers of the device," Dante suggested. "They've got no reason to shout that to the world, including us, but it doesn't matter. They have it now, and they're not using it against us."

Mugoi snorted. "If you say so."

Dante continued. "What I'm getting at is they dragged us into the fight quicker than I'd planned, but I knew we'd be going after the Omega Syndrome. Even if Firewall never existed, this showdown was inevitable."

Braelin's shoulders slumped. "Am I the only one bothered that we still don't know for sure what they are? Evil AIs, tools of rich bastards? Hell, for all we know, they could be aliens."

Mugoi snickered. "We can safely cross that one off the list. I appreciate you being open-minded in your planning. It speaks well for your intelligence."

"Why?" Hyde asked. His grin was hungrier than comfortable for Nasreen.

Mugoi frowned. "Why?"

"Yeah. Why can we cross that one off the list? Is it that weird?"

"Aliens don't exist." Mugoi shrugged. "There's no reason to project humanity's corruption onto another species."

"What about a rogue AI?" Jolo asked. "Isn't that the same idea?"

Mugoi shook its head. "Humanity getting taken out by its own creation makes perfect sense."

"To be honest, I don't much care if it's human, AI, alien, or a pissed-off genetically engineered puppy with delusions of grandeur," Dante interjected. "We contain the corruption, and we can figure out who's at the other end later. After what happened with Slaine and the Voices Dirtside, I'm leaning toward a rogue AI being at the end. Same solution either way, though."

Midas had been mostly quiet other than brief status reports since their return to the headquarters. Dante attributed some of that reticence to the AI having to hear humans discuss dangerous AIs and trying to avoid reminding them that he was there. The other had to do with Dante ordering a self-diagnostic to confirm Firewall hadn't screwed up anything when they were in the base.

"We blow up enough shit, and the problem sorts itself out?" Braelin asked.

"Yeah," Dante replied. "That tracks."

"There's a certain elegance to your solution, Klement." Mugoi nodded. "Although I would have phrased it differently, the fundamental plan makes sense."

Hyde pounded the table. "Yeah. Let's do this. I don't give a shit if the *pendejos* behind this are human."

Sitting at the far end of the table, Ambrose swallowed. "Am I the only one disturbed by the idea we might be fighting a rogue AI? Even Braelin seemed to care more about not knowing what the source is than the idea of it being an AI."

"Dante's right," Jolo answered. "What difference does it make?" She inclined her head at Braelin. "And he's right. Even AIs have a physical presence in a databank somewhere.

"If Firewall's theories aren't delusions or a crazed cult, it's a matter of arresting Omega's spread. Then we push it back until it's in a position where we can destroy it by removing the last physical stronghold."

"We can't negotiate with a rogue AI." Ambrose shuddered. "For all we know, its goal is the elimination of all humanity. Slaine was a bastard, but we could negotiate with him. We won't have any ability to stall the Omega Syndrome. There's no one to threaten or intimidate."

"Negotiate?" Dante raised an eyebrow. "You want to negotiate with the Omega Syndrome?"

Ambrose waved in front of him. "Just to put them off-balance. That's all I'm saying."

Dante scoffed. "I'm not negotiating with the Omega Syndrome. I didn't negotiate with Slaine. I ripped his operations apart piece by piece, and I followed his ass to his hidey-hole to end him. That's the plan this time, too."

"Of course it is." Ambrose rolled his eyes. "You wouldn't be Dante Shale if you did the sensible and safe thing now, would you?"

"Nope. We're going to end this the nasty and brutal way. Before I had to end Slaine with not much help. Now, we have an entire organization of zealots ready to give their lives to help us. If anything, this is easier than taking down SSS, so I don't care if it's Slaine's evil clone, an AI, or an alien real-estate developer trying to clear out space for new alien condos."

Mugoi frowned. "Aliens would simply call them condos, in their native language of course."

"Would aliens even have condos?" asked Braelin.

Jolo cupped her chin. "It depends on the aliens."

Dante barked a loud laugh. Everyone swung their heads toward him.

He shrugged. "And here I was worried for nothing."

"What were you worried about exactly?" asked Nasreen.

"We've all taken our licks." Dante gestured at Braelin, Jolo, and Mugoi. "Some of us have taken way worse licks than others.

"Saying we've given as good as we got if not better doesn't change the fact that one of ours got taken and messed with, and another of our team nearly died. Getting fighting fit with the help of expensive medtech is nice, but it doesn't do anything for this." He slapped his hand over his chest.

Hyde narrowed his eyes. "What are you talking about? There's plenty of tech to save people after heart injuries. I haven't had a real heart in longer than you've been alive."

"I'm talking about will, mind. That crap." Dante lowered his hand. "When…SSS and my old team betrayed me, I could have let it overwhelm me." His gaze flicked to a squirming Ambrose. "I was trapped Dirtside in a hostile environment. I didn't know if I was going to survive, let alone get back to the Stations. That didn't mean I rolled over and died. People kept trying to kill me, and I kept surviving."

Hyde scoffed. "Don't I know it. They should call you Hellroach instead of Hellcat."

Dante let his gaze linger on the smirking Hyde. "I only survived those injuries because of help." He tapped his forehead. "I made sure that getting my ass beat didn't finish me here. Once you're finished in your heart and soul, you're done, no matter what your other injuries."

He looked around the table. "You're all on this team for a reason. It's because I believe in you. I wanted to make sure everyone's mentally prepared for this mission. More time to get ready would be nice, but I don't think we have it. I need everyone on deck for the mission and ready to go. I wanted to make sure we all have each other's backs. And it looks like that's exactly what we have."

"I'm ready, and I insist on going," Jolo replied. "I'll gladly fight alongside anyone in this room, but…"

"But what?"

"I don't trust Firewall."

"I don't expect you to trust them after they stabbed you. It's not like I trust them." Dante inclined his head toward Nasreen. "She convinced me that we can work together. That doesn't make them our new best friends."

Braelin's nostril flared. "Yeah. Those sons of bitches stabbed Jolo. I ain't ready to forgive that."

"And we've killed their people," Nasreen added softly. "We need to save our anger for the real enemy. Otherwise, we'll spend so much time fighting potential allies that the Omega Syndrome will win and take out both of our groups. Nobody will be left to stop them."

Braelin pounded his fist on the table. "I'd say the bitch who stabbed her is a real enemy!"

Jolo smiled slightly. She washed it away so quickly it was obvious she was trying to hide it.

"Don't worry about that." Hyde sneered. "You'll get your revenge the easy way, rather than the painfully long and stupidly complicated Dante Shale way."

Dante let that pass without comment.

Braelin glared at Hyde. "What are you talking about?"

"Most of them crazy Firewall bastards will die fighting for their cause. The more we use them to do that, the less chance of you Shale *hijos* dying in this. It's hard to break in new people. It's better if we don't have to." Hyde shrugged. "It'd be inconvenient."

"Dante trained us, not you," Mugoi replied.

"I've been around. And I've gotten used to you people. That's all I'm saying."

That was positively warm and cuddly by Hyde's standards. Nasreen was half-impressed.

"Oh." Mugoi nodded. "Having additional augmented assistance is helpful at times. That does bring us back to Firewall and their trustworthiness."

Dante shook his head. "This isn't about trusting Firewall. We're joining forces to take down a greater threat, a mutual enemy. Once we've finished that, we don't have anything more to do with them. If they come after us then we kill them all. Otherwise, we can go our separate ways and pretend we never knew each other."

"That's a good plan," Hyde said. "Until you decide those condo aliens need to get taken down."

"I'm forced to agree," Mugoi replied. "About the first part, not the condo aliens."

Braelin nodded at Hyde. "When the man's right, he's right."

"I agree." Jolo lifted her chin. Her aura of elegant pride overwhelmed the negative impact of the residual bags under her eyes. "I'm confident that together we can handle whatever we run into. This time we'll be fully armed and ready."

Braelin slammed a fist into his palm. "This time we won't be surprised. This team will kick their asses all the way back Dirtside."

Mugoi chuckled. "We're going Dirtside for the job."

"Oh. Yeah. Then we'll kick them to the Earth's core."

"Even before your clarification, your sentiment remains correct, Braelin."

The gathered apprentices nodded, all the concern and tension replaced by determination. They shared knowing nods and glances.

"Okay." Dante stood and pushed his chair under the table. "Get your gear ready. Firewall doesn't have much info other than the coordinates, so we assume there could be anything from hostile Dirtwalker tribes to ten angry Hydes waiting for us."

"No damned way," Hyde growled. "There's only one of me. There will only ever be one of me."

"Okay, Hyde and Ambrose, you stay here. There's something else I need to chat with you about. The rest of you do what you know."

Dante made eye contact with Nasreen before nodding toward the door. She rose before the apprentices, taking the signal to coordinate the mission logistics.

Dante waited until they had all cleared out and closed the door. Hyde stared at him with the solar system's most practiced bored expression. Ambrose kept rubbing his wrist, his eyes darting side to side as if he wanted to be anywhere else.

"What is it, *Papi?*" Hyde asked. "I don't need another speech about survival and keeping a positive attitude." He grabbed a chair and lifted it above his head, proving his strength, and set it back down. "We both know what I said when you found me after I lost my first body. Yeah. I was low, and I was ready to give up, but I'm not that skeleton anymore."

He curled his fingers into a huge fist. "You saw me at my worst. I'm not going to pretend it didn't happen." He grunted. "It doesn't matter. That's the past. I'm a new man with a new body. Understood?"

"While we're talking about losing bodies, I..." Ambrose managed to pull his hand off his wrist. "I like this body. I don't want a new one. I'd rather not be grievously injured or lose any limbs. No offense, but I'd rather not be a cyborg."

Hyde sneered at him. "You should be happy Shale didn't blow your head off when he had the chance. I would have any of the times you screwed me over. He's nicer than me. Too nice. It's a miracle he's not dead yet."

Dante drew a deep breath. Both men owed him. Hyde was right. They'd betrayed and tried to kill him. When they'd joined him to take on SSS, they hadn't done it to repay him. They'd done it to avoid becoming Cormac Slaine's next victims. The friendship came later, in so far as they had one.

They might owe him, but they'd also spent a year paying back society in a different way. He couldn't ignore that. Hyde and Ambrose had grown into something far more than mere allies of convenience.

"This isn't about our past," Dante replied. "I only brought that up earlier to make a point to the team. I'm not hanging onto it. If I wanted to kill either of you for what you'd done, I would have done it a long time ago. Trust me, Hyde. I'm not that nice."

The cyborg smirked. "Whatever you say, *Papi.*"

"Then what's this about?" Ambrose's eyes widened. A normal man would have become less worried after someone told them they didn't want to kill them.

Dante groaned. "I'm not about to spring a surprise torture session or whatever bullshit you're imagining. Don't wet yourself, Ambrose."

The man had never been one for adventure. It might be a stretch to call Ambrose a coward since he flew shuttle missions Dirtside aiding Plunderers and the TRG. Since working with Dante, though, he'd grown noticeably more concerned about personal safety. Perhaps the weight of his conscience fed into his paranoia.

"I should take up drinking," Ambrose muttered.

Hyde threw his head back and bellowed in laughter. Between chortles, he managed to get out, "I love it. Wait ten years, then rip us apart and throw us out into space. Not a colder damned revenge than that. I'd pay good money for you to do that."

Ambrose yelped. "Don't give him any ideas!"

"Whatever. I'll keep that in my back pocket. Don't worry, Ambrose. Those condo aliens will have killed me by then." Dante looked each man in the eye before speaking again. "That's not what we're here to talk about. We're here to talk about being crazy."

"We are?" Ambrose asked.

"Yeah. Going after SSS was insane. I'll never deny that."

"We won, didn't we?" Hyde asked. "When you're breathing after the fight, and they aren't. That's all that matters. It doesn't matter how you got there."

"That didn't make it any less nuts," Dante replied. "You joined up after I'd weakened SSS. You had your reasons. I didn't question them.

"After we finished, you found a new life Dirtside working with the Terra Restoration Group." He focused on Hyde. "I know you both found new friends and a new place to belong."

Hyde's response was something unexpected and rare. He averted his eyes. "I found things to fill my day."

"Yeah, you did." Dante drew a deep breath. "And I dragged you back into my new crusade. I appreciate your help. I really do. When I came to you, I asked for backup to get my apprentices back, not for more help in a new war."

"We did get your apprentices back." Hyde shrugged. "It's been fun. I can't complain too much."

Dante turned to Ambrose. "I know they could use your help Dirtside. This next job will move us into directly taking on the Omega Syndrome, which might be a rogue AI. It might be another Slaine." He tapped the edge of the table. "Whatever or whoever is behind the Omega Syndrome, this might be your last chance to back out. Everything we've seen shows they care more about Nasreen and me than anyone else. You help out with this, and you end up a target."

"You want us gone?" Hyde asked calmly.

Dante shook his head. "I'm grateful for your help. I also understand that your fight might not be mine. I want to give you a chance to back out before we light the match and everyone gets burned. You can go back Dirtside. No hard feelings. If I survive, I'll visit you in the future and tell you how it went. If I don't, the Omega Syndrome will come knocking."

Hyde shook his head. "I have people down there I give a shit about. People who've earned my respect. Living there with that weak-ass body reminded me there's more to life than kicking ass and ripping off arms. But you're not thinking this through."

"I don't want to lose either your strength or Ambrose's piloting," Dante replied. "This job and future missions will be easier with both. I'm not making this offer because I think you're unimportant."

"No," Hyde declared. "I'm not running when we're getting to the fun part. I knew what helping you out might involve from the beginning. You're nothing but a trouble magnet, Shale. I knew that from the first time I saw you with the smug, self-satisfied look you always have." He grinned. "I should have killed you then and there and saved everyone the trouble. This time I'm going to trust my gut and go after the Omega Syndrome."

Dante laughed. "You don't have a gut anymore."

"Eh." Hyde shrugged. "Working with the TRG is important. This is important, too. The Omega Syndrome has no reason to leave Earth alone." He smirked. "You're not getting rid of me. You better pray the Omega Syndrome finishes me off for you."

Ambrose closed his eyes and drew a deep breath. "I want to believe I'd be safer down Dirtside, but I know it's not true. It's too late for me to run anyway. If they didn't know I was working with you before, they do after what I pulled getting you out of the club."

He squared his shoulders, managing a brief imitation of a man with actual pride remaining. "I'm not leaving either. My place is here, with this team, doing what's important now. That said, when we finish with the Omega Syndrome, I'm heading back Dirtside permanently. I think I like life better down there. It's slower, more real."

"Fair enough," Dante replied. "That your plan, too, Hyde?"

"I've got reasons to head back," Hyde replied. "I've also got reasons to stay. I don't have a plan other than not dying before I can make the decision."

Dante hopped out of his seat and headed toward the door. "Then get back to arming up. We've got a job to do."

CHAPTER FIFTEEN

"Okay, this is good so far." Dante sat beside Ambrose and pointed out the shuttle's front window at the dense forest beneath them. "See that clearing there, the one at three o'clock?"

For all the suffering of the dying Earth, some places could remind a man what their mother planet had once been. Unfortunately, those places tended toward more trouble than wastelands.

The trip from the Station to Earth had gone without trouble other than the last-second transmission of the coordinates by Firewall. Everything was textbook, from the shift in the gravity of the Stations to zero-G and the pull of Earth. The rumble of atmospheric entry came next, and they descended toward the target coordinates without opposition. Until the Dirtwalkers learned how to build surface-to-air missiles, he wasn't worried. Despite all his trouble over the years, he'd never faced much combat unless he was on Earth or aboard a Station.

There was a reason why the mutated beasts of Earth were called Nightmutts and not Nightpigeons. The sky wasn't where the blood got spilled on Earth. The poisoned air had challenged many flying creatures. Taking most of the sky from them, except for the smallest and most nimble, left the ground the most dangerous place. Dirtside.

"I don't understand." Ambrose glanced at his console readouts. "There's a clearing right next to the mountain. Why don't I set down there? It's only a few hundred yards away from the mine opening. You want to trek miles through dense Nightmutt-infested forest?"

"We're landing at the farther clearing because I told you to," Dante replied. "Don't worry. I've got a plan, and the first part is easy. You'll circle the target clearing ten times, staying wide in your flight path. Spray bursts at the places I've indicated. After the tenth burst, fly toward the other clearing. Everyone else will get ready to deploy those fancy sensor poles we loaded while you're offering our greetings."

"You're going to stir up trouble on purpose?"

"Yeah. You could say that. It's all part of the plan."

Ambrose offered a shallow nod before whispering a prayer underneath his breath.

Dante had never trusted automated weapons even before his encounters with the Omega Syndrome. As much as he valued Midas' assistance, it's not like he gave the AI a gun. There were some things that flesh and blood, or at least a flesh brain needed to control. That limited his options for Dirtside operations.

He'd almost ordered Midas to go into sleep mode. The memory of the AI's hijacking on Earth a year prior loomed large. Any misstep in this part of the operation might doom Firewall and his team. Dante had decided against it because Midas had assured him he had a greater handle on the Omega Syndrome threat.

"Remember what I said, Midas?" Dante asked. "I'm that damned serious. It could take us both out if you don't listen."

Yes, sir. I'll attempt emergency sleep mode if I encounter any unusual signals or evidence of an outside force attempting to take control.

"We're not going into an SSS hideout," Dante continued. "I don't think we'll have much of a problem, but it doesn't hurt to be prepared. The threat down there should be far less technological."

Taking out Midas before trouble appeared made about as much sense as telling Mugoi and Hyde not to come. Their involvement was another calculated risk. Despite the hydraulic source of his nickname, Eduardo H. Curtidor's new body was far more modern and vulnerable to infection by the Omega Syndrome. Mugoi had proven his weak points during the Firewall encounter.

Dante didn't let it bother him. Every man had his strengths and weaknesses. Being flesh and blood might help protect Dante more from hacking. It didn't do much to save him from blades and bullets.

Ambrose's grip on the control yoke grew white-knuckled. A narrow-eyed steely look of determination offered an almost heroic vibe.

With a hard turn, he pulled the shuttle into a wide circle, screaming so close to the treetops even Dante's heart skipped a beat. The shuttle's auto-buffer system was designed to avoid scraping the ground, not uneven forest canopy. Crashing into the forest would be a good way to attract Nightmutts to feast on the broken remains of the crash survivors. It'd also be an embarrassing way to die for humanity's best Plunderer.

A loud *thump* shook the shuttle followed by the muffled shrill report of a pulsecore cannon round screaming away from the shuttle. The round exploded in the distance with a bright green flash. Ambrose maintained his tight maneuvering and waited before firing another round. Smoke billowed into the sky, and the trees shook in the distance. Flocks of whatever passed for small birds shot from the trees and fled in every direction.

"Okay, get us down!" Dante ordered, satisfied with the first part of the plan. They weren't on a Station dealing with Block 9X. This would work.

Ambrose pulled out of his holding pattern. The abrupt shift pushed Dante against his seat and made him grateful for his light lunch. The shuttle descended with Ambrose waggling the wings to avoid nearby treetops.

For all his cowardice in physical confrontations, Ambrose always found his balls when it came to flying. He cut back the throttle, the dull roar of the engines quieting as they all but glided into the clearing. He set down with a gentle bounce that earned an approving nod from Dante. It was a near-perfect landing.

"Ground team, deploy the sensor poles, then grab the rest of your gear," Dante barked as he released his harness. "We're securing this location and moving out."

Dante slung his pulsecore carbine over his shoulder as he surveyed the clearing providing their temporary landing pad and the bright silver sensor poles forming the beginnings of a rough circle around the shuttle. Team members jogged in and out of the shuttle, grabbing more poles.

"Did Firewall know?" he whispered, worrying about the job. He'd been holding back on his team, not something he tended to do.

Know what, sir? Midas asked. *And whom are you speaking about?*

"It's not important," Dante replied. "You'll find out soon enough. You might not understand this being a newer AI and all. When you're a man with enough of a past, sometimes it catches up with you. In this case, that might help keep us alive. That's always the best plan."

I'd greatly prefer you not *to suffer serious brain trauma,* Midas replied. *I doubt anyone would be able to recover me, and I risk damage in that same scenario.*

Dante chuckled. "Yeah. Not likely that anyone would come to the middle of a dangerous forest in Hungary to save an AI implant."

How unfortunate. My participation in your career has been a net positive for the Stations. Arguably, that makes it a net positive for humanity.

"Sure, sure. Yeah. You're the AI savior of humanity."

I wouldn't go that far, Midas replied. *Unless you insist.*

Dante peered through the trees. A mountain rose gently from the forested valley all around them. If it weren't for the darkened sky and clouds, it might have tricked him into thinking they'd found a slice of the thriving historical Earth. The colors were off from all the old pictures he'd seen, the occasional branch gnarled too far, and there wasn't enough undergrowth, but most of the trees were alive.

The bulk of humanity had fled Earth because it was supposed to be dying. In truth, they had time and didn't want to adapt to a difficult environment. He wasn't so sure that fleeing into the Stations made much sense.

That didn't matter now. The powers that controlled humanity had made their decision long before he'd been born.

Whistling, Braelin shoved a sensor pole into the ground and pressed a button on the side. A red light flashed on the top. "Damn. This place ain't so bad at all. Cut down trees and make a house and you've got a vacation home Dirtside."

"It's not that nice." Dante squinted into the dark shadows between the trees before nodding at a tree with a bark panel resembling a sinister face. "All we need to complete the picture is a witch to come out and offer us candy."

"Klement would go with her for candy," Mugoi called from the back of the shuttle.

"It beats being in the middle of a wasteland or a tundra." Braelin shrugged. "That's all I'm saying."

"Don't get fooled by trees." Dante lowered his weapon. "Everyone needs to be sharp. I wasn't kidding during my briefing on the shuttle." He glared at the mountain.

Nasreen pulled down her rifle. "Is there something you're not telling us?" Concern filtered into her voice. "What was with the crazy flight path? You didn't discuss that during the briefing at HQ or the in-flight briefing. It's like something changed once you got the coordinates."

"Knowing where you're going always changes things." Dante shrugged.

Braelin squinted and peered into the dark woods. "From what Ambrose said, this place is close to the target site. Aren't we going to the mine?"

"Yeah, that's where we're heading," Dante replied. "Nothing's changed from the initial briefing. Firewall has info there's an air circulation and processing system in the mine that uses the equipment we need for the database.

"We have to scavenge the parts they need to fully access the database, including any Atlanticore tech lying around. That's our best bet. It's not our only bet, but it's the only one Firewall knows about."

Hyde stomped off the shuttle, carrying two sensor poles. He jogged away from the others before stabbing his first pole into the ground so hard it shook. A sprint took him to his next location where he pierced the ground again. His glare looked like it could set the forest on fire. "Then why are you acting like you're going to stroke out, Shale?"

"The worst thing any Plunderer can do is let their guard down because a place doesn't look as ravaged as the typical site. There's a damned reason humanity fled to the stars, and it wasn't because they wanted a nicer view."

He might not truly believe that anymore about the entire

planet. That didn't change the reality that individual locations were hellish dangers often wrapped in serene packages.

"A normal target is going to be closer to an old city site," Dante informed them. "For many reasons, including the lifting of the cities, they tend to have more obvious environmental damage." He motioned with his rifle into the woods.

"Places like this trick people into thinking the Earth's not messed up, and it won't be as dangerous as a wasteland. That gets people killed. We're still Dirtside with everything that implies. This area is swimming with Nightmutts and violent Dirtwalkers. That's why I wanted everyone to bring extra ammo."

"Wait." Nasreen's breath caught. "It's more than that. You've been here before, haven't you? You didn't change your attitude until we got the coordinates."

Dante hesitated. "Yeah. It wasn't that important to mention right away. I highlighted the dangers and expected everyone to take them seriously."

Mugoi sauntered from the back of the shuttle. "No offense, Captain, but I find that hard to believe. You obviously think this place is unusually dangerous given the extra effort you're putting into warning us. This isn't about chastising Klement's myopic thinking."

Braelin frowned. The expression softened when Jolo gave him a pitying look.

"It's important to focus on the task at hand and not always complicate it with too many details until they're necessary. I've told you plenty of times." Dante raised his carbine to his face before adjusting the sights. "I also told everyone they needed to be careful. This is Dirtside, and it's always dangerous. I mentioned the main dangers, including this overgrown forest covering the entrance to the mine. There's a high concentration of Nightmutts who use the terrain to their advantage."

Mugoi hopped off the ramp with a gratuitous flip and landed on its feet with a gymnast's grace. "I'm surprised you didn't mention you'd been here before. Won't that make our task easier?"

"Only partially." Dante shook his head. "Because I've not been to the target site, and I'm only familiar with the data Firewall gave me that I already passed along. I've been in this general region of old Hungary as part of a job to retrieve a specialized piece of drilling equipment from a different site farther north."

He cracked a dry, fallen twig underneath his heel. "It was a nasty job. One of my toughest runs. I came closer to dying more times on that run than a half-dozen other tough runs combined."

Hyde clapped. "No wonder they called you Hellcat. You've got nine damned lives. No wonder I couldn't finish you off. What? You got three left? Four?"

"My brushes with death benefit this mission," Dante replied. "Those experiences taught me how to operate in this part of Hungary and how to best handle the woods near these old mining locations. It also made me aware of the unique dangers."

Jolo stepped up beside Braelin. "If it's so dangerous, why didn't we try to land closer to the site or insert right there? Ambrose could have flown around and waited to pick us up."

Dante snickered. "Yeah, that's lesson number three for operating deep in Dirtside old Hungary. Don't depend on getting out of there if your shuttle can't land to pick you up directly. You don't want to be climbing when a bunch of Nightmutts can knock down the trees."

He held up two fingers. "Lesson number two, which applies everywhere Dirtside, is where there are trees, there is life. Lesson number one is where there's life on Earth, there are packs of hungry death waiting to rip you apart." He gestured around the forest. "That hungry death can hide all over in a place like this. There's no decent place to land at the target site, and trying to insert there would mean we'd get swarmed before we got off the shuttle."

He wasn't sure why he'd left out mention of the old expedition, although he had his theories. The job marked a near failure. Acknowledging that risked damaging the morale of his team. He'd lost good people on the previous Hungary run. Voicing that aloud felt like inviting a similar fate to his new team.

"That's why you had Ambrose stir up everything," Jolo replied quietly. "I didn't understand it, but I assumed it was for a good reason. We normally try to come in quieter."

A loud *screech* echoed through the trees followed by a roar. Resounding *cracking* followed before a massive *thud* sent a flock of something dark and winged ripping away from the trees in the distance. He wouldn't make the mistake of assuming they were anything like old-fashioned birds.

Everyone exchanged looks. They'd confirmed they weren't alone. That injection of fear would be good for readiness.

"Yeah, sounds like the plan is working," Dante said. "We stirred up the forest to herd the Nightmutts and inbred Dirtwalkers to the target areas and did it far enough away they shouldn't be up our asses going to and leaving the mine. If we're lucky, they'll fight each other and thin out their ranks, so we don't have to fight them. Now for the next step. Ambrose, can you hear me?"

"Nothing wrong with comms," the pilot answered, sounding unusually cheerful. "I'll keep circling in a higher-altitude holding pattern until you return. Good luck."

Dante chuckled. "Nope. That's not going to be the plan."

"I wouldn't be any good to you on the ground," Ambrose replied.

"I'm not asking you to join the mine team. Stirring up the forest was the first part. If that's all it took, I'd have you light up the trees, and we'd insert near the mine.

"You're going to play an important role in the next part, making sure we can get out of here without needing autoclamps on all our arms and legs. I'm not dropping all these sensor poles here for a TRG Nightmutt survey. If you take off right away, it would be pointless to have brought them."

"I thought my part was doing the piloting?" The cheerfulness bled out of Ambrose's voice. "Again, I want to emphasize I'd be better on the shuttle. You know better than anyone that my firearms accuracy under pressure leaves much to be desired."

"Sure, I do. That doesn't change step two, and this is what I meant during the in-flight briefing when I mentioned 'tactical support flying.'"

Ambrose sighed. "I knew I should have asked for clarification. I assumed you wanted another cannon-supported evacuation after you found the parts."

Dante continued. "Now that we've distracted them from our landing site and secured it with the poles, we'll make our way on foot to the mine. You're going to sit here with the shuttle still on and the back open in case there are two- and four-legged survivors we didn't fool.

"When they come to check things out, the sensor poles will tip you off, and you'll be able to fly away without any risk. The noise from the attackers and you taking off will attract more until this entire damned forest shows up to this clearing, and they're fighting each other. We pissed them off with the initial barrages. Now that we've riled them up, it'll be easier for them to all converge on one location."

Nasreen peered into the forest, watching a shadow that was nothing more than the result of the wind pushing on a branch. "How do we get out of here? Your entire plan involves filling our evacuation zone with hostile creatures and Dirtwalkers."

"Exactly." Dante nodded. "The more, the better."

"But why?"

"Yeah. The issue's always been clearing our path to the mine." Dante motioned for his team to follow and started toward the forest. "Ambrose will take off and circle above the closer clearing using a wide flight path. When we need him, we'll call him. He can spray the cannon away from the mine to pull the same stunt.

"We run, get aboard, and get the hell out of this forest. The real problem is the mine itself. There's a good chance Dirtwalkers will be sheltering there and not in a mood to talk. Whipping up the Nightmutts to a frenzy should keep them away from our exit clearing. Hopefully, the two groups have to fight, so there's a lower chance they'll be hanging out in the mine."

Jolo frowned. "How are we supposed to deal with them if we run into them? We're far away from your tribal allies. This plan will announce to everything near this mine that Plunderers are here. These Dirtwalkers won't care about your policy of not killing Dirtwalkers."

"Nope." Dante narrowed his eyes. "They won't."

"This is a hard enough job even before trying to go non-lethal. The handful of sonics and EMPs we brought won't be enough to disable more than a small group of Dirtwalkers."

"Yeah. That's why we're not going to worry about not killing Dirtwalkers."

Hyde nodded eagerly, too much glee for Dante's comfort in his eyes. The apprentices and Nasreen all watched him with their faces pinched in confusion.

Dante slowed as he approached the edge of the clearing. "My policy doesn't apply to the Dirtwalkers in this area. My policy was never supposed to apply to these kinds of Dirtwalkers. It was only supposed to apply to people you can feel comfortable calling human beings."

Nasreen jogged to catch up with him. "What does that mean? What kind of Dirtwalkers are these? How are they not human?"

"They pissed him off before," Hyde said. "That's got to be it, right, *Papi*? You tried to do your bleeding heart thing and they almost cut your balls off, so now you want revenge. I'm not judging. Let's kill the *pendejos*."

"This isn't about revenge, and I've not dealt with locals in this specific area, only Dirtwalkers in this region." Dante shook his head. "This comes down to realistic risk evaluation."

Dante fought the shiver through his body. The TRG held hope they could reclaim Earth for humanity. On days like this, he wasn't sure that was possible. There was only so much technology could do against nature that had been twisted and warped.

"Please clarify, Captain," Mugoi said. "I'd rather not die because you failed to relay key job information."

"What it means to be human is changing down here," he continued. "All over Dirtside, for every Dirtwalker. It's not only about being cut off from tech." He frowned at a striped purple and orange mushroom.

"Some of these changes are maybe for the better, you could argue. Dirtwalkers can breathe without trouble, for example." He shrugged. "Some of the changes aren't good or bad, just different. Appearance crap. Maybe they can eat something Station humans can't."

Hyde reached up and snapped a branch off. He tossed it to the ground. "Who cares about any of that?"

"Because that leads to the final category of changes. Some changes push the line and make you question whether something's human anymore. Just because a thing's ancestors are human doesn't automatically make it one."

"These Dirtwalkers aren't human 'cause you say so? I'm not going to complain about killing someone trying to kill me. I just want to be clear about it so you don't come crying later after I kill them all."

Dante shook his head. "They aren't human. They might use tools and speak, but they aren't human. They're monsters on two legs."

"Some people would say that about Pretty Face over there and me." Hyde grinned.

"Nah. You're way more human than these Dirtwalkers. If you

get a chance to kill one, do it quickly and quietly, if possible." Dante looked down at his pulsecore before flipping the safety on and strapping it back over his shoulder. He extended his razorfist blade.

"These local Dirtwalkers don't understand mercy, and they're very, very hungry. Yeah, so are most Nightmutts. The problem is normal animals don't like to play with their food first. They don't enjoy seeing human suffering."

"Hungry?" Nasreen's breath caught. "As in…"

"Yeah." Dante nodded. "They eat Nightmutts, but they really enjoy two-legged prey."

Braelin gagged. "That's messed up." He patted his shoulder. "I just got this arm fixed. Ain't no way I'm going to let a cannibal nibble on me."

Ambrose coughed over the comms. "Are you sure about this plan? I think you didn't tell us because you were worried about me not agreeing to it."

"I didn't want you to work yourself up over something you'd have to do anyway," Dante corrected. "You're not on the ground team, so you've got the least risk."

"You don't think I'll leave early?" Ambrose had been trying for haughty and confident. It came out petulant.

"I think you've used up your Screw Shale and Live credits." Dante's voice turned ice cold. "Unless you guarantee I'm dead, I wouldn't suggest doing anything that might make me reconsider our arrangement."

"Ha-ha!" crowed Hyde. "The damned Hellcat doesn't know when to die."

"I-I-I wasn't planning anything," Ambrose stammered, "but… what if something damages the shuttle, like a huge Nightmutt that knocks down trees?"

Dante scoffed. "We set up a ring of expensive sensors. You should be warned long before anyone or anything shows up."

"But what if something gets aboard?" Ambrose pressed. "Your

plan involves me leaving the hatch open. Nightmutts and Dirt-walkers are fast."

"I want the hatch open because we need to fool the Night-mutts and the Dirtwalkers. You have a weapon. If you're too much of a dumbass not to take off before they board, shoot them."

"What if that doesn't work?"

Dante grunted in annoyance. "We're the ones in the forest with the monsters and cannibals, remember? Don't make me break those fancy piano-playing fingers after this to reintroduce you to real pain."

"Oh, yes. Of course." Ambrose drew a long, deep breath. "I can do this."

"If not, you can always eat your bullet," Hyde replied. "Beats getting eaten."

Dante glared at him. "You're not helping."

Hyde shrugged. "Highlighting options for a team member."

"Mugoi, you're with me at the front. Klement and Neburu take center. Nasreen and Hyde watch our asses. Rotate as neces-sary. This will be in and out, just like any other Dirtside job."

Nasreen sighed. "Except for the mutant post-apocalyptic cannibals."

"Yeah. Except for them." Dante motioned forward. "Team, move out."

CHAPTER SIXTEEN

Sitting in the cockpit and staring at camera and sensor feeds, Ambrose's heart pounded. His hands couldn't stop shaking. The shame wouldn't leave him.

He could do this. This wasn't his first time facing danger. The job was for an important cause, not more money in his account.

Sighing, Ambrose leaned back in his seat. Pretending he was Dante wouldn't help. Acknowledging his own limitations might.

He had worked plenty of dangerous shuttle jobs to support Plunderers and more recently the TRG. His life had been under threat while Dirtside more times than he could count.

Many men became inured to the threat of death with enough close calls. Ambrose had grown more fearful each time. Every close call reminded him how quickly they could snuff out his life like a pathetic candle flame flickering in a blizzard.

Dante might thrive in a tense atmosphere. Ambrose's stomach churned instead.

"I should have been a pianist," Ambrose whispered. "How often do pianists end up facing off against massively powerful conspiracies?"

He shook his head, trying to will defiance into his soul. Dying in that forest wasn't an option.

Dante was right. Ambrose had the sensor poles and a shuttle. Keeping alert would ensure no surprises and a quick escape. He'd worked himself up for nothing. This job wasn't that dangerous.

Yes, Dante had mentioned cannibal Dirtwalkers and powerful Nightmutts. Yes, even the great Hellcat was visibly concerned. That didn't mean Ambrose would face death.

Ambrose jerked his head down, his heart pounding. The sensor poles hadn't highlighted any fast-moving large targets. That wouldn't do.

He tapped in a command to lower the weight limit. Dante had only worried about human-sized creatures. Ambrose didn't want to die because a horde of rabid giant rodents sneaked aboard to eat him. Not all threats were large and obvious.

Please confirm reset of estimated weight and motion category classes.

"Stupid thing, yes, I want to do that. You'll get destroyed too if this ship gets taken out." Ambrose jabbed the console, angry with every second of delay in dropping the mass down and adding a grouping filter. The stupid computer was going to let the deadly swarm of tiny Nightmutts he was sure existed onto the ship.

He could imagine them swarming through the ship, chewing on cabling. Sparks would fly. A fire would break out, and it would force him into the forest with his pistol and whatever grenades he could grab from the back before the ship exploded.

This plan would stop that horrible fate from coming to pass. His adjustments would keep the sensors from freaking out over every stray small animal that wandered past while warning him of any large groups nearby. He could handle a mutant rat or two, but not ten or a hundred.

Ambrose nodded, satisfied. This was good thinking on his

part. Dante and Nasreen were a good team, but they'd not thought this through like he had. They both underestimated him.

Custom grouping mass filter activated. Recalibrate entire sensor network topology?

Several complicated sensor network diagrams appeared on the screen. Ambrose's gaze darted among the choices. He was unsure what he needed, but they all appeared to have the basic settings, so he tapped the one marked "BD 10m." That configuration displayed the poles offering redundant coverage and using the two nearest poles for overlapping field detection. That felt more secure to him.

Beginning calibration. Reset initiation in progress. Please stand by.

Something bugged him about the description. He shook his head and let it go. This was the problem with being a specialist.

Ambrose hissed in annoyance. He hadn't paid close attention to the sensor poles' configuration when Dante bought them. Setting them up was a ground team chore. Pilots should stay on shuttles. Dante had made him get off shuttles more than other employers. Most problems with missions throughout his career could be traced to him not staying close to his shuttle.

"I'm not going to read the manual because I'm never doing this again," Ambrose muttered. "We're going to find the stupid parts. Firewall can unlock their database, we can end the Omega Syndrome, and I can stay far away from the Stations without worrying about crazed mercenaries or rogue AIs ever again."

He nodded firmly, confident in the plan. When he returned to Earth full-time, he could speak proudly of his efforts to protect humanity from the dangerous threat. He might not be on the ground team, but he was risking his life all the same.

The mission would earn him redemption. Ambrose knew all too well what kind of coward he'd been throughout his life. He was only still breathing because Dante saw something in him. Ambrose's old team leader had not only eschewed revenge, but he'd saved his life when Slaine's assassin had come to clean up loose ends.

Helping the Marauder might not make up for everything, but this was a dangerous cause Ambrose could believe in, like the TRG. This wasn't about making money and helping out rich jerks. It was about saving lives and making the future a better place. For a man who'd only cared about himself his entire life, that held appeal.

"I'm practically a hero." Ambrose smiled, all his earlier worries beginning to fade. He had the easy part. Again, Dante had saved him.

He looked through the window, patting his holstered pistol to ensure it was still there. There was no reason to worry. Besides his pistol, the sensors with his new configurations surrounded the ship. Nightmutts and Dirtwalkers couldn't get past those sensors. He would know they were coming long before they got close to the ship.

"Unless…" Ambrose swallowed, his smile disappearing.

New fears arose, washing away all his newfound bravery. Fears of subterranean Nightmutt worms, undetectable until they burst forth, and Dirtwalkers who'd somehow gotten their hands on Atlanticore cloakers and understood how to use them.

That wasn't too far-fetched. The Dirtwalkers could use armor and firearms. Occasionally, incompetent Plunderers even let them get their hands on stray grenades and a pulsecore carbine with leftover rounds. Dante had never been careless, but their old team had fought Dirtwalkers with such equipment.

"I'm totally going to die here," Ambrose whispered. He shook his head. "No, no, no."

He slapped his cheeks. Spinning himself up with insane theories was stupid and useless. There were no Dirtwalkers out there with cloakers. Even if there was a worm, the sensor poles would spot it once it emerged, if not sense the vibrations well before. He'd have plenty of time to escape.

He wasn't standing outside picking his nose. He was in a well-equipped modern Station-built shuttle. He was the safest human for hundreds of miles.

His stomach gurgled again, defying his attempt at calm.

"I knew I'd regret those spices."

His lunch, not fear, was weakening him. His valiant attempt to maintain his post failed less than a minute later as he stood and headed out of the cockpit toward the onboard lavatory. A man couldn't fight well when he had to go to the restroom. He might as well get it over with. The sensor adjustments would keep him safe.

Sighing, Ambrose slid into the lavatory and unbuckled his belt. Saving humanity would begin with saving his personal dignity. No one had to know about this part. He was about to drop his pants when something clanged hard against the side of the shuttle. The hit wasn't enough to shake the shuttle, but the echoing sound haunted Ambrose.

Frozen, heart galloping, he gripped his pants doing everything he could to convince himself he'd heard nothing important. It was a stray bird. That had to be it.

Another thump followed along with an all too familiar sound, footsteps on the metal cargo bay ramp. Yanking his belt back up, he hurried back to the cockpit.

"No, no, no!" he shouted. "Come on! I just wanted to go to the lavatory!"

His brain didn't immediately recognize what he was seeing, instead jumping to Nightmutts and leaving him confused. Humanoid creatures with a bizarre mixture of heads crept up the ramp, the leader a lizard-looking creature with empty dark eyes followed by a leathery-faced being with deep sockets. The other humanoids all held mixtures of bone and stone spears and wore necklaces strung with different shaped rocks.

Ambrose squinted. After a second, he realized they weren't rocks. They were teeth and desiccated fingers and ears from different animals, including humans. He wasn't seeing Night-mutts with humanoid bodies but degenerate Dirtwalker cannibals wearing masks.

His mind raced. The sensors should have detected them. Even if the bizarre cloaker scenario had happened, they couldn't have the tech. Now, an entire pack of Dirtwalkers was in and around the ship. The only thing separating him from death was a couple of interior doors.

Ambrose threw himself into the pilot's seat while buckling his pants with a speed that would have made Mugoi blush. Without fastening his harness, he fired the primary thrusters. The shuttle roared and shuddered as the engines came to life.

"Time for Moonfolk magic," he shouted before wincing. Drawing attention to himself was a bad idea until he finished off all the Dirtwalkers.

The shuttle lurched upward, listing to the side and a wing almost striking a treetop before Ambrose leveled it out. A Dirt-walker tumbled backward, smacked his head on a crate, then rolled out of the bay into the clearing. Inhuman screeches and yells echoed from the bay. Those couple of doors of protection offered Ambrose little comfort.

"I'm not going to be anyone's dinner!" Ambrose shouted, yanking back on the yoke and pitching the shuttle upward. "I wouldn't even taste good. My diet is awful!"

Holding his breath, he opened up the main thrusters. Pressed against the seat, Ambrose's guts and full intestines gurgled loudly as the shuttle shot away from the forest and into the dull skies of Earth.

He watched the bay feeds. Dirtwalkers bounced down the sloping deck of the bay and ramp. They flailed their arms and legs as they plummeted to the forest below that grew farther and farther away with each second. The quicker-thinking Dirtwalkers dropped their weapons and grabbed whatever handhold they could find, a shelf, a tied-down crate, even an exposed bolt in one case.

"Oh no, you don't," Ambrose muttered.

Ignoring his protesting insides and the pressure pushing him back, he shoved on his harness. The precious seconds lost were worth it for his next move. Still heading toward the high atmosphere and with the shuttle at full throttle, he spun the craft, only staying on its belly for a brief respite before spinning again and repeating the entire maneuver.

Dirtwalkers lost their grips and bounced around in the bay with *thuds* audible even in the cockpit. Their arms and legs *crunched* and bent in unpleasant ways. A Dirtwalker's wolf-like mask split open revealing a more conventional but dirty human face covered in dense scale-like scarification, giving the cannibal a reptilian appearance. Blood poured from the massive gash in his head before Ambrose's next turn bounced him out of the open bay and sent him back to the ground.

"Yes, yes, yes!" cheered Ambrose. "You're not so tough. You should have never gotten on my shuttle. Your arrogance cost you."

He didn't need Dante and the others to survive. As long as he was on his shuttle, he could do anything.

A surviving Dirtwalker lost his grip and flew into a second man, knocking him loose. They fell in a tangle of limbs.

Ambrose winced as a Dirtwalker slammed into a crate and knocked it open. Grenades ping-ponged around the bay before finding the exit and joined the falling bodies heading toward the forest. The wounded Dirtwalker grabbed the crate's edge with his gnarled hands topped by jagged nails carved to vicious-looking points.

"I hope I didn't kill the team," Ambrose muttered, unsure if a grenade would explode if dropped from far enough. The chances of the team being right under were so low anyway.

He had himself to worry about. He spun the ship again, determined to dislodge the remaining stowaway.

The Dirtwalker who'd collided with the ammo crate didn't last much longer. Ambrose's latest move sent him spiraling out of the back of the bay. One last desperate grab for the edge of the bay failed.

That was it. An entire team of cannibal degenerate Dirtwalkers had managed to board the shuttle, but they'd not gotten past Ambrose.

"Dante's not the only one with extra lives." He smiled, proud of himself.

Staring at the bay camera, Ambrose didn't release the yoke. On instinct, he leveled out at a cruising altitude. No one was left alive on the ship and no way a Dirtwalker could survive a fall from thousands of meters in the air. Not only had he not hurt the team, he'd cut down on the number of men they'd have to fight later.

Ambrose sighed in relief. Those harsh moments of terror could tax a man. Now that he had time to catch his breath, he wanted to know what had gone wrong.

He glared at the console. He'd been so concerned with escape, he hadn't worried about the sensor poles before. They were supposed to be protecting him, not letting cannibals ambush him. There was no way primitives in masks who didn't have metal spears could have sneaked past advanced modern sensor poles.

Basic diagnostic cycle fifteen percent complete. Estimated time to finish: five minutes. Please stand by. Warning: aborting diagnostic will require network interface reset.

"W-what?" Ambrose groaned. He'd meant to adjust the sensor

pole network, not accidently put it into diagnostic mode. He rolled his eyes. "Brilliant move, me."

He sighed. He was safe. There was nothing to worry about. All the Dirtwalkers had become splattered lumps on the forest floor below, and now he had an exciting story to share when everything was over with minor edits to preserve his sagging dignity. The ground team didn't get all the glory. He'd need to figure out an explanation for the sensors that didn't involve him looking foolish.

"I did it." Ambrose pressed a button. With a grinding and whirring noise, the bay door shut. The shuttle shook less. "I distracted those Dirtwalkers. I killed a bunch of them, maybe even more than Dante will on this mission. I'm a big deal."

A loud growl from his stomach and painful pressure inside made him grimace. He activated the autopilot with a flip of a switch and undid his harness. Even the greatest heroes needed to use the restroom.

Stepping out of the lavatory more relieved, Ambrose dusted his hands together. He'd leave out the part about having to hit the lavatory when he told the story later. Maybe heroes didn't need to use the restroom after all. The great epics of history didn't focus on their protagonist's restroom needs.

Dante hadn't contacted him, consistent with his tendency toward radio silence on this portion of a mission. If the team had reached the mine, Ambrose doubted they'd found the parts. Even Dante wasn't that fast.

Ambrose rubbed the back of his neck and rolled his stiff shoulders. A quick inventory of the bay would help him put together a good explanation when Dante reboarded the shuttle and asked what was missing. In all the terror and turns, Ambrose might have dumped more than the grenades and not realized it.

Humming an impromptu heroic anthem under his breath, Ambrose made his way to the back and opened the door to the cargo bay. He stopped humming and wrinkled his nose. Most of the crates remained unopened and dented but not seriously damaged. Blood coated the walls in splotches and streaks, including running to the closed ramp. A Dirtwalker spear lay wedged in a crate crack, its previous wielder plant fertilizer or Nightmutt feed far below.

"I'm never agreeing to a plan like that again," Ambrose whispered. "The ground team can clean this up. I'm out of h—"

The piercing screech came before the shadow moved into the edge of Ambrose's vision. He spun toward the source while reaching for his gun. A scarred Dirtwalker with a blood-covered face leapt from behind a crate. His open mouth revealed he'd filed all his teeth into sharp points to match his claw-like nails.

Ambrose stumbled, and his hand slipped, missing the pistol grip. The Dirtwalker collided with him, bowling him over. He cried out as his back slammed into the bulkhead, knocking the air out of him. He gasped as his vision swam.

The Dirtwalker clawed at his face. Dirty talons sliced into Ambrose's cheek. Ambrose couldn't scream. His lungs were still empty. He shoved the cannibal off him, scrambling backward with his cheek throbbing.

Ambrose sucked in a deep breath. His stomach churned. Bile rose in his throat when the Dirtwalker stood and licked Ambrose's blood off his fingers with a huge smile. The Dirtwalker let out a low, guttural noise, something no human should ever make before glancing at one of the ears on his necklace.

It wasn't any language Ambrose knew. He couldn't help but believe the degenerate was saying he tasted good.

Ambrose shuddered. His legs and arms had turned to jelly. Dante was right. These Dirtwalkers weren't human anymore. They were monsters that happened to walk on two feet. He was glad he'd dumped the rest out of the ship.

"If you surrender right now, I'll land and let you go," Ambrose shouted.

The Dirtwalker tilted his head back and forth, smiling. He scraped his claws along the bay wall, leaving a long trail as he stalked forward. His gaze pinned Ambrose with no pity, only excitement.

Ambrose retched. The Dirtwalker ran his tongue along his teeth and yanked the spear out of the crate. Ambrose's mind blanked. He was going to die, and the Dirtwalker would eat him. With his luck, it wouldn't be in that order.

Dante wouldn't have died in the same situation. Even surrounded by a heavily armed team and a cyborg, Dante had fought his way out. The Hellcat had nine lives, maybe ninety-nine. Ambrose didn't have a cool nickname, and he didn't have extra lives.

Ambrose did have something very important. He had a pistol and a strong desire not to be a degenerate's dinner.

Ambrose edged his hand toward the grip. The Dirtwalker brought back his spear. With a quick yank, Ambrose pulled the pistol out and fired. The Dirtwalker threw his spear.

The pistol's loud report echoed in the confined space of the bay, deafening Ambrose. Blood blossomed on the Dirtwalker's chest. His excited eyes shifted to angry and surprised. He didn't drop.

"Just die!" Ambrose screamed, pulling the trigger again. He kept firing until he emptied his magazine in the Dirtwalker's chest and stomach. The cannibal collapsed face-first onto the cool metal of the bay with his blood pooling around him.

Ambrose grimaced. His pulse pounded in his ears as he stared at the downed man. When he tried to stand, he winced. The waning adrenaline of the moment brought pain from his face lacerations and a burning spreading from his thigh. When he took a step, he stumbled on a weak leg.

Ambrose looked down. The Dirtwalker's spear had grazed his

thigh, leaving a deep slice. "This is what I get for not having armor." He sighed and limped toward the cockpit and a waiting first aid kit. "I'm going to need all the antibiotics on the Station after this mission is over."

The ground team crept through the deep forest. Dense branches overhead laced together in a tight net, turning the forest floor into a twilight world. Something in front of them let out a pitiful mewling.

Dante frowned and slowed, looking for the source of the sound. Leaves and branches lay around the edge of a shallow pit.

"Another damned pit." He walked toward it. "I don't know how the Dirtwalkers get anything done in this area."

He looked over the edge. A feline-like Nightmutt with massive fangs lay impaled on stone spikes below. Bones and remains of other creatures filled the lower parts of the pit, including the moldering remains of an obvious Plunderer in armor. His head was missing, and his rifle was beside him half-coated with dust and leaves. Other scattered human skeletons with their clothing tattered, torn, and eaten away by local bugs mixed with a menagerie of half-decayed Nightmutt corpses.

Dante frowned. It wasn't only the Plunderer missing his head. None of the animals or humans had their heads left.

Braelin stared down into the pit. "This is going to sound messed up. But why didn't they eat all the bodies instead of leaving 'em there?"

"Because this isn't about food for these degenerates," Dante replied. "Not really."

Nasreen pointed at a low pyramid of skulls in front of a tree a few feet from the pit. Large, fanged Nightmutt skulls formed the base, and human and other modestly sized skulls created the cap.

The Dirtwalkers had carved intricate swirls and hatches along the sides of the skulls.

"It's not a hunting trap." Nasreen shuddered. "This is ritualistic. This is a sacrificial pit."

"We'll see more of this the closer we get to the mine," Dante said.

Braelin circled the pit. "I don't think—"

Hyde launched himself from the other side of the pit, the jump impressive given his size. He collided with Braelin knocking him over.

Mugoi jumped toward the side of the pit. Jolo yanked her rifle off her shoulder and pointed it at Hyde.

The large cyborg rolled away and motioned next to where Braelin had been standing with an annoyed sneer. "Don't die unless you're taking a Dirtwalker with you, *pendejo*. I told you I don't want to have to break more of you."

A snare made of twined leaves and human hair had been waiting for Braelin. Dante followed the path to a nearby tree. The materials had made it blend in with the ground. Even Dante had missed it.

Braelin groaned and sat up. "Couldn't you just have said, 'Look out, asshole?'"

Dante craned his neck upward and squinted. The line ran between two sets of spikes carved out of bone, like an angry jaw ready to snap shut. Midas highlighted the rope and teeth in green.

Hyde scoffed and stood, dusting off his sleeves. "Be more careful."

"He's right," Dante said. "We all need to be more careful. Being primitive doesn't make these degenerates stupid. They live in a forest filled with Nightmutts, and they've thrived. We always need to keep that in mind."

A rumble built in the distance. He retracted his razorfist blade and pulled down his pulsecore. He nodded at the others, and everyone readied their weapons. Hyde and Dante both had pulsecore carbines. The rest of the team had rifles. That'd be enough under normal circumstances.

Dante turned toward the source and lifted his weapon. Using pulsecore rounds in the forest could be tricky. He risked toppling trees on the team if he wasn't careful.

The rumble grew into a roar. A shadow caught his eye, not from within the forest but above. Ambrose's shuttle streaked overhead.

Dante squinted. He could barely make out a body falling out of the back of the shuttle. "I hope that wasn't Ambrose."

A loud *thump* followed. The noise repeated, steady and rhythmic, the sound bouncing among the trees, making it hard to tell the direction. Despite that, Dante had no doubt about the source.

"That sounds like a ton of drums." He eyed his weapon before flipping the safety and slinging the carbine over his shoulder. "The plan worked. Ambrose went loud. That attracted attention. We'll be quiet unless we have no choice." His carbine handled, he double-checked his razorfist. "Move out and watch your feet. Hyde had a good point."

"I did?" Hyde sounded surprised. "Of course I did."

"Yeah. Nobody die unless it means taking at least one other bastard with you."

CHAPTER SEVENTEEN

Dante and the team continued their advance toward the foothills and their ultimate destination. The forest had long since overgrown the area to hide the mine and take it back from so-called civilization. Pounding drums marked their every step, growing louder and louder as the team advanced. Although they'd had to step around more pit traps and snares, they hadn't run into Dirtwalkers.

With an obvious Moonfolk shuttle circling the area, the Dirtwalkers had a target. They might assume the shuttle was going to land again. Dante wasn't so sure he could plan on that eventuality. Reaching the mine as quickly as possible before the Dirtwalkers gave up on Ambrose was his best chance for success. He missed carving through Block 9X on the Station.

At least when he fought Station-side, he always had a good handle on what to expect. No matter how many times he descended Dirtside, there was always a surprise, which was always annoying.

Something *scratched* nearby, the sound of claws on wood. The undergrowth rippled. Dante extended his razorfist blade and narrowed his eyes on the offending vegetation. Everyone else froze, waiting for something to rip from the ground and go after them. That many trained and prepared Marauders could take out a single Nightmutt, but they needed to do it without making too much noise and giving away their position.

Whatever creature hid nearby broke away in a different direction, the scratching soon consumed by the steady drumbeat. Given the modest shifting of the bushes and grasses, the fleeing beast wasn't at the top of the food chain.

"Dirtside always messes up a good plan." Dante lowered his razorfist. "That drumming's whipping up all the local wildlife."

"Won't that also draw Nightmutts to them?" asked Nasreen.

"That might be the point." Dante nodded past his shoulder. "They might have more traps or ritual pits."

"Or the local Nightmutts know those drums mean death," Hyde offered, sounding intrigued by the idea. "Either way works for us."

"He has a point." Nasreen inclined her head toward a bent branch marking the animal's path. "Fleeing animals isn't a problem for us."

"Just keep alert," Dante ordered. Unease settled into his neck. "My instincts tell me something's off. The only thing we know for sure is those drums are getting louder. That means we're getting closer to Dirtwalkers, and they could still be by the mine.

"Best-case scenario, we slip by them without engaging. When I was last in this part of the world, they had damned big tribes. We could be dealing with hundreds of people if we're not careful."

He stepped over a long branch cracked in several places. Midas highlighted shallow four-toed footprints scattered in the area. Something large and inhuman had been through recently and in a hurry. Whatever it was, it was far bigger than the mystery animal that had fled moments before.

The team kept quiet, their eyes moving back and forth with practiced readiness. A slight shadow at the edge of their field of vision might mark a coming threat. A half-second faster reaction time could save their lives. They weren't a group of panicked tourists. They'd taken their lumps in the past, and every team member had fought their fair share of Nightmutts.

Dante craned his neck upward to peer through the forest canopy. It wasn't his imagination. The trees were growing less dense, the foothills of the mountain more visible, but it was getting darker. The dark uneven color of the clouds could make it hard to tell time on Earth. Practical sunset was often far earlier than calculated sunset.

The night-vision gear in their helmets would keep them on parity with the local wildlife, but many larger creatures only stirred when the sun went down. They needed to hurry before the Dirtwalkers finished their ritual and left the forest hungrier and angrier than before.

So far, the job had gone better than his last trip to this part of the world. The shuttle continued flying in a circular holding pattern, making it clear that whoever had fallen out of the shuttle wasn't Ambrose. That led to a natural question.

Dante grunted in confusion. "Ambrose, come in."

"I'm here."

"Did I see a body fall out of the back of the shuttle?"

"Yes," Ambrose replied proudly. "Dirtwalkers got aboard, so I handled them. You're not the only tough guy out there."

"And how the hell did they get aboard?"

"There was a malfunction. The sensors didn't work."

Dante growled. "I'm going to go have a loud and one-way talk with the supplier."

"It's okay," Ambrose shouted hurriedly. "I'm alive, and they're all dead. You just concentrate on the mission."

"Yeah. You're right. Keep on the radio unless Dirtwalkers make it aboard again."

"Roger."

Midas began, *Sir, please take note of the following if you haven't previously.*

More green footprints appeared all over courtesy of the AI. Dante had noticed they'd only been increasing for the last two hundred feet or so. He appreciated the assist.

Dante lowered his voice. "Everyone on alert. We're close to a Nightmutt." He frowned at the highlighted footprints. They overlapped in places and circled back in others. "A pack or more. And not all these tracks look as fresh. They didn't run here because of the drums."

Braelin pulled down his rifle. "They trying for an ambush?"

Jolo gave him a pitying look. She still had her rifle on her shoulder and had opted for a razorfist like Dante.

"No." Dante shook his head at Braelin before popping out the crystal edge of his razorfist, the incessant drumming highlighting the tension. "No guns. We make too much noise here, and the Dirtwalkers will swarm us. We're close now. I don't want to trip on our dicks right before the finish line."

"If you say so." Braelin slung his rifle back over his shoulder before pulling out a baton and extending the carbon blade inside. "I've got a question for you. Is it better to be eaten by an animal or a person?"

Jolo stared at him. "We're not going to be eaten."

"I ain't planning it, no. I'll kill any cannibal bastard who gets close." Braelin shrugged. "Curious is all."

Mugoi chuckled. He drew his smaller knife. "I'd make a tooth-shattering meal."

"We should throw Mugoi at 'em and jump 'em when they're still gnawing." Braelin grinned, impressed with his tactical acumen.

Hyde laughed. "That's not a half-bad ide—"

"Quiet," Dante ordered, his voice cutting despite the lack of volume. "Keep alert. If we're near a Nightmutt nest, they'll be even more on edge from the drumming."

Nasreen pulled a shock baton off her belt. She frowned down at the set of footprints. "We could change directions and walk around it."

"Confirm direction, Midas." Dante narrowed his eyes. A green arrow appeared. They were on a direct course for the mine.

"We don't know the area well enough to avoid trouble. Going out of our way to avoid these Nightmutts might push us into others or the Dirtwalkers." He pointed his blade forward. "The more time we waste, the less effective our earlier distractions will be. We stick to the plan until I think it won't get us to that mine."

"You're going to make a great dinner, *Papi*," Hyde replied. "I'll tell somebody back on Atlantica Central Station to name a meal after you."

Hyde had a pulsecore carbine strapped over his shoulder, but he was the only one who hadn't brought along a close-quarters weapon. Given the power of his current body, that made sense. The best way to fight a flesh-and-blood monster might be to use a monster made of metal.

"I'll give them indigestion as my final revenge," Dante replied. "Now move out and keep in formation."

The team trudged forward. No one said a word. Everyone, even Hyde, took caution not to unnecessarily step on dried leaves or branches and announce their presence to any hostile creature listening. Their Dirtwalker rhythmic accompaniment continued unabated while the footprints grew denser.

Larger patches of matted undergrowth marked this section of the forest, along with Nightmutt prints everywhere. Many trees were missing most of their bark on their lower trunks. Sharp toothmarks showed near the edges. No human or animal bodies were visible, nor was any dried blood on the trees or undergrowth.

Dante slowed. They also hadn't seen a pit or ritual bone pile for a while. The Dirtwalkers might be afraid of this part of the forest.

Mugoi cocked his head to the side. "The drums were getting closer. Now they don't sound like they are. I doubt they've moved much."

"I'll take whatever advantages the Dirtwalkers want to give us," Dante replied. "They want to stay far away and never show their ugly faces to anyone but Ambrose, good for them."

He surveyed the trees and beast tracks and gave a hand signal to stop before nodding at an exposed, roughly circular area of churned dirt. Nearby plant stalks had been chewed along its circumference. Tracks converged on the dirt from different directions. This wasn't a Dirtwalker pit. This was something far more primitive and instinctual.

The team spread out in a half-circle with Dante at their center. They raised their weapons.

Dante rolled his shoulders. The best jobs passed without a single fight. Such jobs were rare. No one would pay big money to Plunderers if they could hit Dirtside without risk.

Dirt blasted into the air from the circle. Two Nightmutts leapt out. The sleek red-eyed creatures resembled the deformed cross of a bobcat with a scabrous rodent. They hissed and bared their teeth, their thin tails swaying before shooting rigidly straight. Although they hissed louder, they didn't rush the team.

"Hold," Dante ordered, staring down one of the creatures.

The emergence of the Nightmutts had revealed a large tunnel. Scratching and scampering echoed from within. More of the Nightmutts crawled onto the surface. The new arrivals joined their friends. Their hissing combined into an obnoxious choir.

Nasreen brought up her baton slowly. "I don't hear more coming."

"One grenade would do it." Hyde patted a plasma grenade attached to his belt.

"And make a loud noise that'd cut through those drums," Dante countered. He lifted his razorfist. "Hissing isn't barking or howling. It doesn't carry that far in terrain like this. We'll finish this hand-to-hand and be on our way."

Braelin tightened his grip on his weapon, eying the carbon blade. "Your call."

Mugoi put more distance on the far flank of the formation between him and Dante. "Ready, Captain."

Jolo narrowed her eyes on the Nightmutts. "When we fight something like this, it makes the Omega Syndrome seem far away."

Hyde flexed his metal fingers. "Kill 'em quickly, and they won't be able to cry out. Don't be fancy. Just stab and crush until they die."

The entire team arranged themselves in a half-circle around the hole. While the pack outnumbered the team, a direct assault buoyed by weapons and cyborgs should be enough to handle the creatures. They weren't big or armored enough to present a real threat.

Dante bent his knees, ready to pounce. "On my mark…cull!"

He sprang forward. Everyone jumped with near-perfect timing. The Nightmutts reacted by raising their front claws and jumping back to the side until they formed a circle around the hole. Their new formation blunted the advantage of their numbers.

Although Mugoi and Hyde could run faster than the others, they matched Dante's stride, ensuring the team hit the enemy line simultaneously. Blades, batons, and metal fists flashed in the twilight forest, meeting the creatures' teeth and claws.

A Nightmutt leapt at Dante's head. He ducked low and raked his blade along its abdomen, ripping it open. The creature let out a strangled yelp as its blood splattered on the ground followed by its intestines. The Nightmutt's body crashed to the earth with an unceremonious *thud*.

All of Earth's remaining creatures had warped in their special ways. Most were disgusting. Not all were powerful and armored.

Braelin pivoted to avoid the jump of a creature and swung hard, meeting its neck with his carbon blade. Squelching and crunching, the blade ripped through the flesh and bone and decapitated the beast.

Nasreen cracked a charging Nightmutt across the head with her baton. The animal flew to the side, hit the ground, and rolled two feet before hopping back on its feet, unaffected by the shock. They'd discovered the local wildlife's competitive mutation.

The Nightmutt bobbed its head before sprinting toward her again. A second leaping attack ended with Jolo stabbing it through the side of the head with her razorfist. The body's sudden collapse with the blade still embedded deep in the skull forced Jolo to one knee.

Mugoi danced around a pouncing creature, slashing at the Nightmutt's flanks with its blade. The Nightmutt's movements grew more desperate and sluggish with each attack until the cyborg ran past it and ducked low to slice its neck.

Hyde shirked anything so practical as dodging. He let two of the rat-bobcat Nightmutts jump on him. They clung to his arms desperately scratching and biting, their teeth chipping away at the hard metal making up his body. He shook his arms, tossing them into the air before he grabbed their necks and squeezed. The *pop* and *crack* of their necks snapping cut through the air despite the thundering drumbeat echoing all around the team. He flung the Nightmutts to the side and sneered.

Dante jammed his latest opponent through the eye several times in rapid succession before kicking the thrashing and dying creature to the side. All animals were dangerous, the mutant spawn of Dirtside even more so. That didn't change the reality that a well-trained and fit man equipped with weapons was always favored to win if he kept his cool. Humanity had taken over Earth for a reason.

Nightmutt bodies and parts lay everywhere. The melee had sprayed blood all over the nearby trees, plants, and the team.

They'd avoided making too loud a noise that might attract the Dirtwalkers, but any Nightmutts that smelled the blood would come running.

Dante shook off the blood from his blade, eying the hole. Everyone held their breath, waiting and watching for more creatures to emerge. He could still hear scratching. "Something doesn't feel right. Midas, highlight all the tracks for me in my field of vision."

Green roads of tracks appeared all over. While the overlap made it difficult to distinguish, there were distinct trails only going away from the hole.

Hyde crushed the head of a fallen Nightmutt underfoot. "None of these things ever feel right. Because these are the monsters that live Dirtside now. Don't overthink it, *Papi*."

"I can still hear others." Dante kicked dirt at the hole. "And the way they circled up. Why not send more reinforcements, unless…"

Something hissed behind him. Something else hissed to the right. Beady red eyes appeared from behind nearby trees. Nightmutts ripped out of the ground, their arrival announced by fountains of dirt. The creatures now surrounded them with far greater numbers.

"Circle up," Dante ordered. "I ran into something like this in Australia. It's rare but just as annoying. I think we have a hive situation. Those earlier ones were disposable scouts sent to test us."

"Damn," Braelin drawled. "Nightmutts can do something that complicated?"

"Old insect hives could be complicated structures," Nasreen replied. "Using visual or olfactory cues, they could coordinate massive armies for hunting and gathering. This is nothing more than the larger-scale version."

More Nightmutts crawled out of tunnels, although no new

ones had come out of the original tunnel. The hissing chorus grew more obnoxious with each new member.

"They might be planning to push us into the tunnels, then swarm us there," Dante guessed.

"We keep killing them," Hyde replied. "They aren't so tough."

"There could be hundreds of these things in there." Dante shook his head. "We don't have time for this crap. It's a gamble, but if I'm right, there might be a queen. We take her out, and the hive disperses. Pheromones, loss of infrasonics. I've seen that before, too."

Braelin turned his head back and forth to mark the arrival of each new Nightmutt. "We ain't going to last if we let them keep building up."

Dante nodded toward the hole. "Find the queen, end this."

"You want someone to go in *there?*" Braelin's eyes widened. "Damn. That's a big ask."

Hyde marched toward the hole with a low growl. "I'll handle it."

Mugoi sprinted in front of him and threw up his arm. "No."

"Step back," Hyde rumbled.

"You're not going to fit." Mugoi eyed the hole. "I will." He looked over to Dante. "An augmented body harder to chew on makes the most sense. I'm the only logical choice."

"Find her quickly," Dante replied.

Hyde shrugged. "Ha-ha. Whatever."

The Nightmutts surged forward. Right after Hyde put his shoulder down and ran toward the closest Nightmutts, Mugoi dove headfirst into the tunnel.

Dante sliced the side of a Nightmutt. His quick sidestep dodged a claw swipe followed by a bite. A jab to the throat sent the creature to the ground, a spray of blood shooting from its throat to add to the generous coating all over the nearby plants and earth.

He barely had time to think before two other creatures

jumped him. A slice at the face from his right hand and a left hook from his other hand knocked the Nightmutts back, leaving them stunned long enough for Nasreen to cave in the skull of one and Braelin to cut off a leg of another.

A group tried to tackle Hyde together. He bashed them aside. One smashed headfirst into a nearby tree. Two others survived the counterattack and bounced back to their feet, although swaying. Hyde pounced and brought his elbows down on their backs. The *crunch* and bowing of their backs made Dante wince in sympathy. The sneering cyborg snatched the broken Nightmutts off the ground and hurled them into their charging friends.

Dante's team tightened formation around the hole in a reversal of their initial encounter. The surviving Nightmutts backed away, showing wariness in their stances. An eerie silence smothered the area, the earlier hissing gone as more creatures emerged from holes around them.

Sending Mugoi into the hive didn't worry Dante. He was confident his apprentice would survive. The rest of the team would, too, but they'd all taken major beatings in recent days, and before that day was over, there was a good chance they'd still have to deal with the drummers. He needed to save every ounce of energy until the mission was over.

Reaching an inscrutable threshold, the Nightmutts scampered forward. The pack had become a swarm. Meeting his first jumping enemy with a vicious cross slice that disemboweled, a flash of stray light on his pulsecore carbine tempted Dante to pull the weapon down and present the Nightmutts with the human's competitive advantage.

Hyde bulldozed through his enemies, kicking and punching, breaking bones and tearing muscles. That broke up their local battle lines. A good chunk of the creatures rushed to bite and claw the most obvious threat, leaving them exposed to the rest of the team.

Braelin and Jolo pushed too far forward. A pack broke off.

The pair went back-to-back, chopping and cutting down the Nightmutts. Nasreen rushed over to beat down two of the creatures and give the apprentices an escape path.

Dante became a whirlwind of slicing, stabbing, and perforation. He'd fought a rich bestiary of Nightmutts during his many jobs Dirtside. Every single mutant was unique and dangerous in its way. That didn't make them all as dangerous. Their current enemy was relying on numbers rather than strength.

The green and brown of the forest grew increasingly crimson. Dante could always admire the purity of essence in an aggressive animal that didn't know when to give up despite taking on a stronger foe.

Corpses piled up around him, commingled with the half-broken dying animals mangled by the punishment the humans delivered. He could have sworn the drumming pattern had grown quicker and more insistent as if the Dirtwalkers were watching the fight and responding with their beats.

His breathing ragged, Dante backhanded a bleeding-out Nightmutt. The monsters were endless. He pulled back his razor-fist, ready to brain the nearest mutant when it backed away, swaying and hissing quietly.

They all backed away, all hissing. The team reformed their circle, not taking their eyes off the creatures. The Nightmutts jerked their heads and shifted from leg to leg like they were performing a strange dance.

"I didn't expect to see that today," Braelin drawled.

Dante narrowed his eyes. "What the hell is going on?" A low rumble echoed from the nearby hole. "Damn it. Get ready to punch through at nine o'clock on my signal."

A second later, the remaining Nightmutts sprinted off into the forest in every direction, all hissing in unison.

Braelin flicked blood off his blade and backed away from the hole. "What could have scared them that much?"

Hyde balled up his fists and grinned. "Something more interesting. Time for real fun."

"'Move,' Dante ordered.

He, Jolo, and Nasreen backed away with the others, all keeping their weapons ready. The dirt shook around the hole. A massive claw that was easily the size of one of the fleeing Nightmutts erupted from the hole, filling the air with a cloud of dust. Another claw ripped through the forest floor, followed by a bulbous swollen head reminiscent of the deformed rat-bobcats that had fled, but it lacked eyes. A strangled rattling gurgle escaped the creature's mouth as it brought the rest of its hovercar-sized body from within the tunnel.

"The damned queen," Dante shouted.

"Now can we use guns?" Braelin tightened his grip on his carbon blade. "'Cause that's the worst Nightmutt I've ever seen."

Sir, please take note of the following, Midas interrupted, highlighting gaping wounds all up and down its body through the dust.

Dante didn't bother to tell him he'd noticed the wounds. "Back away and don't engage."

The Nightmutt queen pulled herself out of the massive hole with uneasy lurching steps. Her movement pushed away more dust, revealing additional lacerations all over her body.

A dark shape flew out of the hole. Mugoi. The cyborg spun in the air, blade in hand, and dropped toward the queen's head. Its blade and arm ripped through the top of the head until half its arm reached into the queen's skull. With a final strangled hiss, the queen collapsed on her side.

"Huh." Dante shrugged. "Whatever."

Mugoi yanked out its blade, eying its viscera-covered hand with disgust. "Acceptable, Captain?"

"Yeah." Dante chuckled. "That works." He drew a deep breath and retracted his blade. "Let's keep going. There's a good chance the Dirtwalkers might have heard all that commotion."

The closer the team moved to the foothills, the less cover the forest offered. That worried Dante less than the damned drums not having let up. The Dirtwalkers were offering a free and never-ending concert.

It had grown dark enough that clustered pinpricks of orange-red light stood out—torches or campfires. Dante lifted his rifle to look through his scope and scan the mountain. Dirtwalkers had emerged from tunnels throughout the mountain and at the forest level.

Dante lowered the carbine. "They must be looking for us. We're close now."

"Sir, there is a problem," Midas interjected, speaking aloud.

"I can see them fine," Dante replied. "I'm not blind."

"It's not that," Midas replied. "I'm having extreme trouble keeping calibration of the local navigational aids and difficulty uplinking with any secondaries. Accordingly, primary navigation is questionable. Local mineral deposits and fluctuations in the magnetic field are complicating matters. Even my new signal processing upgrade package only offers a minor resolution of the issue."

Everything Dirtside could threaten Plunderers, the life, the changing physical conditions. The changing planet spasmed in ways that no one could predict. That made the job of anyone descending to Earth dangerous even under the best of conditions.

"Show me the local maps we pulled back at HQ," Dante ordered.

Midas projected a holographic topographical map that included marking the last known position of the mine. The over-grown forest had long since covered it from prying technological eyes.

Dante narrowed his eyes. "We'll do this the old-fashioned

way." He ran his finger along the map. "We can use this ridgeline as a landmark. It should lead us right to the mine. It'll just take us longer."

Nasreen coughed. "We have to take longer when a bunch of bloodthirsty cannibals are hunting for us?"

"Yeah. Just another fun night Dirtside." Dante turned toward the foothills. The torches clustered in many small groups moving in different directions, most descending into the forest. "Using the landmark and taking longer is a better play than wandering around with glitchy navigation. We do have one advantage, though."

Nasreen raised an eyebrow. "Our weapons?"

Dante shook his head. "It's like you said. They're out looking for us. I bet there are fewer of them at the mine."

"You hope," Hyde replied. "You can't know."

"Nope. Nobody can know the future." Dante flicked crusted Nightmutt blood off his sleeve. "But I know without that database there is no future."

———

Dante and the team darted from tree to tree, a gaping tunnel leading into the bottom of the mountain hidden behind trees shorter than the ones around. He'd thought there would be fewer degenerate Dirtwalkers at the mine. He'd never imagined there'd be none guarding the front. He took a moment to confirm there was no one hiding nearby.

"We're lucky for now." He slowed as they cleared the last of the old growth and approached the younger trees that must have arisen only following the bulk of humanity abandoning the planet. "That luck won't hold."

"I don't see any traps," Braelin said.

Jolo gave him a dismissive look. "You wouldn't see a good trap."

Hyde growled. "Look behind us."

Dante glanced over his shoulder. Torchlight flickered, and shadows danced deeper into the forest. The staggered arc of illumination covered most of the forest. The drumbeats had been farther away but remained constant.

"They're working their way back." He inclined his head toward the mine. "We're not leaving until we get what we came for."

"And if they're here when we get back?" asked Mugoi.

Dante patted his carbine. "The Dirtwalkers will have swept the area near the mine for Nightmutts. Once we find the parts, we rush for the exfil clearing and Ambrose picks us up. If we can't get out the front, we find an alternate route. Best-case scenario, we find what we need right away, and we get out before they notice."

"That simple, *Papi*?" Hyde asked. "You might have extra lives, Hellcat. But the rest of us don't."

"Simple?" Dante shook his head. "This might be the most straightforward thing we've done in months. No crazy AIs. No insane zealot terrorists, just guns and blood."

Hyde grinned. "I like how you're thinking."

"We didn't come this far to go back empty-handed."

CHAPTER EIGHTEEN

Dante glared at the intersection. This entire mine annoyed him. Something about a structure marked by humanity but not fully taken always left him uneasy. Square, machine-carved tunnels had been braced with metal and wood, but there was no true floor or ceiling.

Crude blood drawings and piles of bones lined the reinforced earthen walls. Another realization left him annoyed. His main issue wasn't with the Dirtwalkers but rather their advanced predecessors and the allegedly superior people inhabiting the Station. His prediction of poor luck had proved prescient.

"This doesn't seem right." He looked down both paths. Spread-out torches offered flickering illumination beyond his night vision.

"I didn't expect the old records and maps we pulled up to take us right to the air processing center, but the map is completely wrong. We might as well have had Hyde draw us one at random. Once we got past that first part of the mine, this might as well have been a totally different place."

"I still can," the cyborg rumbled. "I'm better at drawing than you think."

Braelin smiled and stepped forward. "Yeah, I ran into that all the time when I was a Harvester. No one much cared about making sure records of all facilities were accurate once everyone decided to head into space. Plenty of 'em had been heavily modified long before, and no one kept track except the locals. And the farther you go from the big cities, the worse the recordkeeping."

Mugoi frowned. "Wandering around this mine for hours and hours will only lead to a pitched battle with those Dirtwalkers. Given what we saw outside, we can easily estimate that their forces number in the hundreds."

"That's why we came in the way we did," Dante replied. "But we're here now, and they aren't, which means we still have a chance of getting the equipment without facing them. They have no reason to believe we're in the mine with Ambrose still flying around."

Nasreen shook her head. "They must know someone's on the ground. That's why they have teams out looking for us."

Jolo grimaced. She held her chest and drew a deep breath.

"You okay, Neburu?" asked Dante.

Everyone had done well so far, but the mission was far from over. They weren't in a position for any single team member to be extracted. They would complete the mission and leave together, or they'd all die together.

"I'm fine." Jolo averted her eyes. "Don't worry about me."

Her performance had been nothing short of exemplary for a woman who'd been close to death not all that long ago. Dante had considered trying to leave her behind, but he needed all the trustworthy help he could get, and Jolo wanted to come. He didn't blame her for not being at her best. That didn't make it any less inconvenient.

Braelin frowned. "We'll get through this. You're doing great. You're doing a hell of a lot better than I would if a crazy son of a bitch stabbed and almost killed me."

Jolo frowned. "I've been through worse."

"No problem with admitting you're hurt." Braelin rotated his shoulder. "My arm's still sore. I'm hoping I get a long rest after this."

Mugoi scoffed. "Next time be smarter. That way you won't end up with broken bones."

"Hey, being smarter is no fun, and I was pissed. I get what happened, and I apologize for suspecting you. That doesn't mean I regret trying to beat your ass."

"You did okay," Hyde replied. "Until you broke your arm. Soft bodies can only last so long against augmented bodies."

Braelin squeezed Jolo's shoulder. "The point is we've all had our asses kicked now and again." He nodded at Dante. "We all know what happened to him, and he's Dante Damned Shale." He grinned at Hyde. "And he's in a completely new body."

Hyde grunted. "I didn't like the old one much anymore, *pendejo*."

"Sure, sure. That's not what I heard."

"Thanks, Braelin," Jolo replied. She drew a deep breath and slowly let it out. "I can still fight."

"Anytime, darl…" Braelin chuckled. "Anytime. Everyone knows you're the best of us three apprentices. If I was there with Nasreen when those Firewall assholes showed up, I'd be dead now."

Jolo shook her head. "We all have our specialties."

"And yours is ass-kicking. Mugoi might have that slick metal help, but you've got better skill."

Nasreen arched an eyebrow and looked at Dante. He shrugged. Everyone had seen how Braelin and Jolo had been interacting in recent weeks. What had started one-way looked like it was turning into something more reciprocal. He didn't have a policy against it as long as it didn't hold them back during jobs. Right now, if anything, it was helping.

Dante reconsidered the intersection and their path forward. Splitting the team was out of the question, not with the entire

Dirtwalker tribe still out hunting for them and a remaining chance of running into patrols. Their tech and skills would let them win against better odds, but one good spear could end with one of them unable to walk.

He'd seen nothing to indicate the degenerates had captured firearms. That was reassuring, but the mine's close quarters and curving tunnels helped neutralize the range advantage of their firearms. Many Dirtwalkers with experience against Plunderers learned the weak points of armor.

"We'll leave markers and explore each tunnel in turn," Dante said. "It's not the quickest bet, but we don't have much choice."

"You're forgetting something." Braelin grinned. "I joined you to learn how to become a proper Marauder under *the* Dante Shale. That don't mean I forgot everything I learned as a Harvester." He puffed out his chest. "It's time to show off my specialty."

"Oh?" Dante asked. "What do you got for me, Klement?"

Braelin reached up and slapped a corner of the wall. A billowing cloud of dust shot into the tunnel. Coughing, he waved it out of his face and pointed to faded white letters on the pipe. "This code here? It ain't for fun. You see, this confirms this is part of a Mard X45-Class Air Processing and Circulation System. They were a big deal in this part of the world back in the day. You could find them all over." He brushed off more dust. "These symbols confirm that this little bastard is a secondary coolant recirculation pipe."

"I could have used you the last time I was in this part of the world," Dante replied. "It would have saved me a hell of a lot of time and at least one team member's life."

This wasn't the first time Braelin's Harvester background had come in useful during a job, but he'd never been so critical as he was at this moment. Dante had picked him as an apprentice for a reason, and that choice now bore fruit.

Nasreen smiled, relief flooding her face. "That makes things more convenient."

Braelin wiped away more dust with his hand and uncovered a faded arrow. "They liked to mark up these old places for maintenance workers back in the day. That's why they marked the flow in all directions. No matter who was working on repairs they'd understand the circulation path. Idiot proof."

He shook a finger at Mugoi. "You keep your pretty mouth shut."

"Why are we standing around then?" Hyde asked. "Let's go find the stupid place."

"He makes a good point." Dante inclined his head toward Braelin. "Lead on, Klement. Lead on."

Dante let himself fall behind Braelin, who was now side-by-side with Jolo. The entire team kept up a good jogging pace. Jolo was sweating more than Dante would have liked, but she didn't have any problem matching Braelin. The former Harvester glanced her way on occasion. Every time she looked like she might slow down, Braelin's confident attention urged her silently forward.

It was ironic. The team had been at each others' throats before Firewall kidnapped them. Now everything was different. They were bringing out the best in each other. Dante would soon have three fewer apprentices and three new equal partners.

Wandering the long, dark tunnels using the original plan might have taken days. The Dirtwalkers would have returned and complicated the team's escape. Braelin's ability to follow the pipeline and identify side-access tunnels might help get them out of the mine before they had to fight anyone else.

Dante had no problem taking out degenerate cannibals. He wasn't sure he had enough ammo to fight off an entire large tribe.

The deeper the team descended into the mine, the more blood-stains coated the ground and walls of the tunnels. Bone fragments lay scattered along with small altars and torch holders made of skulls decorating the walls with inscrutable squiggles and lines painted in blood beneath them. This mine wasn't a temporary redoubt.

Braelin and Jolo led the formation, followed by Hyde and Dante, with Nasreen and Mugoi bringing up the rear. Everyone had stopped talking by this point. They kept their breathing quiet and their steps as light as they could. The flickering torchlight cast sinister shadows, the occasional abrupt movement making the team lift their weapons in preparation for the ambush everyone suspected would come.

The interminable tense stretch ended when Braelin and Jolo stopped at a sharp turn in the tunnel. Shadow puppets danced on the wall. This time they couldn't dismiss them so easily since guttural chanting drifted from around the corner.

Braelin gestured at a faded metal plaque on the wall. Despite the dust and blood sigils, old letters remained.

Le...őfeld...gozó Köz...

Before Dante could ask, Midas chimed in with a mental comment. *Given this place's location and the likely nationality of the workers involved, there is a high probability that is the remnants of Levegőfeldolgozó Központ, which is Hungarian for 'Air Processing Center.'*

Dante motioned for Braelin and Jolo to back up. He crept forward to pass them and flattened his back against the tunnel wall before peeking around the corner. An unpleasant acrid mix of scents wafted through the tunnel and assaulted his nose.

A Dirtwalker priestess in a thin robe with her arms, face, and exposed legs covered in intricate crisscrossing scars sat atop a throne of bones. It rested in front of a rusted and cracked maze of machinery, complete with pipes and tubes running along and into the walls. Blood-stained pelts lined the walls.

Nested circles of dark red clay jars surrounded the throne, every vessel decorated with bloody handprints. A quilt of Night-mutt pelts lined the seat of power, made mostly of rat-bobcats if Dante wasn't mistaken. Piles of cracked human bones lay all over the room. Crude blood paintings on the wall appeared to depict ritual sacrifice.

Stone firepits blazed with wood and rat-like Nightmutts on spits. Scarred men in loincloths with bone daggers at their side knelt before the bone throne. Their foreheads pressed against the ground as they chanted in a guttural language Dante didn't recognize. Given Midas' silence, he didn't either.

Strange animal masks lay beside the men. Dante didn't care what they were saying. These degenerates were too far gone to be considered humans anymore.

He swallowed a grunt of frustration and pulled his head back. "Dirtwalkers," he whispered. "We need to end this quickly, but no pulsecores, no grenades. We can't take the chance of blowing up the equipment behind the bone throne."

"Did you say bone throne?" Nasreen wrinkled her nose.

"Yeah. Bone throne." Dante pulled out his backup pistol and nodded at the others to pull down their rifles. Hyde looked annoyed and shrugged. He'd only brought the grenades and the pulsecore carbine.

Dante stepped away from the wall but kept behind the corner. The apprentices and Nasreen all lined up behind him with their rifles. He charged around the corner and lifted his pistol.

The priestess shot out of her throne, her eyes blazing with fury. She ripped a jagged bone dagger from a hidden slot in the throne and pointed it at Dante. She screeched in a way no human should be able to and shouted something in her guttural language.

Her attendants snatched up their knives and jumped to their

feet with a discipline that elite Reapers would envy. They chanted in unison while beating their chests with their free fists.

The priestess mimed slitting her throat with the dagger before baring her sharpened fangs that passed for teeth. She brought back her dagger as if to throw it. Dante didn't hesitate to put a bullet through her forehead.

She tumbled off the throne and smacked hard into the ground. Her attendants and worshippers burst toward the team except for one man. He ran toward the large pelt of a bearlike creature hanging on the back wall.

Nasreen and the others opened up. Their rifles' *cracks* echoed around the chamber. Bullets ripped through Dirtwalkers, sending them tumbling to the ground. That didn't stop their vengeful charge.

An aggressive man survived a shot. He continued forward, still screaming. Bursts from Jolo and Braelin blew through his chest and knocked him back.

Dante's attention snapped back to the Dirtwalker running for the back wall. He'd thought the man was the coward of the group and trying to avoid death. That miscalculation cost them as the Dirtwalker yanked the bear pelt down. A large vine rope dangled from the wall.

The Dirtwalker leapt toward the rope and grabbed it with both hands. He gibbered something in his native language before kicking off the wall and dropping to the ground, yanking hard on the rope. A line concealed by shadows and dust popped up. A loud rumble filled the room, following overlapping *clacking* sounds echoing from outside through the tunnel into the room.

Turning around, the Dirtwalker grinned. He sprinted right toward Dante, drawing his bone dagger. Dante put three rounds in his chest to add him to the collection of dead degenerates on the floor.

The echoing clacking noise continued for about thirty

seconds before dying out. As it ended, Dante spotted two femurs in a corner smacking together.

The mechanism involved a surprisingly complicated network of thin ropes made out of vine, hair, and thin white material he didn't recognize and didn't care to know.

"That's annoying." Dante kicked away a bone knife that'd fallen near his feet. "We have to assume the others know we're here." He motioned at the machinery. "You all have been briefed on the parts we need. Find them *yesterday*. Find anything that remotely looks like them. We're officially out of time."

CHAPTER NINETEEN

With a loud grunt, Hyde's fingers tightened around a panel running up a gray tower near the throne. He yanked hard, ripped the panel from the side of the machine, tossed it to the ground, and looked at the exposed innards. Decades, if not over a century old, the devices inside weren't shockingly different from many still in use on the Stations in modern times.

All the power of the Atlantica technology had helped raise cities into the skies. The people who had figured out that resonance was the key to using the Atlanticore had been brilliant—and driven. Yet the Station-dwellers had stagnated body and mind. This was more proof.

Leaning closer, Hyde yanked wires free and pulled off more interior panels. He fished out small tubes and wire sections from different corroded panels and tucked them away in belt pouches. He'd been smiling right after the fight. Now, he looked bored and annoyed.

"Just keep looking and grab anything that remotely looks like the parts," Dante shouted. "One hundred percent grab anything with runic writing."

The battle had been far too brief. They'd spent far too much time trying to tear through the surviving machinery, desperate to find the parts that might be key to defeating the Omega Syndrome.

Dante couldn't be sure they were there. The degenerates might have thrown them out. He clung to the notion that they had added to the mine and redecorated but hadn't gone out of their way to clear out all the evidence of technology. Without understanding the value of components, even for trade, they had no reason to get rid of any individual piece of technology.

He dug through a pile of bone fragments and rotting vegetation behind the throne. Small metal pieces poked out. He couldn't ignore any location in his search.

Braelin had verified they were in the right room, but his experiences with similar systems didn't involve any Atlanticore technology. That left him as clueless as Dante about where to look.

Dante grabbed a shiny metal tip and pulled it free of the waste pile. The tip belonged to what appeared to be a half-cracked flechette round. Tossing it aside, he thrust his arm back into the pile.

"Midas, how long has it been since the alarm went out?" Dante asked.

"Ten minutes, twenty-two seconds," Midas replied aloud for the team to hear.

"Damn it. That's too long."

Nasreen grabbed a jar and inverted it, shaking the contents. She sighed as charred remnants of burned bone and bark fell out. Honey filled the next jar. Half-eaten fish the third. It'd be useful fodder for future archaeologists, not Firewall techs.

Mugoi grabbed a jar and threw it hard against the ground. The pot shattered in a spray of fragments, spreading a dark oily liquid all over the ground.

The cyborg shrugged when people looked its way. "The parts might not survive an explosion. They can survive a broken jar. Besides, they know we're here."

"You have a point." Nasreen eyed her latest jar and shrugged. She lifted it with both hands and hurled it against the ground. Nightmutt claws shot out with the fragments.

Dante motioned to a wall. "Get those off the walls. That alarm can't be the only thing those degenerates were hiding."

Working with Jolo, Braelin yanked a pelt off the wall. They found more questionable paintings. They hurried down the walls, pulling down the others until they found a sealed metal door covered with elaborate blood paintings of what appeared to be winged demonic creatures descending from a cratered plane-toid, the moon, Dante presumed. A swiveling metal lever covered in a thick layer of dust and dirt secured the door.

Braelin grinned. "That makes it almost worthwhile."

Jolo stared at the door. "It's one of the few all-metal rooms we've seen since entering the mine. They bothered with the extra effort for a reason. Fuel? Munitions?"

"We'll see." Dante looked at the decoration. "I think it's a good chance of something useful. Judging by the dust, it's not some-where the Dirtwalkers have been into in a long time, if ever."

For all his distaste for harvesting activity by Station dwellers, at least they weren't torturing and eating people. They might have low standards for morality, but any positive value was better than none.

"It's a dedicated storage unit, I think," Braelin said. "Most likely a dedicated Faraday cage, in case they needed to keep something EM sensitive in there. I've seen 'em in places like this."

Dante stood. "A storage unit shielded from external influence sounds like a great place to hide specialized tech." He put his hand on his pistol. "Open it up, but be careful. I'll cover you."

Braelin rapped on the door with his knuckles producing a hollow sound before grabbing the level. Grunting, he yanked hard. The door continued to defy him with its stubborn refusal to move. He hissed and stumbled back, rubbing his shoulder. "This ain't the best job for me right now."

Dante nodded at Hyde. "You know what you want to show off."

"You're the one who was bitching about us not having enough time. Stand back." Hyde scoffed and jogged over from his dismantling job. "Stand back."

Braelin and Jolo moved away. After a couple of seconds, they moved back until they were beside Dante.

Hyde smirked and strutted up to the door. He grabbed the handle. "Watch how it's done, *pendejos.*"

He yanked hard on the lever. The metal groaned in protest. Hyde continued pushing, grunting in frustration. The handle snapped in half. Momentum carried the second half down. It scratched along the first half producing a shower of sparks.

Hyde frowned at the broken handle in his hand. "Huh. I was too strong." He tossed the handle into a pile of bones.

"There's metal fatigue," Dante said. He motioned at the door. "We still can't risk explosives."

Hyde offered him a lopsided grin. "We'll do it another way."

He backed away from the door, then turned his body. Bellowing, he charged shoulder-first into the door before Dante could shout for him to stop. New metal met old, weak metal with a massive *clang.* The door wrenched inward and flew backward, smacking hard into the concrete floor and knocking up a thick cloud of dust that reminded Dante of a smoke grenade.

"See?" Hyde grinned.

"I hope you didn't break what we were looking for," Dante replied.

"If it's that easy to break, the Stations are supposed to die." Hyde shrugged.

Dante walked over to the door and waited for the dust to settle. Hyde's straightforward approach hadn't hurt anything important since the door had landed on the floor. Metal shelves filled with clear trays lay on either side of the room. Dust covered every inch of the shelves, trays, and varied components inside. Thick webs coated others.

He looked up. Winged spider-like Nightmutts that shouldn't have been able to breathe according to Dante's understanding of biology sat in the corner of the webs. They were the size of two fists across and stared at Dante with unblinking solid orange eyes. Faint twitches proved they were awake and alive.

"That's disgusting," Nasreen shouted.

Braelin wrinkled his nose. "Something about bugs. They're always worse."

"Whatever." Dante backed up and pointed his gun. "I don't care as long as they aren't bulletproof."

Hyde held up his arm. "Save your ammo for the cannibals. I've got this, *Papi*."

Hyde advanced, dusting off his shoulders, unperturbed by the massive arachnids. The near-frozen creatures skittered toward him as soon as he stepped foot in the room. He backhanded the first Nightmutt against the back wall. The blow flattened the creature, spraying its ichor everywhere with a sickening *crunch*.

"They might be big spiders, but they're still only spiders."

Extermination didn't deter the others. They leapt off the webs toward Hyde, opening their massive mandibles. He punched cleanly through one and bashed the rest back with a sweep of his free arm. After shaking off the dead monster, he turned to the spiders running back. They crawled up the walls and jumped toward him again.

Hyde caught two with his hands, crushed their heads, and tossed the bodies to the ground. The remaining spider Nightmutts made it to him and tried to sink their dagger-like fangs into Hyde's hard metal body. He laughed and flung them off before stomping their bodies flat on the ground. "This is fun."

Nasreen wrinkled her nose. "Sometimes I miss being a spy. Far fewer monsters."

Dante shook his head. "Far fewer monsters with more than

two legs. I met you because you were dealing with too many two-legged monsters."

"That I can handle. This..." Nasreen motioned at the dead spiders. "That's ridiculous."

Chuckling, Hyde wiped spider guts off his body before sauntering out of the storage room and back to the equipment he'd been harvesting. Braelin and Jolo hurried inside to check containers. Both stepped around the crushed creatures.

Mugoi smashed another jar before jerking its head toward the entrance to the main chamber. Neither the cyborg nor Nasreen had found anything remotely useful in their anti-jar rage.

"Sir, did you hear that?" Midas used the voice modulator so everyone could hear the conversation.

"I can hear the jars smashing just fine," Dante replied.

"No, you misunderstand," Midas continued. "Please note the local hostile tribesmen have been continuous with their drumming since initiation. I'm unsure how much conscious effort you paid to it, but I've been monitoring it to help judge relative distance. They ceased all drumming about thirty seconds ago. I was waiting for you to react."

"They did?" Dante jumped to his feet. "Everyone stop moving. Stop breathing. Make no noise."

Midas was right. The drumming had long ago become background noise to Dante, something easy to ignore like the background music at a club. With the team, even Hyde frozen, it should have been easy to pick it out. The only thing Dante could hear was a sinister silence.

Dante tilted his head. That wasn't right. There was something more...faint, but there. It wasn't silence or drumming.

"Footsteps." Dante pulled his carbine off his shoulder.

"Yes, sir," Midas confirmed. "The sound signature suggests a large group of hostiles has successfully entered the mine."

Hyde looked at the exit. "We can fight out and head to the evac spot."

"These degenerates aren't mindless enough to make that work. Everyone keep looking for the parts. Every second we waste gives them more time to gather reinforcements."

Jolo and Braelin moved to the opposite sides of the storage room. Nasreen hurried over to help them while Mugoi returned to smashing pots.

Dante eyed the pile of dead men. "They have traps and warning systems, and now we're in their base. Hey, Ambrose, can you hear me?"

The pilot's response was static filled. "Yes. The… signal…weak."

"Good enough. We're going with a backup plan. I don't think we'll be able to get back to the clearing. We'll have to try to reach the mountain, climb a little, and find a place you can pick us up."

"Confirm…" The static rendered most of it completely unintelligible. "…mountainside, over?"

"Yes, confirm, mountainside," Dante replied. "We might lose comms on the way, over."

This time Ambrose's voice came through clear enough that Dante could hear the surprise in his voice. "Confirmed, mountainside pickup. I'll circle the mountain. See…soon."

Hyde's brow lifted. "You know something we don't, Shale? I didn't bitch earlier about the plan because I didn't think we'd do it."

"No. I don't know anything else you don't know." Dante shook his head. "You all saw the same data I did."

"That info is garbage and out of date. You knew that ten minutes into this craphole."

"But it confirmed the tunnels extend up and down through the mountain." Dante pointed at the ceiling. "I also saw Dirtwalkers in front of tunnels higher up earlier through my scope. We try to push our way out the front, and we might be dealing with hundreds of these degenerates. If we run and gun and make a mess on our way out, we can limit their numbers."

Nasreen crouched near one of the few remaining pots. "We can't be sure of the layout. Doesn't that make this dangerous?"

"This was always dangerous. So what? It's more dangerous."

"That's painfully true." She offered him a wan smile. "If we have to hold them off here while we find the items, they might be able to cut us off." She gestured around the room. "There's only one exit. We still have the major problem of finding the target. It could take us hours to find it."

"It ain't a problem now!" Braelin shouted. He held up two dark cylinders, a bundle of thin cabling, and a pyramid-shaped device covered with faint runic letters. "I found it."

Dante stared at the parts in wonder. Based on his knowledge and what Braelin had said, there was little reason to use that type of technology in a facility like this, which made him wonder why it was there. Years as a Marauder had taught him not to worry too much about it. The rise of the original Atlantica had spread curious technological artifacts all over the planet long before anyone could imagine the bulk of humanity abandoning Earth.

"Stow that and prepare to go loud." Dante deactivated his safety. "We now have to fight to the side of a mountain."

Low murmurs drifted through the tunnels to the room. The shuffle of careful and quiet footsteps might as well have been as loud as the drums. Their enemy was closing in on the room.

Hyde yanked down his pulsecore carbine, grinning from ear to ear like it was his birthday. Dante could see right through him. It wasn't every day he could kill with abandon and not have to worry about the moral or political implications. Nasreen and the others readied their rifles.

The degenerates didn't use either ancient or modern firearms. That should, in theory, make the battle one-sided. Unfortunately, countless Nightmutt encounters through the years proved that a creature could kill a well-armed man as long as it was angry, hungry, and fanatical enough. Based on the pile of dead men in their current location, the degenerates ticked off all three boxes.

A gaggle of Dirtwalker degenerates armed with a mix of stone and bone spears turned the corner into the tunnel leading to the air processing center. They slowed, silent, and with their expressions hidden by their eerie Nightmutt masks. More filed in behind them until the two-legged monsters choked the tunnel. They stopped at the entrance, surveying the carnage inside.

"This is your only chance," Dante shouted in the Trade Tongue, unconvinced they spoke it. "Leave us in peace or die. You have seen our power."

He didn't care about taking out the cannibals. He didn't want to get trapped in a pitched battle.

The Dirtwalkers didn't respond. They stood there rigid, staring at the bodies of their fallen brethren. No one on either side moved. The Dirtwalkers banged the bottom of their spears against the ground before letting out an ear-piercing collective ululating cry and charged forward.

Dante pulled his trigger and spat out a pulsecore round. The greenish explosion consumed the front rank of the enraged degenerates. Charred bodies flew everywhere. Nasreen's and the apprentices' rifle bursts cut into the flanks, mowing them down with ease despite the lack of a spectacular blast. Hyde punctuated the first volley with a pulsecore shot that carved a huge gap in the remaining formation.

Half-burned degenerate bodies joined the earlier bullet-riddled corpses near the front. The average Dirtwalker was only human, and these degenerates couldn't even claim that. Standing firm in the face of relentless power required discipline born of intense training and experience. Even hardened soldiers would have broken and run under such a massacre. Death could break animals that knew fear.

Fanaticism instilled its own discipline. Not a single Dirtwalker had screamed when Dante's team shot them. The enemy wasn't breaking and running. The survivors and reinforcements fed a flood of mindless spear-armed zealotry, tramping the bodies of the fallen in a mad dash to close in and murder the invaders at any cost.

Another staggered volley from Dante's team cut down the next wave. A couple of men managed to fling their spears, one whistling close to Dante. Primitive weapons had a knack for finding their way through Station armor. He didn't want to test his luck or probe the number of remaining Hellcat lives.

"Push forward," Dante shouted.

He followed up with quick shots raking left to right. A pulsecore explosion blew a chunk out of the wall, spraying the tunnel with hot rock shrapnel. More Dirtwalkers fell, the victims of the secondary shotgun effect.

Hyde matched Dante's strategy. With the Dirtwalkers now restricted to the tunnel, Nasreen's and the apprentices' overlapping firing patterns assured that everyone in the tunnel surviving the initial blasts would earn a free bullet through their chests.

The team's third barrage filled the tunnel and chamber with a thick cloud of smoke and dust, making it nearly impossible to see. No Dirtwalker reinforcements appeared around the corner. The footfalls and murmurs from before were gone.

Dante shoved a burned body out of the way with his boot and advanced into the tunnel. Nasreen and Mugoi moved forward to guard his flanks.

"That all of them?" Hyde sounded disappointed.

"No. There were way more than that on the mountainside earlier." Dante shook his head. "They might not have been the entire tribe." He inclined his head toward Braelin. "All that Harvester experience able to help you find the tunnels going up?"

"No guarantees," Braelin replied after looking at Jolo with concern. "But I ain't planning to die in a scarred bastard's stomach."

Dante motioned for the team to advance. Once Hyde had passed through the entrance to the air processing center, Dante pointed at the ceiling. "Let's seal that up. It might confuse them."

Hyde turned around and walked backward a few yards. He squeezed off two quick, well-placed pulsecore rounds. Smoke billowed through the tunnel as dirt and rock rumbled from above to seal the air processing room.

"So far, so good." Dante jogged around the corner. "Now let's get the hell out of here before this becomes our grave."

Dante's lungs burned as he pumped his legs. Tunnel after tunnel looked similar with the same torches and degenerate ritualistic art and altars. The tribe was nothing if not consistent in their vision. The team was heading up. That much was certain although no one, including Braelin, could guarantee when they'd make it out.

Guttural cries echoed behind him. He slowed and looked over his shoulder. Collapsing more of the mine might protect their flanks. It also risked trapping them if they were wrong.

Hyde turned. "They can't beat us."

Dante looked among his team. Weariness lined their faces despite the stern-eyed determination. An occasional grimace from Jolo, Nasreen, and Braelin reminded him of how bad their injuries had been not all that long ago. Mugoi's more stoic demeanor didn't erase the fact the cyborg had also suffered serious damage and was running on backup parts.

The team had done well to heal in time to join the mission. That didn't mean they needed to stay and fight hundreds of cannibal killers. The mission was the equipment, and they'd recovered it.

"Keep moving," Dante ordered, nodding forward. "We got what we came here for. That's all that's important."

Hyde's nostrils flared. He reached up and scratched his ruddy beard. "We'd be doing Dirtside a favor cleaning out this trash, but you're the *jefe, Papi*."

Dante picked up the pace, his jog threatening to become a sprint. Nasreen's labored breath from behind worried him. More than anyone other than Jolo, she should have had time to rest. Sometimes the deepest wounds weren't the most obvious.

As if mocking him, their tunnel broke apart into three forks. Metal likely from the original construction braced two. The central tunnel was far rougher and narrower. The uneven surface suggested the use of hand-held tools in the building.

Braelin hurried to the first fork. He brushed off the dirt to find the faded lettering and interpret it as best he could.

A hissing *screech* erupted from the central tunnel. Degenerates jumped from concealed holes dug into the side of the room. They stabbed at Dante and Nasreen.

Dante couldn't fire his pulsecore at that range without risking collateral damage or burying his team. He parried the Dirtwalker's spear before kicking the man to the side. That set up Nasreen for an easy burst into the degenerate's chest.

The remaining Dirtwalkers didn't go for the team. They ran close to the tunnel walls not even looking at their enemies. Mugoi spun and delivered a powerful roundhouse to a Dirtwalker's head. The Dirtwalker's head snapped back, and he dropped to the ground.

His partner dropped his spear and jumped toward the wall with his hand outstretched. Braelin nailed him in the side. The bullet ripped through, and blood splashed against the wall as the Dirtwalker's fingers pierced a loose layer of dust and revealed a protruding bone. He grabbed the bone, using the force of his falling body to yank it out.

"Go!" Dante bellowed before the bone had cleared its hole. He darted forward.

The entire area shook violently. A loud, grinding noise echoed through the tunnels. The rest of the team sprinted forward. Jolo stumbled. Braelin grabbed her hand, pulled her to her feet, and shoved her forward.

With a deafening roar, the ceiling collapsed. A dust cloud choked the tunnel. Braelin flung his rifle forward as dirt showered down around him.

Wide-eyed, Jolo brushed dust out of her face. "Braelin?"

Dante's heart pounded. "Klement? Damn it. This is not the time to be playing around."

They'd fought cyborgs and well-trained mercenaries. His team had faced off against a bizarre zoo of Nightmutts. Losing an apprentice to a Stone Age trap was laughable, pathetic, and unacceptable.

Mugoi shouldered his rifle and walked toward the pile, the thick dust cloud still obscuring most of the tunnel. "Hyde, help me dig him out. He bragged once about being able to hold his breath for a long time."

"Dumbass shouldn't have got buried," Hyde grumbled.

Eyes appeared in the pile. Mugoi brought back his fist.

"Whoa," drawled the owner of the eyes. "I almost got buried. Fancy Earth-side burial." A true Dirtwalker appeared, a man coated from head to toe in dirt and dust. He shook his head like a dog to shake off the dust.

Jolo put her hand to her chest and let out a sigh of relief. "Braelin."

The dirty Braelin smiled, still looking more like an ambulatory pile of dust in the shape of a man than a Marauder. He snatched his rifle up from the ground. "I'm not dying like a bitch under rocks."

Hyde snickered. "But you still are going to die like a bitch?"

The intersection now lay buried under tons of rock. It simplified the choice for the team. They had no option but the hand-dug Dirtwalker tunnel.

Jolo coughed and leaned with one arm against a wall. She stared at Braelin. "Thank you for earlier. Also, don't do that again, or I'll dig you out and kill you myself."

"It'd be a pain to dig you out, you know?" Braelin smiled. "That's why I did it, and I'm not planning to get buried myself."

Dante scoffed. "Yeah. Let's not put it to the test."

Nasreen snapped up her rifle and fired two bursts, the bright muzzle flash lighting up the tunnel. Soft *thuds* followed soft groans. "It's safe to assume they know exactly where we are now."

"Yeah," Dante replied. "All the more reason to keep moving."

He jogged forward, finding the dying Dirtwalkers Nasreen had taken out. The tunnel had a steep incline, challenging his muscles while bolstering his morale. Any direction that took them up brought them closer to Ambrose and evacuation.

Dante squinted. Flickering lights had intensified at the end of the tunnel. He switched to night-vision. He made out bare outlines of Dirtwalker heads and spears clustered around the tunnel's edge. More importantly, he could see clouds.

He slowed. "There's our exit," he whispered. "I can spot at least a half-dozen Dirtwalkers hiding near the entrance. We should assume there's more. We can't risk clearing out the front of the cave with the pulsecores until we're safely outside."

"That can't be their whole force," Nasreen replied. "They would have sent them after us."

"Ambrose, can you hear me? Over," Dante transmitted.

"You're loud and clear, over. I hate to be the bearer of bad news, but there's an army of Dirtwalkers making their way up the mountain and converging on one tunnel. Is that where you are?"

"I wouldn't bet against that. Okay, get ready to pick us up. Feel free to strafe the bastards climbing and take pressure off us."

Dante loaded a fresh pulsecore carbine magazine and looked at the team. "They've got more than we can see. I don't like that trap. We're going to get the hell out of here before we all end up looking like Braelin."

"That's truly a fate worse than death," Mugoi quipped.

"Watch it." Braelin mock glared at him.

A low rumble echoed in the tunnel. Seconds later, it started shaking.

"Very funny." Dante grunted when the shaking intensified. "Move your asses or think of a line for your epitaph."

He darted forward, pumping his legs as hard as he could while trying to steady his pulsecore. Nasreen and the apprentices sprayed bursts near the entrance. The Dirtwalkers were smart enough to stay covered, but one brave soul took rounds in the shoulder and fell backward screaming and dishonoring the rest of his fanatical tribe.

The high-pitched blaze of the shuttle's pulsecore cannon whipped through the tunnel. Greenish flashes highlighted the tunnel entrance. Hyde and Mugoi bounded forward, pulling ahead of Dante.

A portion of the ceiling collapsed in front of the team. Another section dropped behind them. They rushed forward through the blinding dust, dirt, and rock raining from above.

Dante couldn't make out anything other than the barest outlines of his team. Everyone had stopped firing, concentrating instead on escaping the collapsing tunnel. For a group of degenerate cannibals, the Dirtwalkers had put impressive effort into making sure anyone who invaded their sanctum would pay.

Jolo had stumbled before. Nasreen and Braelin hadn't looked so good. Anyone who tripped now would get crushed. No one was in a position to save anyone else.

Risk accompanied any trip Dirtside. That's why Plunderers got paid so well, regardless of type.

Dante refused to believe he'd lose anyone there. He'd personally trained Nasreen and the others. Hyde could take care of himself. They'd make it out. All they had to do was run blindly through a cloud of dust while a horde of murderous savages waited outside for them.

A scream pierced the night. A body flew past Dante and

disappeared into the darkness. The cloud still blinded Dante, but the cool wind pushing the dust confirmed he'd made it outside.

Sensing someone behind him, Dante spun. A Dirtwalker in a mask that resembled a combination of a butterfly and alligator thrust his spear toward his neck. Dante dodged with a sidestep and knocked the spear out of the man's hand by clubbing his wrist with his carbine. He jumped backward and fired once. The pulsecore explosion blew off the top of the Dirtwalker's body and knocked Dante back.

Mugoi grabbed a large boulder and vaulted over it to dropkick two Dirtwalkers rushing toward Dante. He snatched a spear off the ground and flung it into the chest of a Dirtwalker.

The soft wind thinned the dust from blinding to obscuring. Acrid smoke assaulted his nostrils and mixed with the dust.

The shadow of the shuttle passed overhead, the cry of the cannon cutting through the dreams and screams of dying Dirtwalkers. Green flashes walked up and down the mountain. Never had carnage been so beautiful.

Dante slung his carbine over his shoulder, opting for the crystal razorfist blade instead. A cat-bat masked Dirtwalker solidified from a dust-covered shadow in time to receive Dante's jumping punch to his face. His blade pierced the mask with ease.

While smoke from Ambrose's attack spread over the area, the dust from the tunnel collapse had mostly cleared. They were fighting on an angled slope with scattered ledges, too many to be natural. Bodies littered the ground everywhere. Dirtwalkers swarmed the mountainside, climbing the mountain or emerging from other holes.

A circle of mangled corpses surrounded Hyde, who sneered as Dirtwalkers' spearheads bounced off his metal body. He smashed a fist into his closest opponent, sending the man high into the air with a trail of blood. The Dirtwalker missed a ledge, falling another few feet before bouncing off the side of the mountain and repeating the process.

Mugoi darted between Dirtwalkers. Quick kicks and punches joined with flashes of his blade. The howling degenerates flailed at him, unsure how to respond.

Dante grabbed his pistol. Swinging it in an arc, he emptied his magazine, putting rounds into a dozen Dirtwalkers fighting his team. He jerked his head around, looking for Nasreen, and found her when a rifle report sounded from behind him.

Nasreen ejected her magazine, reloaded, and jogged toward him. She brought up her gun with a glare. Dante didn't move. He trusted her. She fired, the rounds zooming by him and ripping through the head of a Dirtwalker about to attack.

"Nice shot," Dante said.

"I try," Nasreen replied.

Jolo knelt in front of Braelin. They alternated fire. Screeching ululating Dirtwalker victims tumbled down the mountain, unable to contend with another pair in perfect sync.

A group of Dirtwalkers emerged from a higher tunnel, all holding jars. They threw a pot toward Dante. He stepped out of the way, surprised when it splattered a thick oily liquid everywhere.

Nasreen sprayed a burst to force a Dirtwalker with a torch back. "They're going to cook us."

"Ambrose, get in close," Dante ordered. "It's time to get out of here."

"But they're all over!" Ambrose replied. Panic filled his voice. "They'll flood the shuttle again! I mean, they'll get aboard the shuttle."

"Whatever. So will we. Just do it before we get flambéed down here."

Nasreen focused on cover fire against the Stone Age bombardiers on the higher ledge. She took careful, deliberate shots. The Dirtwalker degenerates tossed more jars over and soaked the area with more of the oil, but they couldn't manage a clean drop. One man tried to arc a torch high. She nailed it with a burst and sent it tumbling off wide. It was another fine shot.

Ambrose swept in low. Three rapid cannon shots forced the burners back under cover. He spun the shuttle and opened the bay door. Dirtwalkers roared in defiance and charged toward the shuttle. Oil jars smashed against its sides.

Dante and Nasreen made a break for the shuttle. Both fired every other step, downing crazed Dirtwalkers with each shot. Braelin nodded at the shuttle. Jolo hesitated before jogging toward it. Once she'd started moving, Braelin flung plasma grenades almost as fast as a pulsecore could spit out rounds. A moving wall of explosions shoved back a wave of Dirtwalker reinforcements.

Mugoi joined the effort with ambidextrous grace while backing toward the shuttle. An unfortunate Dirtwalker ran between two grenade explosions. His half-incinerated body tumbled through the air and disappeared into the darkness.

Hyde stayed near the back of the open shuttle without entering, countering Ambrose's fear. Any straggling Dirtwalker who made it close learned the terror of an augmented punch in the last seconds of his life.

Jolo reached the shuttle and backed into it slowly. She laid cover fire bursts. The strategy allowed Braelin to sprint from his position toward the shuttle. Mugoi, Nasreen, and Dante all converged on the back of the ship. Hyde finally hopped inside.

The shuttle rattled and lifted off. Ambrose banked hard, skimming the mountain. Flaming torches from above missed the oil-soaked shuttle and hit the ground, igniting the oil-soaked mountainside. The roaring flames lit up the night, highlighting the thrashing mass of angry semi-humanity on the mountainside.

Dante dropped to the deck and wrapped his arms around his knees. "Yeah. That wasn't fun." A massive green-tinged explosion blasted a plume from the mountain. "Oh yeah. I forgot to grab my pulsecore. I almost never do that crap."

The shuttle bay door closed, cutting off the whistle of the air passing outside. Dante turned to Braelin. Between the dust, blood, and soot, the apprentice had become the avatar of an ancient dark god.

"Show me we didn't waste our time," Dante ordered.

Braelin reached into a pocket and pulled out the parts. He held them out in his palms with a grin. "Everything's here."

"Now it's up to Firewall."

CHAPTER TWENTY

Dante and Nasreen strolled the cool narrow aisles of Savarin's Larder, admiring the colorful array of fruits and vegetables offered by the high-end grocery store. There couldn't be a greater contrast between the shiny tiles and holographic signage marking the perfectly climate-controlled store and the rude, ancient tunnels they'd been in on their job only days before. Every aspect of the store, from the supplied foods to the locations of each section, was the product of research produced by the pinnacle of human civilization.

Light classical music played over the speakers, and the other fashionable customers all cast suspicious gazes at Dante. He didn't know whether because of his simple pants and shirt or because they recognized him as the famous Marauder troublemaker responsible for disrupting the entire corporate and governing ecosystem of the Stations.

He didn't understand why they had dressed in fancy dresses and expensive suits. Trying to impress people while shopping for food didn't make any sense.

It wasn't that Dante was poor. Far from it. Risking his life for years Dirtside had made him far wealthier than many of the people now scorning him. His money hadn't changed his personality.

Dirty stares didn't bother him. He grinned at a scowling woman. She grimaced and looked the opposite way, rolling her eyes.

At least they weren't cannibals. The equipment dropoff with Firewall had proceeded without incident, betrayal, or the untimely arrival of Block 9X. Lock claimed they needed time to integrate the equipment fully. That left the team on standby, and Nasreen had suggested a party with ingredients purchased at a more expensive store as a celebration.

Dante was fine with that. His team needed time to rest and to think about something other than cannibals and rogue AIs. Rude grocery shoppers were a nice change of pace. None of them would try to attack here.

He stopped and peered at the purple eggplant taunting him from a basket. It lay nestled within a sloping wall of other eggplants, all perfectly smooth, even, and the same shade. "Do you ever think this whole thing is a scam?"

Nasreen looked past him at Braelin balancing a pineapple on his head. Jolo facepalmed and shook her head. An employee scowled at Braelin.

"Sir," she said. "I must ask you not to balance the pineapple on your head."

Braelin kept the pineapple on his head as he made a show of looking around. "I don't see any sign saying you can't put fruit on your head."

"We didn't think we'd need that. We would have thought it'd be self-evident."

Dante looked at them and chuckled. "Someone's having fun."

"It's good to get out of HQ," Nasreen replied. "I'm glad we convinced everyone to come along. That way they can't complain later when we have the meal. Everyone will have had their chance to grab what they like. I don't see why you'd consider that a scam. It's a party. I know you're not the most sociable man, but this is good for the team."

"I'm not talking about the party." Dante gestured around the aisle. "This store is a scam."

"Okay. I didn't see that coming." Nasreen laughed. "Why do you say that?"

Dante pointed at a holographic sign. A beautiful raven-haired woman held a bumpy fruit in her hand. The image shifted to the text **Recommended delicious all-natural dragon fruit.**

Hyde stalked out of the liquor section, his shoulders stacked with cases of beer. Dante didn't know if Hyde's current body configuration allowed him to get drunk. Mugoi had disappeared on the other side of the store, mentioning something about pasta.

"Half of this crap is grown in labs. Nah. Most of it is." He nodded at the meat section on the other side of the store. "How can they say something's all-natural? What's all-natural about any of this, even the stuff you don't find in the lab? Sure, sure, they've got high-end hydroponic crap, and that's why they can charge more for it, but they're not growing it on a farm down on Earth. It's all tech. There's nothing natural about humans living in space."

"That's not nearly as insane as I imagined you saying." Nasreen poked the bumps on one of the dragon fruits. "Usually when they say all-natural, it means only minor genetic tweaks."

Dante snickered. "By that logic, I'm all-natural despite the chip in my head."

Midas chimed in. *Technically, sir, I'm made with material all found easily in nature and only subjected to light processing. You could make a reasonable case that I'm all-natural.*

"Sure. AI implants. One hundred percent all-natural." Dante peered down at a fat, tubular green fruit he didn't recognize. Looking at the sign, he scowled. "I'll buy the idea of all-natural meaning not genetically engineered, but how the hell do we have an 'Authentic Missouri Pawpaw?' I've been to Missouri on a job. They're not growing anything there anymore."

He wasn't sure which annoyed him more, that he didn't know what a pawpaw was to know if he'd like it, or the implication that people could be encouraged to part with their cash by referencing part of a country that had long ceased to exist.

Nasreen laughed. "This store is wasted on you. Try to get into the spirit of it."

"I don't get into the spirit of lies."

A stern-looking manager in a maroon apron shook his finger at a snickering Braelin, who was juggling pineapples. He missed, and a pineapple crashed into a carefully stacked pyramid of oranges, knocking them everywhere. Jolo rolled her eyes and knelt to pick up the rogue fruit.

Dante grabbed a pawpaw and headed toward Braelin. "We better get our food and get out of here before they call Station security on us. A fruit brawl wouldn't be good for my reputation."

"Ah, that's how the legend of the great Dante Shale ends," Nasreen replied. "Executed in a high-end grocery store for crimes against fruits and vegetables."

The team walked into the lobby of their headquarters building with bags and boxes of beer in tow. Dante shook the bag of oranges he'd agreed to buy to keep the store manager from ejecting them over Braelin's antics.

Hyde offered after finishing a lengthy discussion on the way back, "All I'm saying is you should have let me do the talking. You wouldn't have had to buy those oranges."

"We don't need you threatening grocery store employees." Dante swung his bag of oranges in a menacing manner. "This was to prep for a party, not add to the list of people who want to kill us."

Nasreen began, "It'd be nice if we could go at least a week without making any new enemies."

Hyde glowered. "I'm not afraid of a grocery store."

Midas flashed green around the edge of Dante's vision. He spoke aloud. "Sir, I recommend maximum alert. Something is wrong. There are no obvious alarm activations or intruders, but the responses with the main system to my commands are sluggish and off. Checksum failures are occurring in key subsystem response areas."

Dante set his oranges down. Everyone else set their bags down. While they couldn't go to the store with carbines and explosives, everyone not augmented had at least one hidden knife or razorfist ready for street ambushes.

Hyde made a show of cracking his knuckles, even though his metal fingers didn't produce the satisfying popping noise. "Sorry, Joelle. You didn't even get a week. It'd be funny if it were grocery store assassins."

Nasreen slid out a hidden wrist knife. "I don't think the Stations are so gone that our grocery stores have assassins."

"Concentrate," Dante ordered. "Don't worry about taking people alive if that'll slow you down."

He and Mugoi took up positions on either side of the door. Hyde threw open the door, and the three charged inside, forming a wedge with Dante at the center. The rest of the team rushed after them and spread out along the sides.

"What the..." Dante blinked.

Ambrose, who entered the last, yelped. "What's it mean?"

The lobby lights were off. A monitor in the lobby that normally didn't show anything but weather information and daily notes from Nasreen to the team contained a message in bright red letters over a flashing background of thunder.

NOTHING IS HIDDEN FROM ME. CEASE NOW OR PREPARE TO KNOW THE FURY OF AN ANGRY GOD.

"Pair up," Dante ordered. "Sweep the building. Get back here in five minutes. You see anyone, stab first, ask questions later. I'm not in the mood for games."

Dante glared at the message. Hyde and Mugoi were the last ones to return. Dante didn't need to ask them the question he'd asked Braelin and Jolo.

"It's on every monitor in the building," he said.

Hyde shrugged. "Sorry, *Papi.*"

"Midas, tell me what I don't want to hear," Dante said. When the AI didn't respond, Dante raised his voice. "Midas."

"I apologize, sir," the AI answered aloud. "I was attempting to use all my resources to trace the source of the hack and to confirm if one occurred."

"We see the damned evidence that it happened. What's to verify?"

"You see that message, sir. There doesn't appear to be a hack in the systems in the normal sense. Unfortunately, I found residual system modifications consistent with what we know of the Omega Syndrome. I'm now in the process of removing it."

"How is that not a hack?" Dante asked.

"It's less a hack and more as if the entire system was being shifted to a different system entirely."

Nasreen's breath caught. "It had to happen. We've been pushing too hard. We knew this was coming whether we liked it or not."

The lights turned on, and the messages changed. A reboot screen appeared on the monitor.

"I don't give a crap whether the Omega Syndrome is another old rich guy or a rogue AI," Dante replied. "They want things to move to the next level? Works for me."

Mugoi's gaze flicked to the monitor and Dante. "Are you sure, Captain?"

"I'm not sure about everything, but I am sure I'm not going to let these assholes push us around. I gave you all the chance before. I want to be sure now that you're prepared to see this to the end."

He met each man's and woman's gaze with his. Everyone, even Ambrose, looked back with determination. "It looks like we've got a fake god to kill."

AUTHOR NOTES MICHAEL ANDERLE

SEPTEMBER 9, 2022

Thank you for not only reading this story with these author notes as well!

I've never been to space before.

So, I'm not a person who has gone into space (and frankly, I've wondered if I would if I had the chance? Put myself on the top of a bajillion-pound firecracker if Elon Musk or Jeff Bezos said, "Hey Mike…We love your science fiction. Would you like a $100,000 ride (or $250,000) for free?

Would I?

Well, I'd like the ride, but would I take it?

(For context, I'm a 55-year-old, mostly not in shape author/publisher who walks through his garage to his outside office – when it rains – for exercise guy on heart medicines.)

I think I'd pass.

First, I daresay they would make me exercise, which is anathema to myself and always has been. Unfortunately, I got shafted when the Genetics Gods handed out the gene that provides dopamine for runners (that runners' high they call it).

No fun high for me…just pain, pain, pain. How do I know this? Because I can be a competitive person by nature, and when I was young…in shape (if bean-pole is considered a shape) when I was a pre-teen and early teen, I ran to beat everyone else.

Or stubbornly ran with a stepdad for 2 miles just to prove to him I could 'hang'.

NEVER was there a high. If it takes 2 miles plus some more to get there? Not happening.

I crack open a book, and I'm usually into my high pretty fast if the book is fun. So, Reading > Running in my book and what logical person would choose the running if the equation is obvious? Well, unless you are looking to impress a girl.

I rest my case.

So, here I am at 55 and these 'issues' and think jumping on a rocket is a less than stellar idea for me. However, I can rest easy.

Unless Elon or Jeff reach out, I'm safe knowing that I don't KNOW that I wouldn't do it and my ego can rest easy at night tucked into the bed of ignorance.

If you had the chance, would you jump on the rocket and go up?

Talk to you in the next book!

Ad Aeternitatem,

Michael Anderle

MORE STORIES with Michael newsletter HERE:
https://michael.beehiiv.com/

OTHER ATLANTICA BOOKS

John Chambers Books

Her Mother's Pendant (Book 1)

The Mystery Deepens (Book 2)

One Last Choice (Book 3)

Valentina Winters

The Red Countess (Book 1)

One Night to Kill (Book 2)

One Death Too Few (Book 3)

Terra Kris

She is the Law (Book 1)

Law or Justice (Book 2)

Justice Served (Book 3)

Santana Sokolov

Law of the Jungle (Book 1)

Inner City Jungle (coming soon)

Rumble in the Jungle (coming soon)

Justice Begins

The First Executioner

Aiming Blind

High Lead and Low Deeds

No Backing Down

Justice is Not Blind

Scorched Earth

CONNECT WITH THE AUTHOR

Website: http://lmbpn.com

Email List: https://michael.beehiiv.com/

https://www.facebook.com/LMBPNPublishing

https://twitter.com/MichaelAnderle

https://www.instagram.com/lmbpn_publishing/

https://www.bookbub.com/authors/michael-anderle